All the kids were in the wedding.

Jane was the flower girl. She'd practiced her role by littering the entire house with bits of shredded paper. Max was in charge of the rings and had slept with them under his pillow last night. Helen's daughter, Libby, had turned down the role of bridesmaid and insisted on wearing a tuxedo and giving the bride away. Cara and Zach were standing in as co-maid of honor and co-best man.

And now, in front of the children, assorted relatives and guests, it was time for Helen to walk down the aisle—between the living room and dining room—toward the man who couldn't see how much she loved him.

Dear Reader,

Merry Christmas! I hope you'll like Intimate Moments' gift to you: six wonderful books, perfect for reading by the lights of the Christmas tree. First up is our Heartbreakers title. Welcome veteran romance writer Sara Orwig to the line with *Hide in Plain Sight*. Hero Jake Delancy is tough—but the power of single mom Rebecca Bolen's love is even stronger!

Terese Ramin is back with *Five Kids, One Christmas*, a book that will put you right in the holiday mood. Then try Suzanne Brockmann's *A Man To Die For*, a suspenseful reply to the question "What would you do for love?" Next up is *Together Again*, the latest in Laura Parker's Rogues' Gallery miniseries. *The Mom Who Came To Stay* brings Nancy Morse back to the line after a too-long absence. This book's title says it all. Finally, welcome Becky Barker to the line as she tells the story of *The Last Real Cowboy*.

Six books, six tales of love to make your holidays bright. Enjoy!

Leslie Wainger
Senior Editor and Editorial Coordinator

Please address questions and book requests to:
Silhouette Reader Service
U.S.: 3010 Walden Ave., P.O. Box 1325, Buffalo, NY 14269
Canadian: P.O. Box 609, Fort Erie, Ont. L2A 5X3

FIVE KIDS, ONE CHRISTMAS

TERESE RAMIN

Silhouette INTIMATE MOMENTS

Published by Silhouette Books

America's Publisher of Contemporary Romance

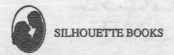 SILHOUETTE BOOKS

ISBN 0-373-07680-0

FIVE KIDS, ONE CHRISTMAS

Copyright © 1995 by Terese daly Ramin

Books by Terese Ramin

Silhouette Intimate Moments

Water from the Moon #279
Winter Beach #477
A Certain Slant of Light #634
Five Kids, One Christmas #680

Silhouette Special Edition

Accompanying Alice #656

TERESE RAMIN

lives in Michigan with her husband, two children, two dogs, two cats and an assortment of strays. When not writing romance novels, she writes chancel dramas, sings alto in the church choir, plays the guitar, yells at her children to pick up their rooms (even though she keeps telling herself that she won't) and responds with silence when they ask her where they should put their rooms after they've picked them up.

A full-fledged believer in dreams, Terese has never wanted to do anything but write. After years of dreaming without doing anything about it, she finally wrote her first romance novel, *Water from the Moon*, which won a Romance Writers of America Golden Heart Award in 1987 and was published by Silhouette in 1989. Her subsequent books have appeared on the Waldenbooks bestseller list. She is also the recipient of a 1991 *Romantic Times* Reviewer's Choice Award. She hasn't dreamed without acting for a long time.

To Mike, Colleen & Bridget, with hope and love.
For the keeper of the K.A. doll who inspired *Helen* in
the first place; and for blended families everywhere.

According to Jewish tradition, each baby starts life with
11,000 guardian angels. This is for all those who feel
like they've grown up too soon and lost theirs:
Reinforcements are on the way; hang in.

My sincere thanks and appreciation to those who
provided me with the information necessary to the
completion of this book: Kathleen Daly,
Med-tech Denver V.A. hospital, U.S. Army veteran;
Les D. Grosinger, M.D., P.C.; Michigan Cornea
Consultants, P.C.; Joan Shapiro, Debbie Vargas
and the Upshaw Institute for the Blind.

In memory of my dad, whose corneas let
somebody else see.

Chapter 1

NAT

Devil's Night

He loved the water.

It was his intimate, his familiar. It slipped around him, cool silk against the fever of his skin. Dark and welcoming, it beckoned him into its depths, urged him forward, stroke against stroke, into its stillness.

For an instant he wondered about the peace that lay at the bottom of the canal's blackness, wondered about resting forever among the garden of lake weeds. Then he cupped a hand and slid it beneath the water's surface, lifted it, streaming with coolness, to his nose. Cradled there, the pungent scent of inland lake exploded against his nostrils, spoke silently of life, decay, continuity. He smiled, dragged deeply on the smell, drew the smoky odor of lake and late Indian autumn into his throat, where he could taste it; into his lungs to hold and savor.

Life . . .

The vigilant, coarse-haired, yellow Labrador-Bouvier mix whose harness lay waiting on the bank plunged joyously through the canal in front of him, playfully snapped a mouthful of liquid at his face. Nat caught water in his hands, squirted it at the spot where the dog's warm breath first eased, then enhanced the chill along his arm. Toby barked at him and bounded away—part of the game—with water flying in his wake.

Zach and Cara would love the game, love the dog, once Nat taught them that harness off meant okay-to-play time, harness on meant Toby was at work.

A sudden splash came from the direction of the bank and a sheet of water cascaded over him when Toby returned and launched his hindquarters sideways, sending another pungent wave and a cheeky *woof* into Nat's face. Spluttering, Nat grabbed for Toby's ruff, caught only a couple of stiff wisps of fur and a bark of canine laughter before the dog tossed another mouthful of water at him and splashed away again. Too late Nat scooped an armful of water at the beast and missed—a fact attested to by the miscreant barking triumphant taunts at him from somewhere out of reach.

"Rotten dog," Nat said with affection.

Toby barked his delighted, "Ha, ha!"

Nat threw back his head and laughed for joy, reveling in the game, the lake and the unexpected late-autumn heat taking pleasure from one of life's ironic quirks: that if he hadn't been in the wrong place at the wrong time what now seemed a lifetime ago, he would never have needed the dog; without the dog, once Amanda had taken Zach and Cara and gone off to marry John, Nat would have forgotten how to laugh. Without laughter, he'd be a bitter, sorry bastard not worth the dust his body would have become if he'd been killed outright almost six years ago the way he'd once wished.

God, he was one lucky son of a gun.

Soon—tomorrow in fact, strange as it seemed to think of Devil's Night as the eve of something so momentous— he would be luckier still, the luckiest Halloween-born bastard who'd ever walked the planet. At 11:00 a.m. precisely, exactly forty years from the moment of his birth, Zach and Cara . . .

All at once happy thoughts deserted him. The smile left his face and he stiffened. Without caring how he knew, Nat realized his parents were hovering on the deck of the house above him, watching, trying not to appear as though they were there to guard him from another misadventure over which they'd have no control. He spun to face the white wall of blankness between himself and them, almost able to see their faces filled with concern, pity, guilt, fear. Phantom eyesight, not unlike an amputee's illusory limbs.

His fists clenched beneath the water. He hated to be watched.

"Nathaniel Hawthorne Crockett." Nat's mother's voice echoed down the long bank, admonishing, cautioning— still underlining his name the way she had when he was six by using all of it. "Be careful. Don't go too far. It's getting dark."

Nat's fists tightened, mouth twisted at the irony. As if nightfall made a difference anymore.

She'd called to him the same way when he was four, eight, twelve, seventeen and twenty-five, as though at thirty-nine he was still some careless kid incapable of finding his nose with a tree-friendly, recycled tissue, some reckless child rushing brazenly forward to get the snot kicked out of him by life. He'd been both a free-lance, then a navy photojournalist, for pity's sake; had survived some of the most violent pieces of the world he could imagine—and some he couldn't. He was one of the most sought after free-lance journalists available even now. That didn't come easy, especially now, but he was old enough, *adult* enough to handle what life had dished out. Particularly now. And hell, he was old enough to be a parent himself.

Was a parent himself.

Carefully he unclenched his fists, unknotting old angers, and let the water sift smoothly, cleanly, through his hands. He was a dad whose ex-wife, Amanda, had taken away his children five and a half years ago, at the same time that an alkali burn had taken away his sight.

An ex-wife who'd told the divorce judge that, despite how much he loved them, how good he was with them, Nat's visits with Zach and Cara should be supervised, since he couldn't actually "watch" his then barely school-age children.

An ex-wife who'd been killed along with her second husband, John—Nat's former friend—by a drunk driver just over a week ago.

An ex-wife who had, at the last, appointed him guardian of his own children in her will.

A few legal tangles had stood in the way of his picking them straight up once he'd gotten the news about Amanda; a few more frustrating tussles had prevented him from collecting them immediately after the funeral—and God, it had fairly killed him to have to walk away from them there. But finally, tomorrow...

With the court's blessings and periodic supervision, Nat, with his driver and his seeing-eye dog and his one-bedroom apartment, would pick them up, bring them home and watch them sightlessly forever.

He hated the way he was finally getting them back, but God, he'd missed his kids.

"Be careful, don't go too far...."

He let the echo of his mother's voice reach him before he turned his back, ashamed of his bitterness, his weakness. He never felt, never behaved this way except when he was here. Despite their best intentions, his parents brought out the worst in him. Seventy years old to his nearly forty, they had begun to need him to parent them sometimes, while needing still to parent him. Especially since the accident. He hated it, but they were his parents, after all. That entitled them to worry, to care.

The same way he loved and worried about Cara and Zach. Would always and forever treat them the way his parents still treated him.

Poor kids.

He grimaced wryly, caught by the irony, trapped in the cycle of the parent-child-parent wheel of life. Hell, where his parents were concerned, he was still a reckless sixteen-year-old taking out the car for the first time. But he hadn't been sixteen for nearly twenty-four years, so, damn it, was it too much to wish that his own parents would do their worrying and caring and nagging somewhere else, and about someone else, like perhaps his younger brother? Was it too much to expect them to acknowledge and respect his capabilities and independence—trust him, finally, the way he'd learned to trust himself in his blindness?

The way Amanda had never done.

Too many emotions were left unresolved by her death.

He squelched canal muck between his toes, listening for the click of the screen door above that meant they weren't watching anymore. Then he took a deep breath and sank beneath the still surface of the canal, into the peace of a blackness where it didn't matter that he couldn't see....

HELEN

Halloween

If she'd known it once, she'd known it forever: God was, at heart, a jokester of the first order. Never in her life had Colonel Helen Brannigan been more aware of that.

She studied the front door of the ivy-colored Queen Anne Victorian manse on Ottawa Street off Huron, threshold to Pontiac, Michigan's historic Seminole Hills. Okay, so here she was—thirty-nine years old with a silver eagle on either shoulder, promoted and decorated for bravery during Desert Storm and afraid to open a little door behind a figurative white picket fence to what awaited her on the other side.

Some heroine she made, huh?

It was a nice house, dark and cool. Not quite her style, perhaps, but her style didn't matter, since she hadn't inherited the house, only the disposal of it and some of its contents as executor of her late ex-husband's estate.

It was the contents of the Queen Anne causing her silent conference with the massive oak doors that hid them.

To ring or not to ring, she wondered moodily. That indeed was the question.

Serenity, not nobility, was the crux of this debate.

Baking banana bread, cutting out Christmas cookies, Thanksgiving turkeys and costume making...going out trick-or-treating tonight! PTA, school field trips with thousands of excited children doing their best to get lost, bingo nights and fun fests...none of the essentials of mothering was up her alley.

Except for love.

Love was good; she could do that. She was, in fact, real good at love, real good at the mother-she-wolf protecting bit. But the real-life, day-to-day, home-and-hearth earth-mother parts of it...

Helen sighed gloomily. There was nothing for it but to admit that Colonel Helen Marie Brannigan, commander of armed men, third of seven sisters, favorite aunt to numerous rug rats of various ages—some of whom now had rug rats of their own—was afraid of a seven-year-old girl.

Elizabeth Jane Maximovich, Libby for short.

Her daughter.

Heart full of qualms, Helen studied the four wavery, leaded panes of glass set at eye level in the door's lovingly kept surface. This wasn't the first time she'd doubted her abilities to handle what lay within the confines of this residence, not the first time she'd wondered at John's sanity in naming her to this position in the event of his—and his second wife's—deaths. But then, it was just like John to choose this sneaky, unopposable means to teach her lessons, expand her horizons—to bring her up short by dropping the daughter he'd taken and fought to keep from her as an infant unceremoniously back into her life.

Lord in heaven, what was she going to do with a child?

Her child. Their child.

Especially one she would always love but, cognizant of her own failings and limitations, had never intended to have?

She hadn't a clue.

For half an instant Helen Brannigan, a woman who'd faced Iraqi artillery without batting an eye and briefly spent time as a prisoner of war without flinching, debated running. What did she know about children—particularly a child she couldn't send home when it fussed?

Not too much, despite growing up with four younger sisters and two older ones, because she'd also had a mother who mothered.

Still mothered, truth be told.

Helen expended another half an instant thinking—wishing?—that perhaps, since seven was supposedly the age of reason, Libby might not really need any more mothering or Halloween costumes or cutout cookies—or anything except guidance, something Helen was *most* adept at providing. Just look at all her nieces and nephews. Not a throwback in the bunch—due, thank you very much, to her erratic but frequent interference in their lives, and despite their sometimes overly conventional parents' efforts to instill them with orthodoxy and decorum in between her visits.

In the shrinking, rapidly changing world they lived in, orthodoxy and decorum were worth less than two cents wholesale, hardly half a plugged nickel on the retail shelf. You had to think creatively to get ahead in this life, be ready to travel and fight, outwit and maneuver, launch a full-scale offensive at your objective at the drop of a whim—live life to its fullest and most-capricious opportunity.

Or so she'd always professed to believe.

Helen sighed. The truth was that mothering, that most conventional and worthwhile of institutions, the true teaching ground of future generations, the proof in the gene pool, was her most stubborn nemesis. Because, like it or not—and the court that had given full custody of Libby to John five and a half years ago hadn't—orthodoxy and decorum had never been hers to command.

A distorted face peeked out through the wavery, leaded glass, and the door to the unknown and studiously feared opened.

"Colonel Brannigan?" a slim, jeans-clad woman inquired.

Helen nodded at the foster care provider and stepped into the house. *Trick or Treat,* she thought.

By all the angels of heavenly glory, she who was about to die saluted you.

NAT

In his sleep he heard the roar, and he woke with his face buried in his pillow, his throat sore from stifled screaming, his lungs strained inside his chest. He knew faded broncos bucked cowboys on his pillowcase, but he couldn't see them, couldn't see the splayed fingers he used to force himself erect.

Sensing movement, the dog at his bedside lifted his head and thumped his tail in greeting. Nat dropped a hand onto Toby's head, gently pulled one soft ear, hoping the animal wouldn't pick up on his distress the way he usually did. Toby nuzzled his fingers, licked his palm, offering affection and calm.

Not enough.

Beside his youth-bed the roar began again. Shaking, Nat made himself sit and listen to the whoosh of air, the tapping sound; made himself smell the dust, put out a hand to feel the blast of heat.

In a minute the roar faded, the tapping receded, dust settled, heat gentled to warmth. Nat shut his eyes and breathed deeply. It was a cool morning and one of his parents had switched the furnace on. When would he be used to it? Sixty-seven months and he still woke up most mornings expecting to see...light, see something... *anything* when he opened his eyes. Expected to go back to work, using the cameras piled on the shelves beside his bed. Expected...

More than he was entitled to, probably.

Unconsciously, he reached out to touch the equipment, absorbing textures in a waking ritual he'd observed since his parents had given him his first Brownie the day he'd turned nine. The cameras were his eyes, better than the twenty-twenty he'd been born with. Through their lenses he'd seen things impossible to see otherwise: beauty and ugliness, unfettered decency and evil. Their shutters had led him to take chances he'd never have taken on his own, to see...

To see. His life, the roots of his soul were housed in sight; without his eyes half his life was gone.

A twinge of anxiety and excitement curled within him. The other half of his life was coming back to him today: Zach and Cara, eleven and nine. It felt like Halloween,

Thanksgiving, New Year's and Christmas all rolled into one, with the trick-or-treating part tonight.

He grinned. He hadn't gone trick-or-treating on his birthday in years. Too grown-up. Hadn't done a lot of things he was looking forward to doing again.

Children made such a wonderful excuse for grown-ups to take pleasure in—and relive—the memories and exploits of their youth.

He opened the watch on his wrist, touched the hands. Hell and damnation, ten-thirty in the morning! Hours later than he'd thought. He had to get dressed, had to get ready, had to go! Just half an hour until the best treats he'd ever gotten in his life could come home with him again.

His fingers convulsed, kneading his knees. His kids were coming home.

He could hardly wait.

In darkness, Nathaniel Hawthorne Crockett sat on the edge of the bed, grabbed for his socks and got ready for his life to begin.

ZACH, CARA, LIBBY, MAX AND JANE...

"I don't care who they are or what the papers say." Zachary Allan Crockett, age eleven, stomped around the playroom, passionate, angry and rebellious. "He didn't even take us home with him after the funeral—"

"He wanted to," his sister, Cara Lauren Crockett, age nine, assured him fiercely. "You saw, he tried. Grandma and Grandpa Sanders wouldn't let him. They made the lawyers tell him he couldn't—"

"If he'd really wanted us, he'd have taken us," Zach retorted. "He wouldn't have let anything stop him."

Elizabeth Jane Maximovich, taller and older than her seven years, put a hand on her stepbrother's shoulder. "Maybe he thought—"

Zach pitched her hand aside. "He didn't *think* anything, he didn't *do* anything, and anyway, what would you know about it? Your *mother* didn't even *come* to the funeral."

"She was in Japan," Libby returned evenly. For pete's sake, they'd covered this territory several times already this morning. She was at the point where she was either going to stamp her foot and *act* seven, or use the martial-arts training Helen had given her for her last birthday and smack Zach good, then get him in trouble for fighting with somebody younger, smaller and more feminine when he hit her back. "It took her three days to get here and then the funeral was over and *your* stupid old grandma and grandpa said she had to wait for the lawyers to talk to her before she could see me because *she* didn't have legal *custody* yet."

"They're *not* stupid," Zach snapped. "*They* were here when Mom and Dad were killed, *they* were here all the time, not my *father*, not your *mother*, just Grandma and Grandpa, so you—"

"Zach," Cara pleaded, eyes tearing with all the sensitivity of her nine years. "Don't fight, please don't fight, there's been enough fighting. That's what we have to stop." She grabbed his arm and hung on when he tried to push her away as he'd done Libby. "You and Libby and I each have a parent still alive, but what about Max and Jane? All they have is *us*. We can't let them split us up—we *won't* let them split us up, but they will if we fight, they *will*. We've lost everything else, but *not* each other, *please*. Maybe we did start out from separate families, but we're *not* separate families now—"

"Family now!" Jane Wallis Crockett-Maximovich agreed firmly. The three-year-old had been named for Amanda's and John's grandmothers when, after much finagling, she'd finally been adopted and brought stateside from Romania as an infant. Nodding vigorously, pleased with both her vocabulary and her ability to participate in the conversation of her elders, she shook a finger and yelled, "No fighting!" She pirouetted in the center of the huddle formed by her siblings, watching the poodle skirt— part of her Halloween costume, which Amanda had finished making the morning before the devastating accident—twirl wide. "Spin!" she shouted, delighted.

"Not now, Jane," Cara said gently, catching her. "Have to talk. Have to decide what to do."

"Do," Jane agreed importantly, though she was somewhat puzzled by Cara's seriousness. "Decide what?"

"Decide what?" John Maximilian Crockett-Maximovich, age five, echoed, his Serbian features screwed tight with anxiety. Max was the most-recent addition to the Crockett-Maximovich tribe—his adoption had been finalized only six months previously—and his English, although progressing at breakneck speed, suffered from a few holes. In his turbulent lifetime, he'd survived the Soviet breakup, civil war, the loss of one set of parents and the conditions of an overcrowded orphanage, only to be found by, then lose, a second set of parents. He clung tightly to Cara's hand, a thin, brown-haired little boy in serious need of reassurance. "Please, don't wanna leave."

Cara put protective arms around him. "Nobody's going to leave. I'm not sure how, but we're all staying right here in our house. Nobody can make us leave."

"Darn right." Libby—very much Helen's Libby despite the fact that she'd spent her formative years to date primarily influenced by her father—planted her feet, hands on hips, and scowled ferociously.

From the wildly curly, shoulder-length, black-brown hair to the high, wide, freckle-smattered cheekbones, stubborn chin, determined mouth and brook-no-back-talk green eyes, she was every bit Helen's childhood duplicate: independent, single-minded, as tough and infuriatingly complex as she was transparent, and hell-bent on doing what she was absolutely sure was right regardless of what her elders, with their wider and wiser worldview, might decide. In short, Elizabeth Jane Maximovich was everything her maternal grandmother, Julia Block Brannigan, might ever have wished on Helen to avenge all the transgressions Helen herself had committed under Julia's parentage and then some.

"So, what are we going to do?" Zach, the smart, tough enforcer, perfectly suited for sergeant but who would never make a general, asked. He checked the clock on the playroom wall—a big blue Cookie Monster. It was babyish by his advanced standards, but Max and Jane loved it, and he tolerated it for them. "They'll be here any minute."

"Oh, don't worry," Libby, the general who went to war filled with the knowledge that there would be casualties and who relished the thought of leaving some, said serenely. A serious student of the Pee Wee Scouts, Nate the Great and the Bobbsey Twins literature all in one, she pulled up her shirt and extracted the two crumpled sheets of heavy legal paper from their hiding place against her stomach. "I'll think of something."

For the first time that Halloween morning, Zach, Cara, Max and Jane smiled.

HELEN AND NAT

"Joint custody?" Helen peered blankly at the woman in the conservative designer pinstripe who posed beside the leather wing chair to the left of the fireplace, a sheaf of legalese dripping through her hands. "We've never been divorced from, or even married to, each other. How can there be joint custody?"

She turned to look at the tall, rambling, active-looking man seated in the deep-cushioned leather chair a third of the way around the heavy glass coffee table from her.

Rough, long-fingered hands contracted on the arms of his chair; opaque blue eyes stared unseeing at the woman holding John and Amanda's will; the generous mouth tightened. Helen's pulse accelerated slightly. It had been over five years since she'd caught more than a passing glimpse of him—before his accident, at the joint "shipping out" party Amanda had thrown for them before Saudi. Who'd known then how far they were really being shipped? Out of their country, out of their homes, their marriages, their children's lives ... But never had Helen seen Nathaniel Hawthorne Crockett appear less at ease with any of his limitations—visual, emotional or otherwise—or less hampered by them.

And sighted or not, there was still no doubt about it: Amanda's ex was gorgeous and had always been gorgeous, pure and simple. From the top of his shaggy, wheat-colored hair to the tips of his beat-up hiking boots, and all points in between.

All points.

Helen fidgeted with the hem of her uniform jacket. Like it or not, there was no harm in feeling that hop, skip and jump in her veins. It wasn't like feeling her pulse puddle laxly around her feet every time she'd seen Nat while she and John were still married. And then it wasn't like she'd ever done anything about the sensation—or even considered doing anything about the awareness. She wouldn't have. It wasn't part of her ethics, her morality or her upbringing. Brannigan girls did *not* pursue other women's men, married or not, in any way, shape or form. Not by thought, word or deed. Ever.

Period.

On the other hand, Brannigan girls didn't always have complete control over their pulse rates. Some things—a great many things, the unfortunate truth be told—had a tendency to take them by surprise. Consequently they often felt guilty for things they didn't do. The refrain went something like this: *Maybe if I hadn't felt, then John wouldn't have done...*

No accounting for culpability sometimes.

Especially not when it was bred in the bone.

Helen jerked the front of her jacket firmly into place. This was neither the time nor the place. Grown-ups got to choose what they did about attractions and where they suffered them. That was the point of outgrowing adolescence. She looked at John and Amanda's attorney.

"I was under the impression arrangements for the children were already sorted out. I just came to pick up my daughter, Libby. Elizabeth. I have to be back in Washington next Monday. I didn't come to stay, only to take care of her and see to the estate. I assumed..." Helen stopped, squirmed imperceptibly, revised the partially spoken thought. No need to remind herself what *assume* translated to. Especially when she'd apparently assumed wrong. "I've hired a nanny, enrolled her in school...."

From his vantage point near the front bay window—the faint stirring of cool air on his cheek, the clean scent of live greenery and loam and the fact that Amanda had once described the room to him told where he was—Nat listened to Helen's voice, heard beneath the disciplined cadence the nuance of panic she'd almost successfully hidden. Long time since he'd heard that voice, the crisp contralto far better at snapping commands than suggesting music, the hidden undercurrent of wry humor never totally absent.

Long and bitter time since he'd somehow had the gall to blame her for Amanda's defection. After all, if Helen hadn't been so career oriented; if she'd objected to her Kuwait posting; if she'd stayed home and kept her husband happier—or at least kept track of him; if she hadn't been so damned attractive to Nat himself, and Amanda so acutely all-seeing...

But what had happened between John and Amanda wasn't Helen's fault at all, not Nat's, not the military's for requiring their services for so many months so far from home. It was John and Amanda who'd made the choices, John and Amanda who'd comforted and supported each other through their loneliness, who'd discovered how alike their goals were, their needs, their plans, their ideas of what made up a family....

Who'd discovered how poorly suited they each were to their own spouses...

Yeah, well. History. It changed nothing. He still remembered Colonel Helen Brannigan when she'd been merely Major Brannigan in vivid, vibrant detail: tall, imposing, sometimes lost when she wasn't hiding inside her uniform; a curly-haired, green-eyed brunette with fair, black-Irish skin and high, surprisingly delicate cheekbones connected to one tough-cookie-stubborn jawline—an effect almost immediately ruined by the laugh dimples set to either side of her wide mouth, two on the left, one on the right. She was the only female he'd ever met who'd made him doubt that Amanda was the one-and-only woman in the world for him. Shook him up pretty good when he'd realized it, too.

Rattled him tenfold more when he'd found himself wishing, even for an instant, that he was the kind of guy whose conscience would allow him to step out on Amanda in order to poach another man's wife.

Made him turn around and run when he'd surprised Helen with the same look on her face—quickly masked in horrified shame—when he'd danced with her, at John's urging, at her and John's second-wedding-anniversary party. Nat and Helen had each made sure not to get anywhere near the other since.

Like it or not, he knew well enough that what took place between a man and a woman often had no basis in logic or persuasion, reality or anything resembling it. He was his own best case in point: while his heart and his eyes had recognized what he wanted in Amanda, it was his soul that knew Helen—still knew her, damn it. It was his body that even now betrayed its affinity with hers when she was in the vicinity, his spirit that hammered at his brain, demanding that he seek her out when this meeting was through.

His mind that had once made him run far and fast in the opposite direction, only to wind up here, now, full circle around the table from her, with nothing but children and history remaining between them.

Nat dropped a hand to where Toby lay quiet and alert beside his chair, absently petting the dog's furry head. Life was a lot more complicated than the black-and-white rights and wrongs he'd grown up with. And if his reaction to Helen Brannigan simply being in the same room, the lawyer intimating something beyond simple custody and the mutinous tones he could hear of children arguing in whispers somewhere in the wings were indicators, then life in all its glory was about to become far more involved than he chose to imagine.

And quite possibly a good deal more interesting, too.

Smothering a grin, Nat sat forward slightly in the leather wing chair and paid attention.

Across the table from him, paying attention, too, Helen caught Nat's half grin and winced. Whatever was coming, she'd get no help from *that* quarter. The dratted man had a true sense of the ridiculous—and got a kick out of it, to boot.

That was her one true remaining weakness when it came to men. Because the bottom line was, gorgeous could cut it for only so long if a man had no sense of humor. Too bad she'd realized this weakness in herself too late to avoid the mistake she'd made in getting swept away by John.

Firmly she yanked her attention away from Nat and past mistakes, back to the discussion.

"Believe me, Colonel Brannigan." The lawyer held up a soft, manicured hand that somehow made Helen nervous. No good ever came out of a situation where someone had to hold up a hand to her to make a point. "I'm sorry if you misunderstood the nature of my correspondence. I'm truly not here to stonewall either you or Mr. Crockett in taking custody of your separate children and getting on with your lives. I'm here only to discharge my duties to this estate, and see to the welfare of *all* the children. And Mr. and Mrs. Maximovich were most specific about this last point. I did, however, think they had discussed all the, er, particulars with you first."

She paused, looking first at Helen, then at the keenly listening Nat. Glanced uncomfortably away when she realized Nat couldn't acknowledge her pointed look. Colored when his mouth tightened and he raised a mocking brow in recognition of the nature of her pause. The man didn't even have the grace to wear heavy dark sunglasses to remind people of his . . . visual limitations.

"Our children's welfare is why Colonel Brannigan and I are here, Ms. Frye." Nat crossed his legs and arranged himself comfortably, carelessly, deep in his chair. "Speaking for myself, I hate the circumstances under which I'm getting my children back, but the situation can't be changed. If we can get on with this? I'd like to be able to . . ." he searched for the right phrasing " . . . get things headed toward normal again for Zach and Cara as quickly as possible. I'm sure Colonel Brannigan wants the same for Libby."

Geneva Frye nodded, colored again when she caught herself, cleared her throat and continued, "I believe you each were granted only visitation in the original custody decrees." She waited for two nods, got none, swallowed. She was out of her depth big-time. "You each fought for more, but neither received it. I've been . . . empowered . . . to offer you the chance you both wanted five years ago to be with your children full-time."

"But there are strings," Helen supplied darkly.

Nat jacked an elbow up on the arm of his chair and covered a grin at the expression in her voice. Before life had changed for them both, John had once told him that what Helen hated most in the world was anything with strings attached—particularly if they were leading strings. A third of the way around the table, she cleared her throat; and Nat heard the glare in the harumph, as plainly as he might have once seen it in her eyes.

Helen didn't give in to the childish urge to kick the former Captain Crockett in the ankle under the table. What the dickens did her pulse find so fanatically attractive about this man, anyway? Besides his ill-timed sense of humor, his physique and that indefinable something that could turn her heart on its ear in a pulse beat.

Geneva Frye inclined her head, gathering composure from familiar ground. "As you say, strings." She consulted her notes. "The...dilemma...here is that Mr. and Mrs. Maximovich wanted the children—all five children—"

"Five?" Helen demanded.

The lawyer nodded. "As I'm sure you must be aware, they adopted a boy and a girl in the last couple of years—"

"Yes, but..." Helen began, then subsided. Clearly there were a few things she'd neglected to take into consideration.

The clipped nod came again. "Five children," Ms. Frye resumed, "and Mr. and Mrs. Maximovich wanted them all to stay together. It was very important to them to maintain this family unit in its entirety—give the children one another to count on even if they had no one else. It's also what the children want. They asked me this morning to let you know that."

Ignoring the implications, Nat prompted, "The particulars?"

"The adopted children—" again she consulted the legal parchment in front of her "—Maximilian and Jane, have no living parents. Mr. and Mrs. Sanders—your former in-laws, I believe, Mr. Crockett—have requested that our firm...explore the possibility of them obtaining full legal guardianship of all five children with intent to adopt. As you know, the Sanderses were first available and became temporary guardians on the deaths of your ex-spouses. From the court's standpoint they are still relatively young, in excellent health, are well-known to *all* the children and have a tremendous rapport with them, as well as having maintained regular contact with the family throughout the years—"

She held up two fingers when Helen would have objected. "—Which is not to say that you, Colonel Brannigan, or you, Mr. Crockett, have neglected the children or failed to maintain as much visitation as you were allowed. From the emotional standpoint, however, your children have not lived with either of you for any length of time in over five years. They have, on the other hand, spent a great deal of time with Mr. and Mrs. Sanders, especially while Mr. and Mrs. Maximovich were in Europe preparing to adopt Jane, and then later, Maximilian. They are, therefore, in a far better position should they in fact choose to seek custody."

"*But,*" Nat interjected, impatient to confirm what he already suspected.

"But?" Helen echoed uncertainly. *But this won't be that simple,* she answered herself. Of course not. Not when John Maximovich had anything to do with the will.

The lawyer smiled tightly. "But," she replied with a nod.

Chapter 2

All Saints Day

For being only three letters long, *but* was one hell of a big word when it held your entire life hostage. Or, actually, nine entire lives, if you counted Nat's mettlesome—and yes, meddlesome, too—ex-outlaws.

And that put it mildly, to say the least.

But if you choose to contest the custody arrangements and drag *all* the children through the hell of a custody battle and destroy their psyches for all time...

But if you choose to move into the house—separate bedrooms, separate living arrangements, of course—and be supervised by the courts for six months to a year, share parenting for all five children, share expenses, disciplining duties, responsibilities...

But if you choose to change your life completely...

The first day and night and day were rough.

"That's not the way my real mom does...did it." Zach, rebellious, tortured, torturing. No tears, because that wouldn't be manly. *"I don't want you."*

"My Grammy Sanders does that better than you." Cara, trying to give Helen and Nat the benefit of the doubt, trying to smile around the ache in her eyes. Letting Helen know the oatmeal she made without swirling strawberry jam through it to look like Mickey Mouse wasn't up to speed. *"Maybe we could call her and she could tell you what she does."*

"I want Mama!" Max, adamant. No tears, no screams, just huddled and cowering in the middle of the night, deep in a corner beneath John's heavy leather-topped desk in the library, holding tight to one of Grammy Sanders's afghans and the worn, well-loved stuffed dog Amanda had made for him. *"Tell my daddy to come."*

"Mother, didn't that army teach you to do anything?" Libby, exasperated and rolling her eyes, holding up leggings that had once been kelly green and were now a somewhat indecipherably streaky red-green-black-brown. *"I mean really, Mum, even I know you have to check the setting on the back of the washing machine and make sure to wash colors in cold water."*

"Why don't you do the wash then?"

"Because you're almost forty years old and Grama Julia says it's about time you learn."

Helen gritted her teeth. Oh, good. Thanks, Ma.

"Mama!" Screamed and sobbed as only a three-year-old can scream and sob: pulled up from the bottom of her toes, painful in volume and pitch, a helpless ache for the listener's heart. *"Mama! Where's my mama? I want my daddy."*

"Shh, Janie, hush." Nat, crooning, gentle. Holding Jane tightly after her restless nap, sensitive fingers stroking her tear-stained face. Gesturing toward where he felt Helen standing. Unwillingly mindful of her presence. Re-

luctantly glad he didn't have to find out whether or not he was equipped to handle this alone. *"We're here, I'm here, shh."*

"You're not Mama! You're not Daddy. You're not, not, not." Jane, hitting at them both, breaking away to run to the encompassing comfort that was Zach and Cara, Libby and Max. *"I don't want you. Go away, go 'way, go 'way!"*

"Sweetheart."

Helen, trying to reach out, to be kind. Not knowing how to do any of it, make any of it better. Wishing she herself could scream and sob so Nat would rock her, comfort her. Wishing she could run to her own mother and cower behind Julia's skirts until the world went away or she could figure out how to handle a crisis that concerned the everyday drama and tragedies of real life rather than the paper protocol of national security.

Wishing she could find humor in the situation the way her office staff had when she'd called and told them to sign her out on an open-ended extended-family-emergency leave and knock off the "real mother" jokes.

"Your mama can't—"

"Just get away from her. Leave her alone." Zach, fierce and protective, stepping between the four younger children and Helen and Nat. *"She doesn't* want *you. She doesn't* need *you."* Turning to herd the others ahead of him into the playroom, pulling the door shut behind him. *"Neither do we."*

Slam.

Helplessly Helen stared at Nat, her shoulders slumped, hands hanging uselessly at her sides. For a moment Nat's face was as blank as his eyes, then his mouth tightened, hands fisted. The dog, Toby, unharnessed and off duty beside him, nudged Nat's fist with his nose. The fingers opened slowly, fanned over Toby's head.

"Show me the door," he ordered softly.

Startled, Helen took an automatic step forward, but the dog had already stood and slid his ruff under Nat's hand, and was soon guiding him to the playroom door. Nat spread his fingers over the wood, slid his hands down until he found the doorknob. Tried it. Swore beneath his breath.

Locked.

"They need time to adjust," Helen offered weakly. Criminy Moses, didn't they all. "Maybe if we leave them be for a while..." Wasn't that what Grandma Josephine used to say? If you ignore it, the thing you want will come to hand? The philosophy had worked to one extent and another with the guys at the Point, with all the other men who'd held the power to let Helen become who she wanted to be.

"If we ignore them, they'll think we don't care." Nat sounded like he knew. He knocked on the door. "Zach? Cara? Please, I just want to help—"

"Take a number," a child's muffled voice advised.

The lock rattled; the door opened wide enough to allow Libby's head egress. "Sorry, no adults, no calls, we're in a meeting."

"But don't you need—"

"We'll get back to you," Libby announced firmly, shutting the door and locking it again.

Nat's jaw dropped and his throat emitted a sound of incredulity. He faced the disturbingly seductive scent of Helen. *Not the time or the place.* The thought echoed years past, time spent warning himself against her even after his divorce, while Amanda and John were still alive. *Never a good time or place...* He beat distraction back.

"Your daughter," he managed to say finally, inadequately.

An accusation if ever Helen had heard one.

She drew herself up and inclined her head modestly—a useless gesture, since he couldn't see it—accepting aspersion as tribute. "So I'm told," she acknowledged. The pride in her voice was evident even to her. No sense denying the obvious.

"Do something about her."

"Why?" Helen's foot tapped the floor, to Nat's perceptive ears sounding more as if she'd said, *"Like what, hmm?"* "She's never lied to me before."

"What's that got to do with it?"

Helen viewed him as though he were daft—another wasted activity. She sighed. Five frightened kids—make that four frightened kids and one Libby—and an overly sexy, blind partner to get used to all in the same day. Was God never going to allow her to fall into anything by halves? "She said they'd get back to us, and they will."

Nat's mouth tightened. It was his turn to foot tap.

Helen sighed again. "Oh, fine." No gracious acquiescence here. She stepped to the door, rattled the knob. Didn't feel the warmth of Nat so near her back, or so she told herself.

This wasn't the first time she'd lied to herself about what she did or did not feel about Nat.

"Elizabeth Jane Maximovich, open this door this instant or I will get a screwdriver and take it off its hinges."

There was a moment's considered silence. Then her daughter said, "The hinges are in here."

Helen gritted her teeth. Who the hell had taught the child political one-upmanship tactics? Oh, yeah—she took a sheepish puff of breath—that would be her. "Yes, but there are screws in the lock plate out here."

"So?" If logic didn't work, fall back on childish response. Libby was, after all, a child.

Exasperated, Helen shut her eyes—the classic long-suffering-mother response, if only she knew it. "Elizabeth Jane!"

Libby's sigh was audible even through the solid wood. "Oh, all right." After a slight clatter, the door cracked open. "What?"

Helen looked at Nat. "What?" she asked.

It was Nat's turn to be nonplussed. Only a moment ago, he'd known exactly why he wanted to follow the children into the playroom—to comfort and console and make sure they'd come out again. But all he said lamely was, "I just want to make sure everything's all right."

"Fine," Libby said, none too reassuringly. "Jane doesn't like strangers after her nap. We've fallen back to regroup—"

Helen cringed at the military terminology. Perhaps she'd spent more time with Libby than she'd realized over the years.

"—So go away for now—"

"Libby."

"—And I'll let you know if you're wanted." She looked up at Helen, green eyes suddenly all anxious, vulnerable little girl. "Okay, Mum? Please, Mum? It'll be better later, I promise. Please?"

Helen felt Nat slump behind her, caving in to her daughter's request before she had a chance to. "Okay." She nodded. "We'll be downstairs—"

"Talking," Libby suggested.

"Oh, undoubtedly," Helen agreed darkly. "But what I *was* going to say before you interrupted was that I'll fix dinner—"

"Not your chili." Libby shuddered. "Jane won't eat spicy stuff and Max doesn't trust you not to feed him something nasty yet and Zach and Cara only like chili made with tomato soup—"

"Fine," Helen interrupted. "No chili." The next question got away from her before she could catch it. "Anything else?"

To her right, Nat snorted, and the dog groaned as if in agreement: she'd left herself open for this one.

Libby deliberated for hardly a moment. "Chicken," she said. "We won't eat chicken. Or peas. Cara hates peas, and you have to make a good impression if you want this to work. Oh, and broccoli, cauliflower, tomato aspic, lima beans, instant pudding, store-bought pizza, anything with tuna fish—"

"Save the dolphin," Nat muttered.

"Exactly," Libby agreed, and went on as though he hadn't interrupted. "Lemon cookies, fish with bones in, ham with raisins..."

The list was long and formidable. Nat took Helen's arm. Fingers shaping themselves to fit just above her left elbow, curving around the fabric of her sleeve, sent warmth seeping through the barrier. Shock rocked them, sent jittery tremors through nerves and pulses, flaunted awareness where it had no right to be. Thoughts rose and hissed rudely between them, shared and disturbing: *No time for this, no place for this, no need for this, no hope for this...*

After a staggered instant of indrawn breath, a moment where their faces turned toward each other—Helen's revealing but unseen, Nat's eye-opening but as quickly masked—she gathered her senses about her, turned blindly and moved them toward the stairs. There she instinctively paused and placed Nat's hand on the banister, the textbook sighted-escort gesture.

Reaction was a book of its own.

Sensation skittered down the slope of already jangled emotions, sent them teetering toward some disastrous brink, linked physically at the same time they were left alone inside themselves, the old recognition renounced but roaring around their ears: *I know you, I want you, come take me....*

Not a word passed between them—the only saving grace in this whole abominable, awkward and uncomfortable situation. If she'd spoken, he'd have known exactly where her mouth was and shut her up with his. If he'd spoken, there was no telling what he'd say among the multitudes of things he shouldn't.

Swallowing, Nat slid his hand out from beneath Helen's, lightened his grip on her arm. God, oh God, just what he needed, to have life reduced to this: a constant physical ache for the carnal satisfaction his body told him he'd find inside Helen's, warring with the crushing emotional need to be the best father he could be to all five of the children who lived in this house. And to have to depend on the woman who turned both his conscience and his libido to putty, whose husband had married his wife... He felt Helen tremble and sway slightly toward him, then grab hold of herself and turn her attention back to the stairs. And to know that within a heartbeat, a single touch of his hand, his mouth on hers...

To know with misgiving that she wanted him, too.

Behind them, Libby's voice continued to chant the "don't like" litany. Concentrating on the hum of the child instead of the thrum in their veins, they descended the stairs.

Dinner was cheese pizza and orange pop from the Little Caesar's down the street, with chocolate-chip-cookie-dough ice cream for dessert. Zach was put out by the lack of pepperoni, but everyone else ate—if not with vigor, then at least without complaint. Jane fell asleep in the middle of her ice cream and didn't wake when Helen gently cleaned her up, then carted her off to bed. Cara and Libby dragged along after her to make sure Helen did everything she was supposed to before turning off Jane's light.

Looking at the three of them before she left the room, Helen felt her frightened heart tug, felt something fierce and determined wedge itself into the gap the tug created. *Mother...* The word whispered through her senses, gummed up the springs in the biological clock she'd ignored since John had won Libby away from her. The clock creaked awake and chimed: *cuckoo, cuckoo, cuckoo... time, time, time...*

She panicked. *God, I'm not ready. I don't know how....*

Too bad, the clock retorted. *Too late. They're here, you're here, it's time....*

She *wanted* it to be time.

Back downstairs, she spotted Nat in one of the big chairs near the fireplace, reading aloud from a children's book written in braille about a dragon who kept getting bigger and bigger until people stopped saying there was no such thing as dragons, then the dragon shrank until it was the size of a cat and lived happily with its new family. At first Helen thought he was simply reading for the exercise. Then she saw Zach pressed tight against a wall near the library door. He was listening hard, his face pillowed on his knees. His shoulders heaved slightly and a light snuffling sound seemed to issue from somewhere in the depths of his chest. It stopped when Helen approached, and she looked down at him, but he glared up at her through defiant, teary eyes, daring her to even try to take Amanda's place. She knew she couldn't, so she went in search of Max.

He was hard to find, but she finally located him curled up behind Nat's chair, fingers twined in Toby's fur, head butted tight against the patient dog's soft neck. Nat smiled once, lopsidedly, acknowledging her presence, but went on reading, his voice quiet and even and soothing. Without changing tones, he inclined his head almost imperceptibly toward the door. Helen looked. From the corner of her eye, she saw Libby and Cara inch into the room and settle into corners near the dog and Max, saw Cara lean toward her father's chair, then pull back, lean in again as though trying to decide which way was better. Carefully, Nat put out a hand toward his daughter, touched her hair. For an instant Cara relaxed, let him slide wayward hair out of her face. Then she pulled away and flattened herself on the floor beside Toby, not quite ready to accept more from Nat.

Sucking in a breath that felt suspiciously full of tears she hadn't even been aware she knew how to shed, Helen retreated to her bathroom, locked the door and cried.

Transitions are the pits, she and Nat agreed later over mugs of espresso so strong it should have wired them to the gills for days to come. But it didn't; they were too distracted, too out of their depth. Too emotionally exhausted. The hot cups warmed their hands, offered a scent of something familiar over which to share...neither was sure what. Long silences, furtive sighs, awkwardness...when it came right down to it, they had little to say. Too much to absorb, and too little sponge left to soak it up.

Helen wished they could exchange glances of support, shore each other up without words.

Nat wished he could touch her face and read her mind, decipher what expressions accompanied the nuances in her voice.

Without common biology to fall back on, they were expected to be parents of the same children, after all. Strangers in unknown company. Strangers with shared history and desires to be sure, but strangers nevertheless.

To each other and the children who stood between them.

If they didn't know enough about themselves to trust each other, how could children who'd lost everything they'd ever known begin to trust them?

And in the midst of everything else, between the two of them lurked that powerful, frightening something—intimacy, awareness, recognition—from which they'd long ago run away.

* * *

It wasn't a great deal different the next day or the day after that . . . and so on.

They tried, but it was a learning process Helen and Nat needed to get right from the start. They had no time to learn as they went; they had no choice but to try to sop up the lessons as they came. Their lives and concerns centered on the children, on the process of gaining trust; their conversations dealt with necessities. . . .

"We're out of milk."

"Did you find the bread?"

"Do you think it's all right for Zach to spend all his time playing video games?"

"I found this in Libby's dresser . . . ."

"Does the dog need to go out?"

. . . And so on, short and clipped. Not unfriendly, merely to the point. There wasn't time to skirt around the edges, come to terms with the underlying heat of their proximity to one another. They were parents without benefit of courtship rituals, dumped together in separate bedrooms without a private place, or a private way, to get to know each other.

Single parents of a group of children who considered themselves, but not Helen and Nat, family.

And so it went.

The children returned to school, to preschool, to routine and faces more familiar to them than Helen's and Nat's. After some debate, Nat, too, returned to the technical photography and darkroom classes he taught parttime at the local community college to fill in the gaps periodically left when his journalistic assignments were sluggish. Routine resumed, he hoped, would make them all easier with each other, give them something to talk about at the end of the day.

Give him air to breathe that was not filled with the eternally unsettling taste of Helen.

Only Helen's normal daily routine remained out of her reach. Which meant she had three hours almost every morning while Jane was in preschool and Max at kindergarten to rearrange furniture—her version of nervous chain smoking—and reflect on her inadequacies, then three hours nearly every afternoon spent alone with Max and Jane having those shortcomings illustrated to her, until the three older children arrived home shortly before four to tell her what she lacked. And that was only on the days she didn't drive the car pool. On car-pool days there were always extra kids around to let her know how far out of her depth she was.

Then, of course, there was Nat she had to get used to. Who knew there'd be so many rules to follow just because he happened to be blind? Who knew logic would have nothing to do with anything when he happened to get near her—in the same house, two floors apart? And who knew that living with a dog wouldn't be such a terrible thing?

Still, life went on regardless of what she did or didn't know.

Parenting and patience came more naturally to Nat than they did to Helen, perhaps, but even he was handicapped by limitations he hadn't expected. The scrutinized time he'd spent with Zach and Cara over the years hadn't prepared any of them for one-on-one, day in, day out, with no Amanda and John waiting to sort out the pieces when Nat and his children parted. He realized with an ache in his heart that the time he'd had with them before now had been fun time, limited time, presents and fa la la and dreams of the future, without remembering that dreams and reality are often two separate things and that meshing them was, more often than not, a whole lot of work. None of it had prepared him for this.

But it would work, he assured himself and Toby fiercely, night after night when he went, exhausted and torn, to his bed at the rear, southern side of the second floor. He would make it work. No matter what. And little by little, things would get better. They had to. An increment at a time, the children—all of them—would get used to him, to Helen, to the current state of things. They would learn to accept, to move forward, to trust. They had to.

No matter *what.*

On the front, north end of the second floor and completely overwhelmed, Helen couldn't whip up the mental energy to think that far ahead. A day at a time was the only way she knew how to play it—just like her first weeks in the army, at the Point. Getting through, getting by was the name of the game until the day arrived when she'd figured out the rules. And if there weren't any rules here, that would be fine, too, as long as she knew there weren't. Then she could make them up as she went along, change them if they didn't work, organize a plan.

Organization and preparedness were the keys to life.

After nearly twenty years as an army officer, with all the rules neatly written down—which didn't mean she always followed them, only that she had a list in front of her that she could ignore when she chose—she was lost without a plan.

What was it she'd thought on Halloween, standing on the porch waiting for someone to answer the door? That she was just a little concerned about how well she'd do as a single parent to the child actually born of her loins? That she was, in fact, scared to death of the prospect of failing and screwing up one child's life as a military, move-around mom? And now she had to figure out, what?—how not to screw up the lives of *five* children, while trying to get her military career shifted to *Michigan,* which was not exactly the hub of army life or promotional opportunities for a recently promoted, full-bird colonel with her eye on eventually achieving a generalship.

Which wasn't what this was about by a long shot. Her career was merely a sidebar, a comment on the moment.

In the blink of an eye, the crunch of steel and fabric and bone, all their lives had changed—Nat's, the children's, hers—and there was nothing any of them could do to change things back, retrieve moments that were lost. All they could do was forge onward as best they might. But with her? A mother impersonator? Of *five?*

She rubbed bleary, sleepless eyes with shaking hands. Lord-oh-Lord-oh-Lord. When John Maximovich made the effort, he sure did know how to wind up and throw the ball hard. She should have figured she'd have to face her fears eventually—whether she was prepared to or not.

But as... Colonel Mom?

Propping her elbows on the vanity desk beside her new bed, Helen stared at the face the mirror reflected back to her in the moonlight. Sucked in a tight breath and let it out slowly. Well, nothing else for it. Between here and the third floor were five children who needed a mother—or a reasonable facsimile thereof—and needed Nat. She wasn't what they were looking for, but, God willing, for the next six months or better she was what they had. She and Nat and the psychological observers and the courts and the Sanderses, with the proof at the end to be found smack-dab in the middle of whatever kind of pudding the baking period brought.

A good pudding, she hoped. Thick and rich and not soupy, with five mostly happy kids floating in the middle of it and Nat in the bow shouting directions and her at the rudder steering around the lumps he couldn't see.

Oh, God—she slumped, head in her hands—she'd gone completely punchy. She didn't even know enough about kids and kitchens to be able to come up with a simple analogy. And as far as desserts and puddings were concerned, Jell-O Instant Pudding, add milk, shake and ready to eat in five minutes was about as good as she got.

Just her luck it was near the top of Libby's list of things the kids wouldn't eat. Which meant she had a lot to learn.

Big surprise, huh? But so did they.

Damn good thing, then, that determination and stubbornness were two of the things she was best at.

And damn good thing God kept a special eye on children and fools.

Especially fools who wanted to slink down the hall and crawl into bed with Nat.

Chapter 3

Still rattled after almost a week to get used to being here, being the "mom,"—currently, for reasons she preferred not to recall, synonymous with pariah—Helen stood in the middle of the laundry room surrounded by mountains of multicolored clothing with nary a dry-cleanable garment in sight. Her pen wavered above the grocery list.

"Toilet paper, milk, bread, cream cheese, pudding, a packet of shoes for My Pretty Pony..."

She squinted and tapped the pen clicker against her teeth. She'd forgotten something important; she could feel it in her bones. "...Hamburger, hot dogs, soup, frozen waffles, frozen pot pies, Hamburger Helper, fluoride rinse, antiplaque rinse, cookies, fruit, a wedding dress for Malibu Barbie..."

Nope, she couldn't think what it was. Ah well, she decided philosophically, it couldn't have been important. Well, at least not *too* important.

She hoped.

She shrugged. If they didn't write it on the list, she couldn't very well be expected to know they needed it, could she? She'd simply pick up extras of everything—except the Pony shoes and Barbie clothes, and she was only buying those because she was so entranced that Cara and Jane had come out of their shells and offered to trust her enough not only to ask her to buy something for them but to find the right things to boot. Better than standing here stagnating in front of this apparently personality endowed washing machine—and a bitchy personality it had, too—waiting for cows to fly.

Libby, of course—*her* Libby—didn't do dolls. She was into other things: planning chaos, sorting mayhem, telling her mother how to do all the things her mother didn't know how to do—speaking of which...

Yawning and guarded, dressed in a Tasmanian Devil T-shirt and a pair of plaid flannel boxers, Zach stepped through the laundry-room door.

"Colonel..."

Helen winced at his use of her title. Damned rank sounded too blasted military, too tightassed and stringent to be used by children in their own home—especially when The Observers were around to hear it.

She could just imagine these young, idealistic, usually single and childless social workers sending each other skeptical glances, making notes in their reports: *Not integrating well. Poor adjustment to situation. Recommend more-frequent visits.* And this in a state whose programs served as a national model for the preservation of The Family—read parents with biological offspring—at all costs and in all situations in order to maintain a trimmer state budget under the compassionate guise of "Families First." Helen only hoped that the ideal of family conservation would work to advantage for her, Nat and the rug rats—to which end she'd been trying unsuccessfully for days to come up with something for the children to call her besides the "Mom" everyone but Libby strenuously avoided.

Naturally, Nat was already "Nat" and sometimes "Dad," but even Max and Jane had begun to address Helen as "Kern'l." As though she were some forbidding Dickensian entity—which, if the reactions of her nieces, nephews and Libby to her when she was being her sternest were to be believed, she was pretty sure she wasn't. *They* had a tendency to giggle.

"Colonel, have you done the wash yet?" Zach's tone was faintly accusing, faintly hopeful, as though something as meaty as trust hung in the balance. Perhaps it did. "I need some clean school pants."

Helen sighed. Zach might not know what to call her, but at least he was speaking to her. That in itself was a vast improvement over yesterday.

"Ah..." Dubiously she viewed the jumble of laundry—some of it clean, most of it dirty—on the floor around her. School pants. Now where had she... Light dawned; she looked at Zach. "Navy blue Dockers with reinforced knees, right?"

"Yeah."

"Thought so." She opened the dryer, plucked out the needed item, feeling like a magician producing white doves from thin air. "These do?"

"Those're Libby's."

"Oh." Deflated. Magic exposed for the trickery it was.

Zach held out a hand, almost conciliatory. "Almost" being the key. "She needs some, too, so I'll take 'em anyway. What about mine?" A hint of belligerence mixed with the accusation this time. "And Cara's?"

Helen could almost hear the unspoken *or didn't you wash clothes for anybody but your own kid?* circling like a buzzard over road kill.

It didn't help that she was only *almost* certain that she had. With all this parochial-school navy blue to wash, who could tell?

She reached into the dryer, scooped up another handful of dark blue. *Be pants and be big,* she prayed, and brought the items into the light. A school uniform vest and two pairs of pants—each in one piece and of one not-even-bleach-dabbled color. Zach took them from her, sorted the tangle of cotton legs and Orlon knit.

"Mine, Cara's, mine," he announced finally, examining vest, pants, pants. "This'll do. Thank you, Colonel." He turned to go.

"You're welcome." Helen hesitated, called him back. "Ah, Zach?"

He looked at her. "Yes, ma'am?"

She made a face at the formality. "Well, I was just thinking that, um, 'Colonel' and 'ma'am' are a little too, um, *protocol* for, er, family use, don't you think?"

Zach shook his head. "My mom told me I should always show respect for my elders, whether I respect them or not. And my dad—I mean, my *other* dad, not this one—"

John, Helen thought, surprised by the accompanying pain.

"—Said military people should always be addressed by rank, not name."

"Well, that's true, but—" she clutched the grocery list, not wanting to think what he'd implied about respect—or his lack of it for her "—it wouldn't be disrespectful if I told you you could call me, say—"

"You're *not* my mother and I *won't* call you that." Violent, adamant, instinctive.

"Oh, God, Zach. No." Helen shut her eyes, swallowed. Sweet Mother Mary, another insensitive mistake. Would she never stop making them?

She reached for him; he shied away. "I didn't mean—I wasn't saying—I meant, well, maybe you could call me Helen or something instead of Colonel is all, you know?"

"Oh." A measure of fierceness left his face. The wariness remained. "Yeah." He considered her a moment, then shook his head. "No," he said. "I can't."

She was astounded. "Why?" she asked, unable to help herself.

Zach shrugged. "It just wouldn't be right." He tossed the pants and vest over his shoulder. "I gotta go get dressed," he said, heading out the door.

Helen stared after him, the words *It wouldn't be right* clanging painfully inside her heart, echoing in her ears. Rejection hurt, damn it, no matter how deeply embedded in lead your ego was.

She shook herself, drew herself erect. *He's eleven,* she thought tightly. *What does he know?*

He's eleven, her heart responded softly. *He's been through a lot. Give him time.*

Time...

She drew a cleansing breath, brushed the moment aside. Yeah, time. Speaking of which, she had a lot to do with hers. Grimly she eyed the laundry, which seemed to have multiplied while she stood there. A pair of Sesame Street pajamas, a load of yellow Big Bird sheets and a rubberized bed protector dropped into the puddle of mixed fabric at her feet.

"Mom?" Libby's voice thundered hollowly down to her through the second-floor laundry chute. "Mother, are you down there?"

Oh, bother, not now. Couldn't she simply crawl into a hole and lick her wounds in peace? "Yes," Helen hollered back, knowing that where Libby was concerned there was no sense in denying where she was. No matter where she hid, young Miss Maximovich was bound to find her out. "What do you want?"

"Jane wet her bed last night. Cara and I stripped it, but don't forget to make it. Oh, and Max put on the same clothes he was wearing yesterday. I think you should prob'ly make him change 'em so he doesn't wear dirty stuff to school this morning."

"It's almost time for school. Are you dressed yet?"

"Not yet."

"Well, get dressed and get down here."

"But don't you want me to tell Max—"

Helen dropped her hands to her hips, viewed the laundry chute through narrowed eyes. "Libby," she said firmly.

"But—"

"Now."

"Okay." The response was disgusted and resigned. "I will. But he's gonna smell." The laundry chute banged shut.

Helen rolled her head, easing the tension in her neck, looked at the pile of somewhat fragrant sheets at her feet. Shut her eyes and sighed. One more load of laundry and one more "to do" to add to today's list.

Grimacing, she bent and picked up the yellow—and yellowed—percale with two fingers at arm's length, dropped it into a pile closer to the washing machine. This wasn't like anything she'd ever had to do in her life—if you didn't count the years her mother, Julia, had spent trying to domesticate Helen's GI Joe, gung-ho self, and that had been a disaster—so what the dickens did she know about doing laundry for an unfriendly mob that got upset if you accidentally put their green stuff in hot water with their red, and the resulting—albeit *clean*—mess turned out a sometimes Christmas striped but generally uniform brown? And then told Nat, who wouldn't have known otherwise—until he got to class and a student told him what he was wearing?

On the kitchen side of the laundry-room wall, the phone rang. Helen grabbed for the instrument, accepting the reprieve with alacrity. In a moment she wished she hadn't been in such a hurry to get out of doing laundry. She shut her eyes, trying not to sigh when she heard the too-familiar voice at the other end of the line. The children loved Amanda's mother to death, and she, in her defense, would have died for them, but as far as Helen was concerned, Emma Sanders was a worrisome impediment to the situation's general bliss and recovery.

"No, he's on his way out the door, Mrs. Sanders, and—"

"The hell he is," Emma interrupted sharply. "He's there, I know it. He's just avoiding me the way he's done for the last—"

Familiar with the diatribe, having heard it several times during the past six days, Helen interrupted without a qualm. After all, this wasn't *her* former in-law, so why should she deal with her? "Why don't I see if I can catch him, shall I?" Helen asked quickly, pulling the telephone away from ear and mouth. Hauling the white, twenty-five-foot cord across the kitchen with her, she bellowed down the front hall, "Na-at, phone. It's your mother-in-law."

In the front foyer, harnessing Toby for his morning walk, Nat winced. Adjustments were part of life; no one knew that better than he. But why the hell was it always necessary to deal with the complications all at once? Wasn't it enough that he was trying to live in an unfamiliar house with three floors—not counting the basement and attic—and umpteen million rooms? Wasn't it sufficient for him to struggle for the patience and understanding to deal with five kids in varying stages of grief, denial and distrust without putting them in the same domicile with Helen, who not only played havoc with his pulse, but who moved things around when she was nervous? And not just little things, not simple rearrangements of things; she transported furniture from one room, one floor, one *house*—in this case, his apartment—to the next so often that he had to use his cane *and* Toby so he wasn't constantly tripping over things the way he had the first couple of days. Wasn't all that plenty enough for anyone? So did he *have* to deal daily with the former in-laws who wanted to take his children away from him on top of it? Was that fair? Was it necessary—

His pulse leapt suddenly as a hint of something intrinsically feminine invaded his nostrils, filled his lungs.

"Nat," Helen said again, this time from a point so close to his left ear that he jumped and backed into her. The damned woman moved more quietly than any cat he'd ever met. Maybe that was why he was having such a hard time dealing with his nether regions around her: because she engaged—or perhaps that was *enraged*—his mind, then snuck up on him when his self-control was elsewhere.

"Sorry," she said now, steadying him with a hand on his arm, the other at his back, ignoring the current, the desire to turn "steadying him" into an embrace. "Didn't mean to startle you. Thought you had ears like a bat. Emma needs to talk to you...."

An odd sensation fizzed inside Nat; he couldn't quite nail down its source. "Is that some kind of blind joke?"

"Pardon?" Her change of emotion was evident in her voice: puzzled, distracted, and then suddenly embarrassed. "Oh, ah, you mean, ah, as in 'blind as a—'? Ah, no, I'm sor—I didn't mean—"

The chuckle that had been building inside Nat broke loose. He grinned.

Helen made a sound of disgust, ignoring the intriguing set of responses his grin elicited: the restless fuzz that skimmed her shoulders and across the back of her neck, the hypersensitive feel of the prickly cling of clothing on skin just before a thunderstorm. The desire to lift her arms, bare her body and stretch to meet the storm head-on. It would be a warm storm, full of thunder and lightning, but with a delicious rain that refreshed and renewed at the same time that it laid waste—or was that waist, as in Nat's long-fingered hands sliding along hers, first up, then down, around....

Her mind snapped to attention with a silent raspberry. Oh, for the love of... Like she didn't have anything better to do than fantasize about hedonistic pastimes. This proximity thing her mother used to talk about when she and her sisters were teenagers—as in "too much proximity to the cute boyfriend, or even boy friend, leads to temptation"—was getting way out of hand.

She breathed, shutting the door on uninvited reverie before the subject in question—Nathaniel Hawthorne Crockett wasn't *nearly* as blind as he might appear, and anyway, the whole idea of him reading her in braille was simply far too evocative for daytime consideration—figured out what she was thinking about.

"Not funny, Crockett. Besides, anybody with any trivia background at all knows bats *aren't* blind. It's a misconception, the same way lemmings rushing to the edge of a cliff and throwing themselves into the sea by the thousands as a means of population control is a misconception, or like—"

"Like blind people needing someone to get fire trucks off the stairs or wanting their furniture to stay where they left it the night before is a misconception?" The question was calm but pointed.

He'd gone down on his knees over a Tonka hook-and-ladder truck last night trying to keep his footing on the second-floor landing.

Argumentative.

He'd tripped over the wing chair she—or, to be fair, *someone,* but let's face it, who else in this house was stubborn enough to hoist the damned thing—had moved into his bedroom sometime between when he'd gone to bed last night and when he'd risen this morning.

Challenging.

No military mind—especially Helen's—could fail to miss this gauntlet, chain mail that it was and flung coolly at the side of her face. Especially not when Nat had been delicately alluding to the issue without once stating it all week.

Helen herself subscribed to the "If there's a problem, state it, don't eat it" school of thought and had a little— well, okay, a *lot*—of trouble being sensitive to other people's needs if she didn't know what those needs were, specifically.

She pursed her lips in consideration. "Well, yeah, I guess so," she agreed, deliberately dodging the point by figuratively grabbing hold of the end of the stick and shaking it. "Exactly like that. Besides, I thought that's why you have the dog."

Toby pricked up his ears and wagged his tail. The phrase "the dog," when used by Helen, was often accompanied by illicit handouts and surreptitious ear-scratching worthy of his response.

"Pardon?" The flung gauntlet, returned with unforeseen force, caught Nat off guard. The fact that his dog seemed willing to desert him for Helen even while in harness disconcerted him further. "Excuse me?"

Helen sighed, martyred but exuding patience. "To get you around obstacles in the dark."

Nonplussed, Nat felt his jaw go slack—with shock or wonder, he wasn't sure which. He had a few friends, coworkers with whom he was comfortable enough—and who were comfortable enough with him—to make light of the darkness he occupied, but this was... unexpected. Especially in the current circumstances.

On the other hand, back while they'd still been friends, before his wife-stealing had intervened, John had told Nat a little of what Helen—and living with Helen—was like: incendiary, organized, impractical, righteous, surprising, curious, decisive, without ceremony, challenging, never boring. And that was putting name only to what lay near the surface. Now Helen, with all those qualities—and a great many Nat had a feeling John had never taken the time to recognize—was living with Nat and his kids-her-kid-their kids in a house where stasis, if it had ever existed, was certainly now a thing of the past.

In other words, he thought, surrendering without being sure there'd ever been a battle, *better get used to it.*

But so had she.

From the kitchen behind them rose the faint squawk of someone ignored too long on the phone. Entrenched in the middle of something far more...current...Helen and Nat confronted each other and continued to neglect Emma.

Nat's jaw firmed, mouth grew thoughtful, face calculating. Forewarned by years of dealing with people who reacted to her in ways they didn't expect from themselves, Helen armed herself with ready answers and watched him warily.

"When you're dropped someplace where you don't know your way around in the dark, what do you do?" His voice was mild.

Helen wasn't fooled. "Get out my night-vision goggles," she replied promptly.

Sightless or not, he should have seen that one coming. She was military and unpredictable, after all. He gritted his teeth and growled.

"Okay, all right," Helen said, resigned, but not quite giving in. "That wasn't what you meant—I understand. Whether they'd fit or not, you want me to put on your shoes and see what it's like to be you living in a house with five kids and someone like me."

"Okay," Nat agreed. "For starters," he added darkly.

"Well," Helen mused, "let's see." She thought for a moment, tapping one toe loudly enough to be sure Nat heard her mental wheels turning. "Okay, I've got it. The army trained me to never let down my guard—especially in the dark—in a combat zone, which, now that I think of it, this whole situation sort of is. So, I have a tendency to be pretty careful moving around in the dark, particularly if I'm somewhere with people I don't know, like you."

That was a novel thought that hadn't occurred to him. He let himself be sidetracked. "You're careful moving around in the dark here because of me?"

"Of course." Helen nodded. "I never have any idea where you'll leave the dog...."

Toby's tail thumped; he looked up at her hopefully. *I'm starving. No one feeds me. Please, can't you slip me something before he takes me out and works me to death?*

Helen rolled her eyes at the beast. "A likely story," she said without sympathy. "I know how well he treats you. Better than me, that's how."

Toby nosed her hand, working the crowd.

"Don't fish," Nat said automatically—to both of them—as Helen palmed the dog's bearded chin and mouthed, "Later."

"I heard that," Nat said.

"I told you." Helen shrugged. "Ears like a bat."

"Which," Nat suggested meaningfully, "if I remember correctly, is where we were before you started talking to the dog, who, by the way, is in harness and therefore not to be distracted—"

On the table below the entry-hall stairway, the cordless phone rang, the light on the second line flashing. Helen picked it up, punched it on.

"Hello?...Oh, Lord, Emma, I'm sorry...were you holding all that time?....No, I—we—no, we just wound up in the middle of something...." She grabbed the sleeve of

Nat's jacket before he could edge Toby closer to the door and make his escape.

"No, no, everything's fine...no, the kids are just about on their way to school...no, no, it's my fault. Take me out of Washington and I turn into a flibbertigibbet...no!" She was offended. Why couldn't anybody who wasn't family ever spontaneously know to reduce the exaggerated metaphors she was prone to using to their proper proportions? In this instance, "flibbertigibbet" equaled, say, "a tad frazzled." Maybe even monumentally out of her depth. She sucked in air, harassed out of habit—and perhaps for the fun of it.

"Of course I'm not a flibbertigibbet in front of the children, why do you ask... It's an expression, Emma. Everybody in my family...well, I'm sorry you feel that way. I was brought up by a pack of occasional flibbertigibbets and I think we all turned out splendidly, and so do the people who entrust a portion of the security of our sovereign nation to my capable hands. Here's Nat." Helen took a deep breath, hit the mute button and pressed the phone against his hand. "Talk to her before I say something drastic."

"Oh?" he asked mildly, entertained no end. In addition to what she did to his lust levels, the woman was a font of things he'd never met in anyone else. "What drastic statement might you make that you haven't already?"

His voice was innocent and interested.

Distracting.

Once more diverted from her purpose, Helen shrugged. "Oh, I don't know, something like..." She caught herself digressing, shook the phone at him. The rubbery antenna bounced on his chest. "Oh, no you don't, buster, you're not sidetracking me again." Damn the man; he'd found her fatal flaw. She was a sucker for conversational tangents. Fell for them every time he found one. "She's *your* children's grandmother, and she has certain inalienable rights, so you're talking to her whether you like it or not.''

"Take a message?" Nat suggested hopefully. "I'm on my way to an important meeting?"

Helen snorted. "Not a chance, bud. I've been taking messages for you all week. I quit. Haven't had to play anybody's secretary since I was a captain, and I'm not going back to it now." She pressed the phone into his hand, unwisely gave his jaw a friendly, chin-up jab. The contact made her fist tingle, jarred her train of thought. She brought herself back to business with an effort. "Besides, what have you got to lose? If you talk to her now, maybe you won't have to do it again for a while. It's got to be better than being stuck with the laundry."

"Optimist," Nat muttered. He took the phone, punched it on. "What can I do for you, Emma?"

In lieu of a grin, Helen gave his arm a light jab, laughed aloud when he grimaced and turned his back on her, gasped when he suddenly spun about and grabbed her hand, pulled her toward him.

"Hey—" she began, automatically resisting, then shut up and gave ground at the sight of his intensely expressive face twisted first with disbelief, then with outrage. Then it went utterly and completely blank.

The hand around hers tightened and trembled.

A sudden prickle of misgiving traced her skin; her insides went cold. "What?" she asked.

Nat shook his head, silent, listening. Leaning in close to him, ear against the phone, Helen could make out Emma's voice, cold and shrill; the words eluded her. In the middle of something that sounded particularly vindictive, Nat pulled the phone away from his ear, released Helen and felt for the Off button, terminating the call. For a moment longer he stood silent, holding on to the receiver. Gently Helen took the phone from him, set it on the table, made him face her.

"Tell me," she suggested quietly.

Nat's jaw worked. He sucked in air, expelled it slowly. "Apparently one of the kids said something yesterday when Emma picked them up from school—I'm not sure what, she wasn't very coherent—and she...must have misunderstood or taken it wrong...."

Thunder rose inside Helen without warning, like an unexpected summer storm that boded only ill. She caught his arm, shook him. "Get to it, Nat, damn it."

"Emma and Jake called children's services and filed an emotional-abuse complaint against us. They've gone to court to contest custody and take the kids."

Chapter 4

"Emotional abuse?" Helen asked in disbelief.

Mouth tight, Nat nodded.

"*Emotional* abuse?"

This time Nat didn't nod, but merely tightened his jaw. The stain of angry color in his cheek was confirmation more damning than his silence.

Disbelief gave way to outrage as she thought about it. "Their live-in parents died, let's see..." She squinted, counting. "Six, eleven, twelve, thirteen days ago. They spent seven days with Emma and Jake, being told that you and I don't care about them and aren't fit to be related to them at all, let alone be their default parents, at the end of which they spent two days being questioned and observed in-home by custodial services, at which point we got here, completely unprepared for what was going to happen because Emma and Jake neglected to let anybody but their lawyer know so he could get a head start preparing for a custody battle. This is the same day that the kids find out they actually *aren't* going to be split up the way they thought, but will be living under the dubious guardianship of their other parents—us—and *we've* had a complaint filed against *us* for emotional abuse?''

Again Nat nodded, swallowing a crooked smile. She sounded for all the world like a she-bear with cubs, bellowing and snarling a warning to any comers. Knowing how little she thought of her aptitude in the mothering area, he couldn't help but feel some bittersweet enjoyment of her reaction. She was a Mother with a capital *M*, whether she realized it or not.

"If I followed it," he told her, "it's got to do with something one of the kids said about us living together without being married, which Emma interpreted as being overly confusing to young minds brought up with traditional family values, not to mention detrimental to their psyches. And somebody being forced to eat peas—"

"That doesn't make sense. Peas are *good* for them."

Nat gave a helpless shrug of agreement, then continued, "—Who always gags on them—"

"Nobody gagged on them. Nobody said anything *about* them. Nobody even hid them in a napkin and fed them to the dog, and he *loves* peas."

"—And it would be laughable if it weren't so damned serious...." He stopped, his train of thought arrested when Helen's observations caught up with him. "He does?" Hell, now she knew things about his *dog* that he didn't.

"Yes." Helen nodded, sidetracked in spite of the furious adrenaline flowing through her veins. "He prefers raw broccoli, but frozen peas'll do in a pinch. He won't eat 'em if they're canned...." She shuddered. "'Course, neither will I." She came straight back to cases. "What about the kids? They can't *take* them from us—we don't even *have* them yet."

Nat's mouth twisted. "That's the problem—we don't have permanent custody yet. Even if we did, protective services would have to start a file, investigate, but we'd have some legal place to stand. As it is—" he shrugged unhappily "—more than one judge decided we weren't the right parents to have even shared custody of our own children after our divorces. And if Emma's right, extenuating reasons won't matter, only the results will show in court."

Protest was instinctive. "That can't be right."

"No."

"A custody battle won't be pretty, and it'll be hell on the kids."

"On all of us."

Helen's chin came up; Nat heard it in her voice. "I'm not losing Libby again."

"Me, neither." A promise and a warning.

She caught his sleeve, gave his arm a shake, a threat of her own. "I won't give up Zach and Cara, either."

A grin twisted his mouth, faded. "Or Max and Jane."

"None of 'em," she said flatly.

"They're family," he agreed. "*We're* family. We're just a bit snarled at the moment—"

"And untangling the knots takes time—"

"Right."

"—Which we're apparently out of."

"Yes."

They were silent for a moment, hardly breathing, squared off opposite each other not as adversaries, but as nations that had never been at war calling a truce, forming an alliance. The fact that they had no blueprint to follow perplexed, but did not deter, either of them.

The silence ended when Helen inhaled deeply.

"I'll fight," she said finally, ferociously, stating it for both of them. After all, she was a bang-up U.S. Army colonel, with a degree in military logistics and a breastful of well-earned decorations—including combat medals, thank you very much—and it hadn't been easy getting here. It had been hard work, with an overabundance of manmade impediments and some really rotten hours, but she'd done it. It would be silly not to utilize the skills she'd spent twenty years of her life honing. "There's a lot of things being in the army might not have taught me, but I know how to do that."

Nat shook his head, smiled grimly and supplied what she left out. Years spent living navy and Pentagon protocol had taught him well, too. "We'll fight."

She gave a clipped nod. "Whatever it takes."

"Except—" Nat took her hand off his sleeve, held it with her attention "—except we keep the kids out of it as much as possible."

"Of course," Helen agreed, surprised. "That goes without saying."

"No." Nat shook his head. "It doesn't."

"Well, it should."

"True, but it didn't, and now we both know that we both know."

"Yes," Helen said, smiling tightly. "We do." She turned her hand to clasp his. "One for all?" she asked.

Nat squeezed her hand hard. "And all for one," he said.

Between them, where their palms touched, awareness burned and scorched and augured dilemmas of its own, while from above them, children dressed for school flooded down the stairs.

Ice-forming Moon

There had to be a solution.

Restless, Nat stalked the night, unable to sleep, stuck in a limbo not of his own creation. Images of Helen-Zach-Helen-Kids-Helen-Emma-Zach waylaid his dreams at every toss and turn, accosted his wakefulness with every step. He knew there had to be a solution, but what?

Using his cane to make sure Helen hadn't moved any furniture to ease the day's frustrations, Nat felt his way to the French doors leading to the screened side porch, then went out.

The air was brisk, the slate tiles cold beneath his stockinged feet, and he tapped quickly east, searching for the thick rug he'd helped Helen drag out of the basement, hang over the backyard barbecue and beat to get the dust out. They'd laid it out here only this afternoon. Working through a conglomeration of rising tensions, she'd called it. Making herself tired enough to sleep tonight so she'd wake in the morning with *The Plan*. A grin worked its way across his mouth. Even in memory, her voice around the two words made them sound capitalized and faintly evil.

She'd then flatly announced that they'd put up the storm windows out here tomorrow to be sure no piddly-minded keeper of Emma's complaints could come in here and mark them down for leaving the screens up so late in the season, thus ensuring the house would not be warm enough for the children's health and well-being, even though Emma herself had admonished Helen from the start to be sure to leave the children's windows open a crack at night so the air could circulate. This despite the fact that Max had been clutching his inflamed left ear and complaining that everything connected to it hurt.

Fortunately, a quick trip to the doctor, a course of antibiotics and some children's nonaspirin analgesic had relieved the worst of Max's misery, but it had not improved relations between Emma and Helen—or him and Emma, for that matter. Especially not when Helen deliberately marched off, found the storm windows for the boys' room, put them up, then closed the inside windows, locked them and caulked them shut for the winter in front of Emma while the woman read Max a story and soothed him to sleep. Nat and Zach had done the same thing to Jane's nursery and the older girls' room.

Again a grin toured his face. He could just imagine the tight line of Emma's mouth, her lips pursed with insulted disapproval, as she tried to ignore the open attack, the blatant changing of the guard—or guardians, as the case may be. No doubt about it, some of the battles were probably a trifle petty, but . . .

The grin faded. But it was the petty things that could so easily be distorted and blown out of proportion—the way they'd been at the end of his marriage. The seemingly inconsequential things—like Emma's choice of the verb *forced* to describe the children's consumption of a simple vegetable at dinner—that could undermine the construction of this family—his family, Helen and all—for good.

His cane struck softness; his feet found the edge of the carpet, cushy and warm. The air through the screens was frosty by comparison; it was a clear night, by the feel of it. He turned left, reached out with the cane to find the rattan couch, made sure of its location behind him and sat. In his imagination, the sky was full of stars, visible despite the city lights, and the porch and yard were full of shadows. According to the calendar page Cara had turned to and read them this morning at breakfast, tonight was November's full moon, at one time known as the Full Beaver or Ice-forming Moon, winter's warning of the freezing weather to come. He could feel the truth in the tale—less, he suspected the result of the season than of the cold war he and Helen were unwillingly being brought into.

He understood why Emma was doing this: she was afraid, somehow, that despite the fact that neither he nor Helen had denied her and Jake access to the children so far, they would eventually; afraid that despite the laws protecting grandparents' rights, the fact that Nat would not—without real and extreme provocation—prevent any of the children from seeing any one or more of their four sets of grandparents, that she and Jake would somehow lose the last pieces of their daughter that Zach and Cara in particular represented.

The fear and bitter distrust that pervaded so many divorces was truly a horrible thing. The fact that Nat and Amanda had managed to make their divorce civil and cooperative regardless of the custody arrangements had nothing to do with how Emma dealt with it now or ever. The devoutly Catholic Sanders family simply did not get divorced. That Amanda had done so and remarried must mean Nat was the Worst Person in the World; it was the only possible justification.

Understanding did not make Emma's actions easier for Nat to swallow.

A gust of wind swept autumn dust through the screens, brought the sounds of skittering leaves and branches scratching roof tiles to his ears. He lifted his face, shut his eyes to taste the draft more clearly, the irony of succumbing to a habit no longer needed not lost on him. The tang of winter coming, holidays approaching, tingled on his tongue, slightly bitter with the fragrance of cloves mixed with the tartness of apples from the dish on the rattan table beside the settee.

A lot like life these days.

Sighing, he traced a pattern in the tapestry cushion beside his right knee. He hated inactivity, thought without action; forced himself to remain seated rather than pace uselessly in a space he wasn't completely familiar with, knowing that to do so risked crashing into any number of things that hadn't been there yesterday and waking the entire house. He was a man for whom movement was second nature, for whom passion and chaos and being in the thick of things was synonymous with life. He understood these things about himself, dealt with them daily.

Understood that sometimes life also required idleness and tolerance, thought and indulgence, however much he often equated the lack of physical activity with standing still.

He also understood, whether he wanted to or not, who had punched Emma's buttons, caused her overreaction: Zach.

Unhappy, rebellious and filled with the lack of self-esteem and resulting insecurities that being eleven carried, Nat's son was at the stage prone to misinterpretation and unintentional misrepresentation, an age where he believed everything that didn't go his way was a personal attack. An age where nothing was his fault, where personal responsibility and accepting the consequences of his actions were somebody else's lookout, where the nature of hormones and physical growth spurts frequently left him at odds with himself and almost everyone else.

It was a phase, Nat's mother and those of Helen's sisters who had older boys assured him; Zach would outgrow it within six months—probably. And Nat himself had passed through it. But in the meantime it was Zach whose intense unhappiness over Amanda's and John's deaths, whose general discontent with the world he inhabited but didn't really want to change, whose thoughtless exaggeration of what it was like for the children to live with Helen and Nat had provided Emma with the... *excuse,* for want of a better word, she'd been looking for to question Nat's rights to her daughter's children. Nat's children.

Zach, who'd given his grandmother the fuel to try to take him and his siblings away from his father—in part simply because Amanda's will dictated that, in order to gain guardianship of his own kids, Nat had to live in the same house with the single woman in the world who visibly, publicly ignited sparks and made his body zing by merely stepping into a room.

A woman to whom he was not married.

The specter of an idea ghosted through his consciousness, fled with the unexpected scrape of leaves on concrete—or perhaps slippered feet on slate.

"Nat?"

The voice was soft, a part of his thoughts or borne on the wind. Wishful hearing, or was she there?

He turned, expecting the former, finding the latter when her fingers grazed his shoulder, seeking him in the darkness. He started at her touch, caught off guard by her again.

He'd tried to keep her out of his mind, tried not to think how near her end of the hall was to his by sitting out here in the cold and thinking of other things, other people. But she'd found him anyway.

"Helen?" If chaos bore another name, he was sure—judging by the hyperawareness of every nerve and instinct he possessed—it would be Helen.

"You couldn't sleep either?"

"No."

They were silent a moment, not quite awkward, but hardly on an even keel. Nat cocked his head toward her. She had something on her mind; he could hear it in the way she rubbed her hands together against the cold, then smoothed them down whatever fabric covered her thighs. Terry cloth, perhaps. It had been a long time since he'd made—wanted, taken—the opportunity to pay close attention to a woman in dishabille in the night.

He heard Helen loose a breath, then there was a plop near his feet and the cushions beside his knee depressed beneath her weight.

"Heard you sock-foot-it down the stairs and brought you your moccasins," she said mildly, using a foot to shove the fleece-lined chukkas against his feet where he could find them. "Figured your feet ought to be about frozen off by now."

Nat laughed quietly, reached for the footgear and slipped them on without asking her how she knew he hadn't simply carried something downstairs with him to put on his feet. In less than a week he'd already learned better than to ask her things he wasn't a hundred percent sure he wanted to know. "They are, thanks. And sorry, I didn't mean to wake you."

"You didn't." Helen's laugh was rueful. "Took care of that my own self, thinking too much."

"Emma?" he asked.

She sighed. "Among other things."

Restlessly she rose, wandered the porch, returned to stand in front of him.

"I have to ask you," she said, "and I don't want to do this."

He lifted his face to her—a courtesy. Felt for her hand, squeezed her fingers in a gesture that was friendly and without deeper import.

Deeper import burned his palm, anyway.

He ignored it—sort of. "Talk," he said softly.

"Don't do that." She yanked her hand away from him, put space between them. "I can't think with you touching me."

Surprise coiled and shuddered inside him. She'd violated the unspoken cardinal rule, the only thing that had helped them endure the last week so close to the fire they'd dismissed for years: don't speak of it and it won't exist, we won't have to deal with it.

Keep it light, he advised himself. And ignored himself immediately. What the hell, advice was cheap.

"You can't?" he asked. Easily. Carelessly. Attentively. He couldn't help himself; something in the way she'd said it encouraged his . . . response.

"You know damned well I can't," Helen said flatly. "I've never been able to. You know that, too."

So much for hoping she'd back away from the flame first. Or that she'd pull on the "tough colonel" facade and pretend she'd said nothing at all. He should have expected that "tough" for Helen would be facing the truth first, last and in the middle, whether anyone wanted her to or not.

"Yeah, I guess I do." The admission was harder than he'd thought it would be. Too much depended on them not losing their heads over one another now. Yet.

Maybe ever.

He rose and moved toward the sound of her voice. "You know the same thing about me, don't you." It wasn't a question exactly. More of a query, an experiment. A chance to see if either of them was as blind as they sometimes appeared. "Do you really want to go into this now?"

"No, Nat, I don't." She tossed up her hands, let them slap helplessly against her thighs. "But it was third on my list when I came down here." She flicked her thumb against the first three fingers of her right hand, ticking off the items. "Emma, Zach, you and the impossibility of remaining a sane woman—"

He swallowed a grin he hoped she didn't see. He wasn't about to tell her that half of his attraction to her lay in her, er, *unique* perspectives and her apparent, er...close associations...with life's lunatic fringe despite the straight-arrow eagles she'd earned the right to wear on her collar.

"—Or getting a good night's sleep with you down the hall. In that order. And wanting to, um, *discuss* any of those subjects with you or not has nothing to do with anything. When you're preparing for battle, it's best to—to..." She hesitated. "To acknowledge the—the flaws in your defenses beforehand. We can change the order, but we have to cover them all."

"Emma, Zach, me." The grin was in his voice now; he could hear it: inexplicable melody in the discords of chaos, rhyme in cacophony. Helen making him sense something in the madness—the sadness of John's and Amanda's deaths, Emma's fears, Zach's forlorn exaggerations of the truth—that he hadn't before; something that, if asked, he couldn't yet explain, could only say he was glad that it existed. "I see."

She heard the laughter in his voice, too. "It's not funny, Nat." Impassioned, pensive, hopeful. She wanted there to be something to catch hold of, hang on to. Even a single frayed thread would be better than the nothing clutched in her fist at the moment. "This is our lives here, the kids' lives—"

"I'm not laughing, Helen."

"—And Emma's and Jake's, and my mother's, and your parents', and John's parents', and if you'd told me ten days ago that I'd be standing here at all, let alone standing here in the moonlight saying this to you, of all people, I'd have called you a liar. Or worse."

"Me of all people?"

The laughter was simmering now, inappropriately close to eruption, the thing inside him causing this irreverent response chuckling like a madman out of control—like the photographic artist he'd once been, pursuing pictures through his lenses whatever the danger or the cost because he had to, because the vision, whatever it was, kept breaking through, looking for a means of expression. He almost didn't recognize himself, it had been so long since the vision had been upon him, but he didn't care; humor felt good, far better than sitting in the dark alone, grinding the salt of recognition into his own wounds.

Throwing caution to the night, pursuing the sound of her voice, her scent in the air, he advanced on her carefully, hands at his sides, intent—for reasons not quite clear to him—on not spooking her. The ghostly idea that had eluded him before flitted back toward him now. He breathed gently and ignored it, willing it to come close enough to catch.

Helen's slippers scraped the rug when she backed up a pace. "What are you doing?" she asked.

"Satisfying my curiosity," he returned, canting his head to zero in on the location of her voice. "Indulge me."

Helen backed into a chair, edged around it. "I don't know you well enough to indulge you."

"You've known me for years. We simply weren't on speaking terms for a while." His shin found the same chair the backs of her knees had found. Ah. He grinned, dragged his hand along the chair arm to guide himself around it. If he had himself oriented correctly—and judging by the strength of the wind along his right arm, he did—she'd be stuck in a corner soon. Fine by him. "We've been living in the same house for a week—"

"Six days," Helen corrected, a stickler for details, especially when they didn't matter. "And between kids and chaos and lawyers and laundry and what-have-yous, I don't think that counts."

"Six days," Nat agreed. "Whatever. And I've spent almost all of it wondering—"

"Oh no." Helen gulped. "Not that." Not if he'd been wondering the same thing she'd been wondering, anyway. Life was plenty complicated enough without either of them speculating about *that*. Truly, she was certain, the better part of valor would be to leave *that* well enough along.

Despite how much she really rather wanted it.

She edged out of the corner behind the chair, keeping it between them, desperately trying to change the subject, regain control of a situation over which she'd apparently never had any. "Zach said something to Emma that set her off, didn't he?"

"That'd be my guess." Nat nodded and switched directions in turn. "Don't change the subject."

"I thought that was the subject."

"Not anymore—or at least, only indirectly."

"Indirectly? Probably at least twenty thousand—" an exaggeration, but that's how she felt "—lives are at stake right here in this house tonight and a good five of them are minors and they're only *indirectly* the subject?"

"Yep," Nat agreed. "That's what I said. Is there an echo in here?" Instinct caught the sound of her starting to move before she made any move at all; reflex swung him about, had him lunge across the arm of the chair to snag her when she did. "Hi," he said, using her hand to guide himself the rest of the way around the chair, keeping her in the corner behind it.

She was breathless, giddy, a little ticked and wishing she was in uniform so she wouldn't have to behave like a civilized civilian. Wishing his nearness didn't make her feel so out of control. "I thought you were supposed to be blind."

"As a bat with radar," he confirmed. "And no 'supposed to be' about it. I thought you came down here to figure out a solution to our problem."

"This isn't it."

"How do you know?" He reached for her, slid his hands up her robed arms—terry cloth, as he'd thought—and held her by the shoulders. "It might be."

"No." Helen tried to hang back as he drew her forward, but it was a losing battle she didn't really want to win. "This is just asking for trouble—in fact, it's buying trouble retail. It'll put us right in Emma's hands."

"Not if—" Nat let his fingers glide up her shoulders, drift into her hair. She lifted her face and leaned into him because she couldn't help herself. He brought his mouth close to hers. "—we're married," he said, and kissed her.

She heard the words and tried to struggle, but his mouth was warm, he tasted rich and sinful and heavenly, and her hands, instead of settling on his biceps to push him away, fluttered weakly for a moment, then caught at his elbows and hung on. The thunder inside her head reproved her: *Colonel, you are out of your gourd.* But the soft rain, the mist of melting ice following close behind, smiled gently and said, *Call me Helen. Please.*

"Please."

The word sighed against his lips when he released hers. Smiling crookedly, he nuzzled her mouth.

"I thought sin was what you'd taste like, but I was wrong. You taste a lot more like Eden."

"Adam and Eve were tossed out of Eden and had to put on clothes because of what they knew."

"Yeah, and now I know why Adam didn't mind knowing or going."

He cupped her head and bent to her again. The taste was richer, sweeter, headier than before, her arms around him, her mouth opened to his inviting him deeper.

He went there and knew immediately that he shouldn't. Not yet. Not while the danger still lay in them being single.

The soft purr of need from the back of her throat, the intense, instantaneous tightness in his jeans, the groan of desire in his chest told him everything he'd wanted to find out and then some. He should stop this now, take his tongue out of her mouth, his hands off her bottom, and push her away. He should also convince her to marry him as soon as possible, take their mutual desires out of the public eye and bring them legally into the bedroom. It was the only way—for the kids' sake—to remain in the house with her without turning himself into a sexual time bomb.

Pulling together reserves of strength he hadn't been aware he possessed, he broke the kiss and moved Helen to arm's length, shut his eyes against the uneven breath shuddering in his lungs. As though in a dream, Helen eased herself toward him, let her hand rest on his cheek.

"Nat?" Her voice was thick and curious, drugged with desire.

He resisted her with everything he had in him. "Marry me, Helen."

"What?" She was a sleeper awakening, disoriented, pulling away from him, trying to figure out where she'd been. "What did you say?"

He swallowed, a little disoriented himself, trying to keep his priorities in order when all he could think of was opening her robe, taking her down to slate and losing his mind. "Will you marry me?"

"Will I what?" Fully awake now, she shoved out of his reach, saturated with disbelief. "Are you out of your mind?"

"Yes," Nat said, "and no."

Helen snorted, disgusted.

"No, that's not exactly what I meant." He held out a hand. "Please, it's for the kids. Let me explain..."

Three heads bobbed behind the parted curtains on the French doors.

"What are they doing?" Cara whispered, trying to peer around Libby's head into the sun porch.

"Kissing," Libby whispered back.

"Kissing?" Cara asked, shocked. "I didn't think they were supposed to do that if they're not married."

"No, that's sex, you stoop," Libby informed her. "Kissing doesn't have anything to do with sex."

"Huh," Zach grunted above her head. "If you think kissing doesn't have anything to do with sex, then you either need to watch more eight o'clock TV or have a talk with your mother."

"I've talked with my mother," Libby whispered, "and I know exactly what kissing has to do with sex—it's called foreplay—but *just* kissing doesn't make babies. Besides, you heard Dad—they're getting married."

"The Colonel doesn't seem to think so."

"Oh, the *Colonel*." The whites of Libby's eyes gleamed when she rolled them. "Trust me, the *Colonel* will marry him. My aunts will see to that."

"How do you know?" Zach was skeptical as ever.

"Dad—*your* Dad, I mean—said nobody ever made the Colonel do anything she didn't want to."

Libby grinned. "You don't know my aunts very well. They're good at revenge. Besides, my guardian angel will take care of anything they don't, she told me."

"How—" Zach started to argue, but Cara put a hand over his mouth, interrupting him.

"Shut up," she hissed, pulling him away from the French doors. "They'll hear you." She caught Libby's arm, drew her back into the living room. "You really think it's working?" she asked.

Reluctantly Libby turned away from the porch, headed for the front staircase. "It's working." She nodded, hiked up her pajama legs and started up the steps. "I hope." Fingers crossed, her voice trembling, she added, "It has to."

Chapter 5

Veteran's Day and Teachers' In-service Day,
No School—5:06 p.m.

"Marry him?" Helen's oldest sister, Alice, sat at the Crockett-Maximovich's big dining room table, mouth gaping. "Is he out of his mind? Does he have any idea what he'd be getting himself into if you said yes?"

Helen's other sisters—all six of them had shown up uninvited bright and early with their children "to play" while they went to work or whatever, and were now back to pick them up—nodded agreement.

"He's lived in the same house with me for more than a week," Helen snapped, defensive and irritated. "I think he probably has some idea of what I'm like by now."

"I lived in the same house with you for eighteen years," her second-oldest sister, Meg, pointed out, "and I wouldn't marry you if you paid me."

Helen sniffed, dismissing Mary Margaret's observation with a flip of her fingers. "You're only saying that because you and Tim are separated right now and marriage of any kind is way down on your list of things to write home about. Besides, we're too closely related. You *can't* marry me—it's against the law."

"Law, schmaw." Edith, fourth in line and right behind Helen in the Brannigan birth order, rolled her eyes. "Marrying you would be like trying to give birth to a barrel cactus without anesthetic, and none of us would do it if we were men, not related to you and desperate for female companionship after ten years in prison with only sweaty bodybuilders to look at, and that's a fact."

"Nobody asked you," Helen said smartly.

"No," Sam—Samantha to anyone who wanted to lose an ear or any other unprotected portion of her anatomy—concurred. She was fifth of the girls. "But according to you, Nat asked you to marry *him*, which leaves us with a little doubt as to his overall sanity and, consequently, his suitability to be our next brother-in-law and uncle to our children—"

"Like Kevin was completely in his right mind when he married you."

"—And as I recall," Sam continued, unperturbed by the aspersion cast on her husband's mental fitness; his alleged lunacy was a good part of the reason she'd married him in the first place: it helped keep people from noticing her own, "the last man you brought into the family didn't work out all that well."

"Ah ha!" Helen slapped a hand on the table and rose. "That's it exactly! I'm glad you agree. John *didn't* work out, and you all were behind him marrying me one hundred percent."

"Well..." Twink, Brannigan number six, waved history aside with a flutter of her fingers. "Everybody makes mistakes when they're desperate."

"And we were pretty desperate," Grace, youngest of the sisters, confirmed. "You kept thinking up *scenarios* and making us *act* in them. We had to do *something* to make you stop screwing up our lives for a while."

"So you screwed up mine?"

Grace shrugged. "Not intentionally. Besides, if I remember, you were a willing participant in the crime."

"And you did get Libby out of the thing," Twink reminded her. "It couldn't have been all bad."

"The lust was great," Helen admitted cautiously, not sure where they were headed with this, but knowing that, if she herself were on the giving instead of receiving end of this situation, the danger would lie both in fessing up to the truth and in not doing so. They had a tendency to get you both coming and going, Brannigans did. "But—"

"But it wasn't the end-all it might have appeared to be at the time," Meg finished for her with a touch of pain.

Silent, the sisters eyed Meg, troubled and sympathetic at once. They would meddle in her heartache when her bruises were less fresh, her sense of humor on the mend and her first holidays apart from Tim gotten through. For now they would distract her as best they could, not let her wallow too deeply in the mud pit she was digging herself into and try to appreciate their own sometimes-imperfect-but-always-there husbands a little more.

But at the moment they had Helen's life to rummage around in, and the complications contained therein were, without doubt, delicious enough distraction for any of them, including Meg.

"But..." Helen cleared her throat, drawing attention from Meg. Verbal harangues aside, they cared about each other deeply, after all. "But what I was going to say is that Nat's proposal has nothing to do with lust."

Alice choked.

Sam snorted involuntarily.

Edith rolled her eyes.

Meg swallowed a disbelieving snicker and looked at Grace, who coughed and eyed Twink, who said it all in a succinct, incredulous, "Ha! We've seen the way he takes notice when you're in the room. Not to mention vice versa."

"But it *doesn't.*" Helen was working hard to convince them. The muscles near her right eye twitched with guilt. "We'd only be getting married for the sake of the children, anyway."

"Oh, right," Twink agreed dryly. "Like I'm so sure. Then why's your eye ticking like mad?"

Helen opened her mouth, shut it with a snap. Blasted tick gave her away every time. Still, what could she say that wouldn't sound like further bluster—or that would change the truth? *Never trust women you grew up with to let you lie to yourself when you needed them to,* she thought gloomily.

Still, she'd be damned if she cried uncle yet.

"Well, it doesn't," she repeated. Stubborn to the core.

She rose, busied herself with the seemingly endless preparation of food to feed a crew that apparently required a different amount of fuel every day. Some days more, some days less—she couldn't get a handle on their needs. And she was too chicken to leave the kitchen to Nat despite his assurances that he knew his way around a kitchen blindfolded, cooked for himself all the time and was healthy as a horse.

She wasn't sure if it was some kind of minor bigotry against his blindness that made her feel she had to manage the cooking along with the laundry because of his "handicap," or if it was some kind of long-buried gender guilt acquired through her genes that made her keep herself in the kitchen because "men hunted, women gathered"—she glared at her sisters—in droves. Or maybe it was cowardice, pure and simple, because she didn't want to taste some of the throw-it-in-a-pot-and-pour-it-over-pasta "surprises" Nat had told her were his specialty.

"How do they taste?" she'd asked him dubiously, considering the offer. *"Will the kids eat them?"*

"Taste?" he'd responded, drawing his eyebrows together quizzically and raising them. *"Kids?"*

He'd probably been laughing at her, but it was difficult to guess without a light in his eyes to confirm or belie the assumption, and she hadn't, at that point, had the gall—or the forethought—to ask, so that had been the last discussion she'd had with him about who would fix the meals. She rationalized it to herself now as a civilian extension of her military duties: Gastro-intestinal Defense as opposed to Global Defense. Simple.

Now, if only she didn't feel she'd been had...

She turned her back on the stove when a minor commotion broke the lull in her sisters' conversation.

"Me do it, me."

Moving as fast as her chubby legs would carry her, Jane burst through the kitchen door, a brace of Brannigan cousins hot on her heels and Toby in close pursuit.

"No, I get to do it."

"No, me!"

"Hey, hey!" Helen stepped in front of Jane, stooped and brought her to a stop, nieces, nephews and dog piling up behind her. "What did I tell you guys, huh? No running in the house. Somebody'll get hurt." Oh, for pity's sake and horrors above, she sounded just like her own mother. Ah well, no way to take it back now. "Now..." She settled on her haunches, caught Jane about the waist and tickled her. "What's up, short miss? Where're you goin' so fast?"

Jane giggled, but still managed to eye her competition aggrievedly. "Toby—"

Hearing his name, the dog attempted to wedge himself into the huddle between Helen and Jane, lavishing kisses on them both. Helen lifted the dog's chin out of the way to no avail. Struggling and sputtering, Jane shoved at his head, stamped her foot.

"Toby, sit."

Toby sat, then shoved his muzzle forward, snuffling Jane. She pushed his nose out of her way.

"No," she said severely. "Not now." Still aggrieved, she looked at Helen. "Tern'l, Toby needsta doe out, Nat say me do it."

"No he didn't." A cousin, two years older and male. "He said *we* could do it."

"Yeah."

"Nat's home?" Helen asked no one in particular, knowing he must be, since Toby was here. She wished her pulse would stop hammering with the knowledge. Was glad that the children, at least, were too concentrated on their own affairs to pay attention to hers. She brought her focus back to Jane.

"No, me." The three-year-old shook her head vigorously, earnestly placed her hands on either side of Helen's face, willing her to hear. "My job, Tern'l, *my* job."

"Your job," Helen agreed, hugging her, "because in a big family like we have, everybody is important and everybody has to help and nobody is too little to do something, right?"

"*Not* too little." Jane nodded emphatically. "*My* job."

"Absolutely." Helen straightened. "You do it, but let Ben, Chris and Erin help."

Jane wiggled out of Helen's grasp. "Okay."

"Can you get the door all right?"

Already twisting the dark brass knob on the door that separated the kitchen from the basement landing and the door to the backyard, Jane nodded.

"Be careful on the stairs." Oh, God, Helen was a mother, wasn't she? Born to be the sayer of *don'ts* or *be carefuls* or not, she was saying them and meaning it.

But of course, that had never really been the problem at all, had it? No, the problem wasn't that she was afraid of being a mother, it was that she was afraid of having children she couldn't send home, afraid of the awesome responsibility of raising them to be well-rounded, healthy adults. That was what bothered her most of all: she questioned her ability to raise happy, healthy children who would eventually become happy, healthy, fully functional adults.

Disturbed by revelations she hadn't intended to become acquainted with, Helen missed the looks her sister gave her, the compressed lips that smothered smiles, the knowing eyes, the thoughtful faces that recognized opportunity when they saw it—and knew what to do with it.

"Well." Edith cleared her throat, whether covering laughter or another emotion, Helen couldn't tell. "Jane seems to be adjusting to the new order around here."

"Most of the time." Helen nodded, craning her neck to watch her toddler carefully negotiate the stairs and the doors. "She's pretty great."

"How're the others doing?" Alice asked gently.

"Oh, you know..." Helen shrugged. "Some days better, some days not. Zach's on an emotional roller coaster that's starting to be fueled by hormones. He's the hardest. I never know what to do, where Nat and I stand...."

She stopped, regrouped. "Libby, of course, was born to stand on her head and have her world turn upside down every now and then. She charges forward without looking back the same way she's always done.

"Cara's trying, but it's not easy for her. I don't do things the way Amanda did, and sometimes I forget to check and make sure Cara knows that I know she's the oldest daughter and that I depend on her as much as her own mother did. I catch Nat looking like he's trying to..." she paused, sought out the word "... *see* Cara sometimes, then looking like he's glad he can't. She looks so much like Amanda already, I think he's half-relieved he can't see her grow even more so.

"And Max..." She smiled. "Nat has Max reading the calendar to him every day so he knows who's got what appointments, and Max knows he has a very important job to do because if he doesn't, Nat won't know about stuff and gets left out of things. It seems to be good for them both, because I think Max wants to trust us, but he's afraid we'll leave him the way all his other parents have. I haven't said yes or no to Nat yet re The Marriage, but—" she slapped a fist into a palm for emphasis "—that's a real reason in favor right there."

"Yes, well, hmm." Meg coughed, cleared her throat. "Marriage is a huge commitment to make because of a kid who'll grow up and be out of here in twelve or fifteen years," she suggested at last. "If you and Nat find out too late that you can't get along and split up, it'd be even harder on Max and the other kids. At least if you're only living in the same house, you don't have to make the same... pledge to each other, you don't have the same reasons to grow to hate each other. The kids might actually be happier.... You ought to think about that."

"I know, but well..." Helen hesitated, sorting through reasons that sounded like excuses, excuses that sounded like a car salesman's snow job.

In a pan on the stove, tomato sauce bubbled and spit, splattering red dots across the almond enamel. Glad for distraction, Helen turned, stirred, then absently dipped a spoon into the marinara, touched it to her upper lip, concentrating a moment on the taste. Needed a dash of... She rolled the flavor around on her tongue. Cilantro, maybe a smidge of... *Worcestershire*, yes, that was it!

Opening the fridge, she scanned the contents standing on the shelves in the door, found the Lea & Perrins; opened it and added a bit to the sauce; tasted again. Shut her eyes and savored. Ah, *perfecto*.

Behind her, her sisters nearly choked to death, holding in their laughter. She ignored them; it was the only defense.

"I mean," she continued, as though there'd been no gap in the conversation, reaching for an offhandedness that didn't fool them—or her—for a minute, "as long as we're supposed to...raise...the kids together, it'd be more...convenient to be married, that's all. We could adopt them, they could all have the same last name, there'd be less confusion and fewer questions to answer all 'round, and..."

She hesitated, because the next piece of rationale didn't sound as good to her today as it might have, say, a week ago; she didn't necessarily *want* to go back to Washington five days a week, but she hadn't come up with any other solution to managing the career half of her life yet while keeping the kids—and Nat—ensconced in theirs. "And if we're married, we could really split the responsibilities, have legally sanctioned obligations to each other. It'd be easier for me to hire a housekeeper and spend weekdays in Washington, weekends here with the kids...."

Her voice trailed off, sounding unconvinced. She looked at her sisters. They looked back.

"Ah," Alice finally said wisely, managing with difficulty not to roll her eyes.

"Well, that makes perfect sense then." Meg nodded, hiding the follow-up *not!* she mouthed at Edith behind a strategically placed hand. "And I suppose distance *might* help it to work."

"Oh, a marriage of *convenience,*" Edith agreed. "That's completely different."

Sam snorted and said it for all of them. "If he thinks marrying you for the kids' sake would be *convenient* and you agree with him, you've both lost your minds."

"Yeah," Twink said, "I mean, I've heard of people not getting *divorced* because of the kids, but to get married? Isn't that like expecting the cart to pull the horse?"

"Oh, I don't know," Grace disagreed. "People get married all the time for kids—look at all the teenagers who get married because they 'have to,' because she's pregnant and somebody doesn't want the baby to be illegitimate. I mean—" she looked at Alice "—*you* did it. You were only seventeen and you got the marriage annulled right away, too, but you *did* get married because you were pregnant *and* you kept the father's name so Allyn and Becky wouldn't wind up illegitimate Brannigans."

There was dead silence for a millisecond while they all digested this. Then Alice exclaimed, "Helen!" Aghast, she glanced furtively around, making sure no children were in earshot. "Are you *pregnant?*"

"Oh, Helen," Meg murmured, equally appalled, equally furtive. "You're almost forty years old. I thought sure you understood the principles of safe sex by now."

"Yeah, Helen," Twink scolded, not the least furtive. "You're the one who always reported us to the condom police and now you didn't? I'm *shocked.*"

"Oh, *God.*" Helen buried her face in her hands, groaning. Why did they always insist on jumping to the wrong conclusions in spite of the fact that in doing so they were rarely right?

Because messing with somebody's head is fun, she answered herself. *Same reason you do it to them.*

"I am *not,*" she announced aloud with some force, caught herself, scanned the area for eavesdropping ears and lowered her voice. "I am not," she repeated in a whisper, "and be advised, you'd better hear this now before someone with big pitchers walks in here and mistakes your *ass*—" she stressed the syllable "—umptions for gospel and spreads the non-news to the family tabloids. I

am not, repeat, *n-o-t* pregnant now nor will I be at anytime in the future by Nat or anyone else.''

"Well, of course not," Sam agreed, disgusted. "Who
said you were? We all know you had your tubes tied after
John divorced you because you were afraid you'd meet
another guy, fall in love marry him, have another baby and
lose it in the next divorce. Which, by the way, is another
good reason to *think* before plunging headfirst into marital waters that look a little shallow to me.''

"She had her tubes tied?" Grace was dismayed at having been left out. "Nobody told me.''

Twink patted her hand. "Well no, of course we didn't,
dear. You were pregnant with number three at the time and
we didn't want what Helen did to influence you in any
way.''

"Oh, fine," Grace snapped. "I'm twenty-eight years
old, I've got four kids and you guys still think of me as the
baby—''

"I told you that in *confidence*." Helen turned on Meg.

Meg shrugged. "They're confident. Besides, they weaseled it out of me.''

"Nobody weasels anything out of you, Mary Margaret,
unless you want it weaseled out. You're the original
'mum's the word.'''

"I didn't tell Grace," Meg retorted.

"Oh, like that excuses you.''

"It doesn't?''

"No, it damned well does not—''

"Girls, girls!" Edith murmured placatingly. "Fighting
won't get us anywhere, and we still have to figure out Hel-
en's wedding. What with the holidays coming up and
all . . ." She shook her head. "It's a little tight.''

"What wedding?" Helen asked. "I didn't say anything
about a wedding. Marriage, yes. Wedding, no. Not with
you guys planning it.''

"You have to have a wedding, Helen," Sam said, "with a shower and a bachelor party and a rehearsal dinner and relatives and everything else. Otherwise it doesn't count." She rubbed her chin, thinking. "Now let's see, if you're doing this for the kids and to get Amanda's parents off your back, you'll want to do it soon, so you won't have time to get a priest—"

Twink nodded. "Waiting requirements, six months at least. What religion is Nat?"

"Ah..."

"Why don't we ask the judge next door to perform the ceremony?" Grace suggested.

Sam tapped her chin. "What about a church deacon? Could he do it sooner?"

"I don't think so," Edith said. "I think they still have to ask about whether or not you love each other and all that stuff and make you wait to make sure the vows'll last and announce bans, and I don't think we want to get into that."

"Oh, yeah, I forgot, you could be right there, but hey, what about a woman Episcopal minister? That might be nice—different, but apropos."

"I don't know." Alice shook her head. "I think you've still got the questions."

"True, and I don't think they want to be asked if they love each other. Do you?"

They all looked at Helen.

Her mouth opened and shut soundlessly. They were pushing all her buttons, and they knew it. She hated that; life was far better when she was pushing theirs.

Alice nodded. "Thought so. You know, you can't consummate the marriage if you don't love each other."

"That would be wrong," Edith agreed.

"Says who?" asked a curious male voice from the front-hall doorway.

Oh, great, Helen thought, mortified. *Speak of the devil.* Hunkly Gorgeous in the flesh and no place to hide.

Literally.

She watched her sisters stare as Nat, holding his cane, slouched comfortably against the doorjamb—all seventy-three magnificently well developed inches of him showcased to perfection by a barely belly-length, cutoff, sleeveless Wayne State University sweatshirt, a pair of comfortable, well-worn sweatpants and bare feet. He was a man very definitely in his element and enjoying it to boot. In front of him, six unembarrassed Brannigans outnumbered the one, Helen, who would have sold her soul to sink through the floor and fade to black even though *he* couldn't see her and especially because *they* could.

"Says who about what?" Twink asked, innocence personified.

"Says who we can't consummate the marriage—if there is one—for any reason at all?" Nat returned patiently.

"Oh, *geez*," Helen moaned.

For a moment silence reigned while the Brannigans digested male challenge and contemplated response. Then Alice looked at Meg, Meg turned to Edith, Edith nudged Sam who raised a you-take-it brow at Twink who clicked a thumbnail between her teeth and figuratively passed the gauntlet to Grace. Wrinkling her nose in disgust, the baby of the family planted her elbows on the table, her chin in her hands and said, "Well..."

"That's what I thought," Nat said—smugly, to his discredit.

Sam sent him a glance of withering disapproval, glanced at Helen. "You're going to have to watch him," she advised.

"Got an answer for everything," Meg concurred.

"Too tricky by half," Edith affirmed.

"Got to be a flaw we can exploit there somewhere," Grace said puzzled, "if only I could decide what it is."

"Well, *I* like him," Twink stated flatly, "and that's a good point you made, Nat. I think he'll be good for you and you should marry him immediately, Helen."

"I agree," Edith added. "Alice?"

"Oh, there's something definitely flawed with his argument," Alice said, "but there's something flawed in Helen's, too, and since they've obviously thought this out just about as far as they're going to think it, I think they should pick a day and worry about the after-marriage details later."

"Ah..." Well out of her depth, Helen looked around wildly, hoping to find an opening that meant escape. There wasn't one. She eyed Nat in the doorway, the only way out that didn't mean going through herds of children. As though anticipating her, he casually straightened, then slouched again to block the entire passage.

"Time to play truth or dare," he told her quietly. "How 'bout it, Helen?" He held out a hand. "Marry me, won't you?"

"I—I—I don't—"

"The judge next door is a woman," Grace suggested again, speaking up while the speaking was good. "She won't ask anything except to see your marriage license and the certificate that says you took an hour of AIDS counseling and understand the consequences of unconsidered actions."

"Thanksgiving's on its way," Alice said. "All the relatives will gather, so it would be a convenient time to stage a marriage of convenience."

"Give you the two weeks you need to get blood tests back, too," Sam agreed. "Even though you don't *have* to have 'em, it might be a good idea, show a little planning to Emma...."

Helen blanched, knowing without doubt that several of the misdeeds she'd once sowed upon her sisters had just come home to roost. "I don't—I don't—"

"Dad, Dad!"

There was a sudden stamping down the back staircase, and Zach, Cara, Libby and the older cousins appeared, big-eyed and out of breath.

"Dad, Colonel there's—"

"—Two police cars and—"

"—Police and one of those social workers—"

The front doorbell buzzed; all the children except for Libby froze.

"—On our porch," she said.

Despairing, wondering if Amanda and John could see what they'd wrought, Helen reached for Nat's hand. His fingers twisted around hers, lips thinned grimly. As expected but hoped against, they'd come.

"Better answer the door," he said.

Chapter 6

They didn't take the children, but it was a near thing for a while.

With eighteen kids and six sisters gawking from doorways and the staircase, Helen and Nat together let the law in, ushered the two women and one man through the frankly curious—and somewhat hostile—family and into the living room. When the protective-services representative requested a private area in which to interview the children individually, Nat—grim faced and with a sinking heart—guided them into the library, where they sorted Zach, Cara, Libby, Max and Jane out of the gathering. The male police officer herded them away from everyone else into the dining room while the social worker set herself up in the library. When she was ready, the female officer collected the children in random order, starting with Jane, and led each off to talk with the woman who held the power to determine whether or not to leave them in their own home or remove them into protective custody, where they would spend time at Children's Village until the court decided on disposition.

Because of some peas, a thoughtless interpretation and a grandmother's fearful love.

Regardless how small or inconsequential it seemed at the time, like dominoes set up to illustrate the workings of a chain reaction, every little thing you did affected your life forever after.

It was better this way, Helen and Nat tried to convince themselves, each other—tried to persuade the sisters, who wouldn't leave no matter how late it grew, no matter how hard Helen attempted to reason with them to get them to; "reason" and "family" never had had anything to do with each other when it came to Brannigans defending or supporting other Brannigans. It was better that the system worked too hard to ensure the safety of their children rather than vice versa.

Better, that is, except when it didn't work at all, when it tried to protect children who didn't need it, failed to protect those who needed safeguarding either from their home lives or from themselves—or, in tragic, too-oft-reported instances, failed to shield their communities from them.

Mostly, though, Helen and Nat didn't talk, they paced or stood tensely outside either the dining room or library doors, comforting each other without realizing they did it with a brush of the arm here, a squeeze of the hand there.

At one point Helen suddenly remembered the marinara, got her sisters to feed their kids, made the cop watching hers—and they were *hers,* she realized all at once; that was how she thought of them, as hers and Nat's, unplanned but fiercely wanted all the same—feel guilty about how hungry the youngsters must be since their normal dinnertime was six and it was now seven-thirty and they had school tomorrow. Then she offered to feed the officer, too, because she could hear his stomach growling and her dead ancestors would roll in their graves to think that one of their descendants had been so uncharitable as to let a hungry man remain so.

The stern-faced officer in question unbent a bit at that, almost smiling, and accepted the plate he could hardly avoid when Helen handed it to him. Then she fixed two more plates and had the next child to be called through the library door—Cara, as it happened—deliver them to the policewoman and court officer on the other side.

"Nothing ventured," she muttered under her breath, rocking on her heels and watching the door as she might a window, looking for revelations on a foggy day.

Nat, listening, chuckled in spite of himself and the circumstances. Trust Helen to work out the logistics of a situation and turn it on its ear. Even before he'd met her he'd followed her military career—as had most of the officers who'd ever had occasion to deal with the adjutant general's office after she'd been posted there—with some amusement. Though she'd never admit it, Helen had a certain innate genius for taking any faulty but overly stuffy and ordered department, slicing the red tape around it to ribbons, shredding all the outdated forms and organizing the resulting chaos into a more-genial, more-efficient, people-oriented unit. Enlisted personnel loved her as much as the non-coms, and junior officers bulldozed out of her path hated her—until they needed her on their side again.

This time when Helen passed him in her pacing, Nat reached for her, slipped an arm around her shoulders and kissed her temple.

She leaned into him for an instant, almost hugging him back, then moved quickly on her way.

A short time later, when the interviews were finally finished, the determination was made that in this instance the complaint against Nat and Helen had been filed in error—the children appeared well if not yet completely readjusted, and thanks for dinner. The children's services rep, who had implied but not formally offered an apology, hesitated for a moment on her way out the door.

"Look," she said, turning uncomfortably back to Helen and Nat, "I don't usually make this kind of observation to people I'm called out to investigate, but, ah, in this case... I get the feeling this whole thing is some sort of internal family dispute, ah, former in-laws against their late daughter's *single* former husband and, ah, I kind of wonder if things, er, might not go more, ah, *smoothly* for you both in that regard if you were married instead of just, um, living together..."

Nat shrugged. "Thanks," he said, "but we—"

Helen hushed him with a finger against his lips. "Thanks," she said, "and we will be married—" she looked at Nat, slipped an arm about his waist "—by Thanksgiving."

Nat touched her face, absorbing the smoothness of her skin through his fingers, feeling the tightness of determination along her jaw. Wished he could see her, read her eyes. "Really?" he asked softly.

"Yeah," she said firmly, "really."

"Well, good, congratulations," the children's services rep said, and seemed to mean it.

In his turn, Nat hugged Helen hard and whispered, "Good," and hoped neither of them would find any reason to regret such a hasty decision.

Thanksgiving

Turkey day dawned bright and clear, with sun glittering in prism colors through the frost on the windowpanes and a light dusting of early snow on the ground. The house smelled from days' worth of preparations for a feast—of cinnamon and cloves, pumpkin and apples, yams and corn bread stuffing and the luscious, heavenly scent of turkey.

Feeling like she was about to leap into the chasm between herself and reality, Helen was up before dawn, with *Webster's Unabridged Dictionary* flopped open to the *C*s on her bed, nervous as the proverbial bird about to be beheaded, stuffed, basted and devoured.

Convenience: [Latin, from *convenire,* to come together, join suit.]
1. The absence of that which annoys; personal well-being; comfort.
2. That which gives ease or comfort or makes work less difficult and complicated; a handy device.
3. A condition personally favorable or suitable; advantage. *At one's convenience:* at a time, or in a place or manner, suitable to one.

As, she thought, moodily supplying her own example, *a marriage of convenience.*

Which definition, after all, said nothing about the word *mutual.* And brought to mind *convenient*'s antithesis, *inconvenient,* as in disharmony, discord, dispute and hassle.

Scrutinizing herself under the bright lights at the bathroom mirror, Helen grimaced and sighed. No, no matter how hard she looked, she still couldn't see anyplace where she twinned Alice, so why did she feel like she'd turned into her oldest sister?

Because somewhere along the way, when her impending marriage to Nat inevitably failed for lack of a finger to stick in the dike of *convenience,* then they would undoubtedly get it annulled—as Alice's first, very brief marriage had been. Only theirs would be annulled for lack of consummation.

After an appreciable amount of discussion and a great deal of thought—which included kissing and a little light, over-the-clothes but really blood-boiling petting, let's face it—she and Nat had finally, albeit reluctantly, agreed that the fewer complications they allowed in this "marriage," the more likely it was they'd be able to *stay* married at least until Jane was through high school.

Lust alone, they'd decided, was no place to start a life— or at least fifteen years of a life—together. Especially since they didn't have time to work through all the baggage that unavoidably accompanied a new sexual relationship, enough time to simply be together and absorb each other, pay attention to the pleasure of discovering themselves by themselves. Especially since this wasn't about *them* at all, but about—and for—the children.

It would be easier, they told themselves, each other, to remain friends, keep emotions steady—to hold the doubt that inevitably arose and eroded a purely sexual liaison at bay and maintain the level of... companionship, to which they were rapidly becoming accustomed if they merely went on as they'd begun: in separate bedrooms, as platonic partners, with a shared love for, and commitment to, their children; confederates with some heartfelt vows between them.

Shipwreck survivors aboard the same life raft with five children in an unstable sea, depending on each other alone to protect the kids and their futures, to make it through.

Because if they didn't get this thing right from the start instead of hurting only herself and Nat when reality invaded and good intentions and emotions hit the fan, they'd be hurting five vulnerable little kids as well.

Better, perhaps, to let Nat's former in-laws take all the children now, and save the pain, than to let the kids believe they'd found a magic, holiday-style solution to a dilemma that could only be solved by all of them working together to make happily ever after an option, not by one single appearance of a miracle that lasted barely a few days.

The fact that Helen thought she might *like* being married to Nat—especially if all the marital fringe benefits were involved—had nothing to do with anything. Nor did the fact that she was—secretly—beginning to enjoy the constant chaos of five kids with needs to be filled. Nor the fact that she really didn't think she wanted to return to Washington; despite the constant mayhem of family existence, life was far more...satisfying...here. Far more interesting. Far more complicated and less theoretical than the politics of "guarding" national secrets and paper shredding in the capitol. Far more involved and involving.

Far more real.

Despite the doomed Christmas pageant she'd so enthusiastically—and stupidly—agreed to help the children's school and parish music minister produce. Like she had nothing else to do what with her wedding today, five variously excited to stoically apathetic kids to think about and all the relatives her sisters had invited to, er, "pay their respects" to Helen and "welcome" Nat and the children to the family over the upcoming Christmas season.

Sighing, she stuck out her tongue at the mirror and turned off the bathroom light, slapped the unhelpful dictionary closed in passing and went to stand in the glass-enclosed porch off her bedroom—which also happened to be the master suite. It was cold outside, less than twenty degrees, and she was glad when her bare feet found the thick rug she'd laid over the tile, thankful for the icy slap in the face when a draft came in from somewhere and threw particles of frost to sting her cheeks.

She needed a cold dose of weather this morning, an awakening from the premonition that things had been going just a little too smoothly the past couple of weeks to be believed. Even Zach appeared to have settled into a kind of...pattern of acceptance...since Helen and Nat had told the kids they were going to get married today and all of them could help with the wedding.

Jane would be flower girl, in a new long dress Aunt Alice had whipped together for the occasion. The three-year-old had practiced her role by littering the entire house with bits of shredded paper—much to Toby's delight and subsequent upset stomach, since some of the paper Jane shredded had once held candy or margarine or other equally delightful and edible things. She had been thoroughly rebellious when Helen had required her to clean up the "bootifool" mess.

Max was in charge of the rings and had slept with them under his pillow last night after insisting that someone set his alarm for six-thirty so he'd be ready in his rented tuxedo in time. They'd worked hard to convince him that 4:00 a.m. would be *way* too early to get up, that eight would be plenty soon enough and then, at the crestfallen expression on his face, had compromised.

Libby, naturally, had turned down the role as one of Helen's bridesmaids and insisted, instead, on wearing her own tuxedo and giving the bride away. Had to be more comfortable than a dress, she'd said, then refused, despite evidence during her fitting to the contrary, to change her mind.

Cara and Zach, too young to be considered legal witnesses, were nonetheless standing in with Helen's sister Meg and Nat's brother Jed as co-maid-of-honor and best man respectively.

The judge next door had graciously consented to leave her own Thanksgiving festivities long enough to perform the ceremony. Jake and Emma; Helen's former in-laws, Henry and Ida; her mother, Julia; and Nat's parents and brother were all coming and staying for dinner after. And Helen had ultimately convinced her sisters that less was more and gotten them to agree *not* to invite all the relatives to come both today and for Christmas. Indeed, on the face of it, everything looked well-ordered and proceeding as scheduled.

But it was usually best not to judge a day by its appearance.

His dresser drawers were missing and he couldn't find the sweatpants he'd hung on the bathroom doorknob before climbing into the shower.

With an annoyed, "Damn, she's at it again," Nat felt his way cautiously around the room, trying to discover what Helen, in her infinite mystery, had done with his stuff now.

His tuxedo was, of course, right where he'd left it over the back of the wing chair Helen hadn't yet moved out of his room. Again. The monkey suit—bright red cumbersome-bund and all—was a grudging concession he'd made to the occasion at Cara's insistence that he needed to "spiff up" to get married. This despite the fact that Helen had assured them both sincerely—under her breath, but Nat heard it—that Nat looked plenty spiffy enough as it was in his one good gray suit with a rose in his buttonhole. But his daughter had her heart set on the penguin look, so there the blasted thing was in all its questionable glory.

Not, he thought dryly, that he could see it anyway, and wasn't that the point? How it *looked?*

Well, perhaps not entirely. Perhaps it was how it felt, too. Formal and credible. Pomp and circumstance.

And a little bit unreal.

He hadn't worn a tux since his high school prom; the last time he'd gotten married he'd been in uniform. There hadn't been a great deal of call for formality since his discharge, and when there was, he put on his suit and tie and let it go at that. But this was Cara's request. And Max had told him gravely that they were all dressing up, even the Kern'l, like at the dancing scene in *Beauty and the Beast,* because getting married was special and you had to look that way, too.

A man would do a lot for his kids.

Shoving wet hair out of his face, he continued his search. Only his drawers, his sweatpants and the contents of his closet were missing. Everything else was exactly where he—or rather, Helen—had left it.

Muttering something colorful under his breath, he made his way back to the foot of his bed, reached for the robe that should have been there—but wasn't. For almost a minute he stood stock-still, trying to figure out whether he'd truly lost his mind or someone else was merely messing with it. Then swearing on a stack of bibles what he intended to do to the miscreant who'd left him skivvies and nothing to cover them with, he grabbed his quilt—nope, that was gone, too, damn it. And no cane where it should be, either.

Thoroughly annoyed now, he tore the sheet that remained on his bed off of it, draped the percale about his waist and went in search of Helen.

There was a kids-trying-to-be-quiet commotion in the hallway outside her door, and someone tapped lightly. Before Helen could step in from the porch and respond, the door eased open and Libby stuck her head into the room, glanced furtively around. Without knowing why she did it, Helen instinctively remained silent and out of sight, waiting out events; Libby obviously did not want to be seen.

Probably a wedding-day surprise, Helen decided, amused in spite of her premarital jitters. *Probably fixed me eggs and candy corn on a bed tray. Well, I won't spoil it. I wonder if they did the same for Nat.*

"Coast's clear," she heard Libby breathe to someone behind her. "Come on, hurry up before she comes back."

"I can't," Cara's voice whispered back. "Zach's standing on this stuff and I can't move."

"Well, tell him to get off it and come on."

"I am off it, you stupid dork." Zach's voice, low but audible, decidedly sarcastic. "She's standing on the junk herself. Tell *her* to get off it, and hurry up, why don't you."

"Shut up, both of you, and get off it and hurry up," Libby retorted in a stage whisper. "It won't be a surprise if she catches us."

There was a squeak and the door eased the rest of the way open; the floorboards creaked with the tiptoe of little feet across them. Curious, Helen leaned against the wall, poked her head far enough around the corner so she could see what was going on. She was just in time to catch Libby dumping a load of Nat's clothing on her bed, spot Cara and Zach dragging Nat's quilt and blanket piled with his dresser drawers across her floor, parking them next to the bed.

"I'll hang these clothes in the closet," Libby hissed. "You guys go back and get the dresser."

"Are you crazy?" Zach demanded. "It's heavy. We need you to help, too—"

"Hey." Helen stepped out from behind the partial wall that divided the sitting area-balcony from the bedroom. "What are you guys doing with Nat's stuff?"

"Huh?"

Startled, they turned to her, three less-than-innocents caught with their hands in the cookie jar. Libby recovered first.

"Mom." She was impatient and disgusted. "You spoiled the surprise."

"Oh?" Helen asked. "And what surprise would that be?"

"Well, we were just—"

"Helen." Furiously feeling his way through the doorway, Nat stalked into the room, chest bare, sheet gathered in a fist at his waist out of the way of his feet. "I thought we'd worked out this you moving stuff around on me without giving me the guided tour first. What the hell have you done with my clothes?" He stopped, felt with his foot the distinctive texture of the fabric he was standing on. "Is this my quilt on your floor?"

"Nothing, yes and don't swear in front of the children." Lord, he had a nice chest. She allowed herself a split instant to wonder what the rest of him looked like bare. Equally good, no doubt—and that was probably an understatement.

"Children?" He tilted his head from side to side, listening. "Which children?"

"Da-ad!" Cara exclaimed, dismayed and aggrieved. "What are you doing here? You know you're not supposed to see the bride before the wedding. It'll jinx it."

"That's a superstition and—"

"Did you see Mom before that wedding?" Zach asked, almost casual, mostly pointed, a little sad.

"Yes, as a matter of fact, but—"

"There, see!" Libby, triumphant. "Divorced, so it's a bad thing and you have to leave right now."

"Maybe," Nat said dryly, "if I could see *anything* it would be, but since I can't actually *see* the bride now or later, only hear, smell—" he turned to where he'd last heard Helen's voice "—you smell great, by the way—" returned his attention to the children "—touch or taste if she was close enough, so what's the—"

"Some-antics," Libby retorted, making Helen need to clear her throat and swallow a grin at the child turning some of the adult's favorite discussion-winning phrases back on him. "Don't be so literal, and 'sides, you *could* see her if you had an operation like the one we watched on the Learning Channel where they take off, um, that part of your eye that makes you not see and put in one so you can—"

"Elizabeth Jane!" Helen interrupted firmly. The flaming, mortified color on her face was reflected in her voice.

Libby turned to her earnestly. "Well, he could. I heard you tell Aunt Edith you wondered why he couldn't—"

"It's not nice to eavesdrop, Libby," Helen said feebly, chagrined beyond her wildest imaginings. "Nat, I'm sorry. Speculating 'what-if' is what I do for a living, but if I was going to 'what-if' about you, I should have at least made sure our informer wasn't within hearing distance first." She whipped back to Libby before Nat could respond. "Speaking of which, my miss, why don't you inform us about what you guys are doing in here with Nat's clothes?"

It was Cara who answered matter-of-factly, "Married people sleep together."

Which Zach promptly punctuated with a "Duh" that dripped with all the disrespectful how-did-you-get-so-old-when-you-are-so-dumb sarcasm his eleven-year-old voice could muster.

And Libby finished, "And you didn't have time and this is the mom's and dad's bedroom, so we decided to move Nat in so you wouldn't have to."

And Nat reacted with a startled chuckle, and Helen sat down on the arm of the sitting-room couch, her jaw hanging.

They were right, of course.

Which only goes to prove the theorem that it's *always* best not to judge the drift of a day by the smoothness with which it begins, and to remember that, regardless of what decisions two adults make between themselves, when there are children involved and the adults in question are parents, it's best to remember that children raised to have minds of their own usually do.

* * *

The wedding, of course, went almost as smoothly as Nat's and Helen's plans for maintaining separate bedrooms after it.

The bride got cold feet and suggested to the groom that they call the whole thing off, since there were obviously a whole lot of things the kids expected of them married that she and he hadn't thought to discuss yet.

The groom, suffering his own jitters, agreed with her in one breath and in the next told her they'd have to discuss a lot of things later because he needed some serious help "getting into that damned monkey suit" and he hoped to hell that when someone finally described her freaking dress to him it was worth him getting into the shoes that were sure to kill his feet instead of the hiking boots he'd have preferred to wear, and did she, perhaps, need any help getting into it and would she mind terribly helping him?

Emma and Jake arrived too early with their attorney and a yam-with-colored-marshmallow casserole in tow. Jake, looking sad and uncomfortably like a guilty little boy with a secret he didn't like keeping, fidgeted nervously with the knot in his tie; Emma, bitter but beautifully coiffed and dressed in black, stuck a cigarette in her mouth the moment she stepped through the door, put it politely away when Zach hastily told her she couldn't smoke in the house because one of the colonel's relatives had brought an oxygen tank and was using it. When her grandson's back was turned, she eyed Helen with daggered loathing and made the tight-lipped accusation, "You did this on purpose."

Which Helen hadn't, but her sister Twink unfortunately had.

Emma was, Helen tried to remember, a woman in mourning, a grieving mother who'd lost her only child less than a month ago, long before Amanda's natural time—never easy for any parent, doubly hard for a woman like

Emma who'd been, Nat had told her, unable to carry another pregnancy to term and had wanted to, desperately.

Helen's former in-laws, the frequently reality-deficient Henry and Ida Maximovich, arrived true to form, fifteen minutes early, intending to be forty-five minutes late and bickering about whether Henry had been driving seventy miles an hour down I-75 from their home in Lovells—too fast—or merely sixty-eight miles an hour—too slow. Ida, looking as usual like she was somehow wearing a bird's nest on her head, brought in from the car with her two covered dishes, one filled with the child-dreaded tomato aspic, the other which she urged Helen to "stick right in the oven, dear, so the stewed prunes with noodles will be ready for lunch."

When Helen accepted the dishes and leaned in to brush the lightly weathered cheek with a kiss, offering sympathy for the loss of her ex-husband, Henry and Ida's youngest adopted son, Ida shook her head briskly, patted Helen's shoulder and held her at arm's length, saying, "Now, now, none of that, dear. God must have needed him and Amanda in heaven very badly to take them that way, but we've done our crying and this is your day. I'm just glad we can be here for you and the children and that John came to his senses and finally decided to share Libby with you as he should have from the start."

Touched by the unexpected sentiment from her usually ditsy-seeming former mother-in-law, Helen blinked back startled tears. As a duo, Henry and Ida had always appeared somewhat caricaturish, but apparently her memory and long-ago estimation of them was wrong. Having decided this, she turned to greet Henry, who gave her a distracted arm squeeze, then hit his head on the hand-held television he was carrying when he tried to dive headfirst into it in order to recover the ball some college football player had fumbled.

So much for poignancy and revised estimations.

The "normal" grandparents arrived next, simultaneously.

Helen's mother, Julia—dressed appropriately for the occasion in a new, dark red sweatsuit covered with clowns and the names of all her grandchildren—greeted her daughter with a hug, a narrow-eyed, critical, up-and-down assessment and a considering, "Uh-huh." Handing her a loaf of bread and a can of mackerel, she said, "Well, you've stepped in it now, so I guess you'd better suck it up and feed the masses." Then she offered her arm to Nat and led him away, telling him in detail what he should be prepared to encounter that he probably hadn't already if he went through with today's "I do's," and, if he wanted to back out, now was the last chance he had to do it.

By contrast, Nat's parents, Katherine and David Crockett, were reserved and quiet, drawing their son aside to pass on a message that had been left on their answering machine by mistake, about calling his oculist. Then they greeted the grandchildren happily, but withheld comment on the day's festivities even when Helen's sisters descended on them, ostensibly to commiserate with them over their acquisition of the Colonel as a daughter-in-law. His brother, Jed, less reticent, took one look at Helen and pumped Nat's hand in effusive congratulations. It was he who finally divulged the secret of her appearance to Nat: harried, tousled, glowing, scoop-necked, slim-fitting, lots of *little* tiny buttons and a knockout.

Halfway down the aisle created by a frightening number of people he didn't know—relatives, uniformed and civilian friends, opposing attorneys, the children's-services caseworker and the two cops who'd come with her when she'd interviewed the children on Veteran's Day and a few people Helen was later sure had simply wandered in off the street—an overly anxious Max threw up onto the pillow holding the rings, and a buzz went round the room that Helen had stuffed the turkey raw, undercooked it and given Max salmonella poisoning when she let him eat some of it before the ceremony.

Four grandmothers, half-a-dozen aunts and a couple of uncles were there in a trice to take care of him, but it was "Kern'l" and "Nat" from whom he sought comfort, whom he finally allowed to lead him away to get cleaned up after receiving assurances that the wedding couldn't possibly, and wouldn't, proceed without him.

And it was an indignant Libby—naturally—who, on learning from Zach what her mother was being accused of this time, enthralled, appalled and thoroughly entertained the shocked, gasping, snickering and mirthfully tearful spectators by climbing up on a chair, tuxedo and all, and leaping to Helen's defense with an incensed tongue-lashing, informing her listeners her mother couldn't possibly give anybody Sam-and-Ella poisoning by stuffing a raw turkey because she didn't have any idea how to make real stuffing and besides had had a ton of other things to do with her time than to stick it inside anything, much less a dead bird, and anybody who didn't believe her could just follow her right out to the kitchen and see all the boxes of Stove Top waiting to be fixed. And not only that, but the turkeys, all three of them, were in the oven right now, and Libby herself would show anybody who wanted to see them that the birds had oranges, celery, onions and a little flour in the oven bags with them, but not one of them had anything inside it except their carcasses.

So there.

And Cara, hands on her nine-year-old, beginning-to-form, taffeta-covered hips, nodded her head hard and said, "Yeah."

And Jane, without understanding anything except that Libby and Cara were mad at a whole bunch of people, stamped her precious little foot, stuck her bottom lip out as belligerently as her sisters and said, "Me, too."

The crowd roared.

The actual exchange of vows was somewhat anticlimactic after that—except to Helen and Nat.

Their vows to each other were thoughtful and circumspect, halting and dry mouthed. Helen's hands trembled inside Nat's; his wrapped around hers, hard and strong and tight even as his voice went hoarse and he had to clear it several times in order to articulate all the things he needed to say to her.

They didn't use the word *love* they used *respect*. Instead of *honor* they chose *trust*. In place of *cherish* they put *appreciate, care for, shelter and defend*.

They hadn't, and didn't, lie to each other or themselves or those gathered. They held each other's hands and didn't pretend; they made a contract. Their reasons for getting married were as plain and unconditional and irrevocable to them as they were to their multitude of witnesses—so plain, in fact, that nobody had offered to take the children so they could honeymoon.

Convenience or not, they were getting married for the same reasons settlers and immigrants had chosen from time immemorial: because marriage suited the purpose, filled the need and protected the children.

That they were neither settlers nor immigrants, but modern people in modern surroundings with modern careers and personalities, was something they simply promised to try hard not to let get in the way.

And in the end it all came down to the same thing: a signed, witnessed and notarized piece of paper and a judge who proclaimed, "Now by the powers vested in me by the State of Michigan, I pronounce you husband and wife...."

Together they drew a tremulous breath, smiled, laughed a little nervously. Then Nat framed Helen's face with his palms and drew her toward him while he leaned toward her.

Their kiss was warm and dry, tentative and careful—a plain and simple seal on their pact.

Nat's pulse leapt anyway, something inside him cried out, heat coursed in tatters through his bloodstream. He wanted more, but he forced his rebellious body to take less. Accept it.

With the touch of his lips on hers, Helen felt her heart thud and race, then splinter and shrink inside her chest; felt suddenly afraid of the power of a thing so chaste it might be shared between siblings. She wanted less, oh God, please, because it would be so much easier that way. Found herself instinctively leaning into Nat for more.

They parted, breathing a bit frazzled, and Helen was glad Nat couldn't see her face, couldn't read what she feared he'd find printed there.

He was glad that his blindness prevented her from seeing what lay inside his soul, afraid of revealing something to her that he had no intention of revealing even to himself.

This had nothing to do with them other than peripherally; this was for the kids.

Holding hands, they faced the assemblage, smiled and laughed self-consciously through the applause, the calls of welcome to the Colonel and Mr. Crockett. Then Nat took Helen's arm and they retreated down the aisle amid back-patting congratulations and a confetti of rose petals.

And they both knew with misgiving that neither of them had gotten what they wanted out of that kiss.

Nor what they needed.

Chapter 7

Thanksgiving—Part II

"I'll sleep on the couch in the sitting room," Nat volunteered much later.

Reluctantly.

It was late and it had been a long day—longer even than it seemed on the surface, and that was pretty long—filled with...*incidents* masquerading as family, but he was hardly ready to sleep.

He was ready to tear apart a granite wall with his bare hands to relieve his tension.

He'd been standing or sitting near, talking with and about Helen all day. Her perfume was in his lungs; the infinitesimal taste he'd had of her mouth lingered on his lips. The husky, not particularly musical quality of her voice seemed to have affected the balance of his inner ear, leaving him light-headed and preoccupied with waging a battle to control the behavior of the more uncontrollable aspects of his anatomy.

The occasional feel he'd had of her skin, the contact with wisps of her hair against his cheek when they'd cut the wedding pumpkin pie together, the sensation of all those "*little* tiny buttons" going up the side of her dress and resting under his palm when he'd slipped an arm around her waist during their wedding pictures had made his fingers itch with longing to undo them, to count them, to find and taste the heat he could feel building beneath them. And he knew intimately that Helen hadn't failed to note his reactions to her, that she hadn't failed to react in kind, because when the photographer had arranged them so they were spooned together, standing with Nat's arms wrapped around Helen's waist and his hands resting on her belly, her rump tight against his fly... he'd been hard and aching, had become even more so when she gasped slightly and shifted a tad to place air between them and he'd held her where she was.

He'd felt the fluttery quality of her breathing beneath his hands, the staccato rhythm of her heart pounding like primitive drums against his chest, and the constant awareness of her and his cognizance of the civilized "forbidden" clause in the contract they'd made between them had driven him slowly mad with want.

Now, alone with her in a room that not only housed a bed but came equipped with a lock on the door, remaining civilized was the last thing he wanted to remember.

"You can't," Helen informed him—also reluctantly, equally as aware of him as he was of her, equally wanting.

Equally determined to maintain the distance she felt was the only hope for this... liaison's success.

She'd spent the same time near, thinking about or speaking with or about him as he had her. He'd teased her and she'd enjoyed the teasing. He'd touched her, naturally—a hand on her arm, trusting her to guide him around obstacles in his path; his hand covering hers when they'd cut the pie together; his fingers at the small of her back while they'd stood in the receiving line and collected knowing and, once or twice, somewhat snide and perfunctory congratulations.

She'd liked the feel of him—his arm about her waist, his fingers on those stupid side buttons on her dress. Liked the restiveness in his hand when he'd moved it, trying to find a place to light where he wouldn't accidentally undo the buttons; when his thumb strayed north once and grazed the very outside edge of her breast while the photographer tried to take their picture. Liked the feel of his hands on her belly when the photographer repositioned them, the flood of heat that centered there, the sensation of him at her back, warm and solid and secure—and horny.

Been horrified and mortified when, feeling the evidence of his desire against her rump, she'd moved to put a comfortable space between them and found herself instead edging back to settle more firmly against him, while his hands shifted, splayed and tightened at her waist, holding her there. While his cheek rested against the side of her head and his breath created sensory havoc near her ear.

And she'd wound up wanting more of the same and more beyond that until "want" had created its own universe, become its center, was at present a craving.

"It's only a love seat," she continued now. "It's way too short for comfort, and what if one of the kids gets up in the middle of the night and comes looking for us? Jane looked a little flushed when I put her to bed."

"Tell 'em we had a fight?" Nat suggested, peeling out of his tuxedo jacket, knowing he'd much rather be peeling Helen out of her dress and, subsequently, her senses. "You kicked me out of bed?"

"D'you really think that'd be the best way to begin?" Helen eyed the jacket he flung carelessly aside and turned her back on him, went into the bathroom. He might not be able to see *her*, but she could certainly see *him*, and the desires on his mind were printed as plainly on his too-expressive face as she was sure her own frustrations were printed on hers. "It's a good idea, but I'm afraid the kids will think the way we've begun is the way we'll go on, and if we begin with a disagreement that lands either of us on the couch the first night we're married, how long can it be before they're afraid we'll have a disagreement that lands one of us out on the street?"

Carrying her wedding dress, she came out of the bathroom, robe belted snugly about her waist. "No," she said with a notable lack of eagerness. She was an in-charge-of-herself, disciplined woman, but everything had limits. "There's no help for it. We have to sleep together."

There was a moment of silence while they weighed the pros and cons, the value of honesty versus the practicality of starting here and now to lie to themselves and each other.

"That's asking for trouble," Nat said baldly. "I dream about you when I sleep as it is, and make no mistake, they're hardly celibate dreams. They're lewd, lascivious and a whole lot debauched. Let me into your bed, turn it into *our* bed...however innocently we intend, I'm afraid..." He shrugged and left the probable consequences unstated but plain.

Helen's usually autocratic imagination fastened on the unstated, etched vivid mental illustrations that sent anticipation and heat searing from somewhere near her diaphragm down into her belly and left her unable to breathe through the fire in her lungs. She worked to wet her suddenly dry mouth and swallowed.

It was a big bed—king-size, in fact, with a firm, relatively new mattress and no low spot formed in the middle yet. There was plenty of room for each of them, no reason for them to wind up anywhere near each other in their sleep.

Unless they wanted to.

Or instinct did it for them.

She was not a big fan of inevitability. She preferred a little choice to anything labeled Fate.

"This isn't going to work, is it?" she whispered.

"Not unless we change the rules," Nat agreed.

"To accommodate lust," she murmured.

"And relieve it."

Again the silence, concentrated with inexorability, broken by the hum of the furnace and the sound of Toby quietly digging himself a bed in the carpet outside the door.

"No," Nat said sharply at the door, and the digging sounds ceased. The groaning dog circled his spot three times, collapsed audibly, comfortably and fell asleep. Nat returned his attention to Helen, tipping his head from side to side and reaching out hard with all his available senses for clues he couldn't see.

She looked at him, forgetting his blindness for a tick, expecting him to look back and see...

Instead she saw his head tilt, angling for the best vantage not to miss anything she did in the dark; watched his fingers seem to touch the air, gather it, collecting it for sensory analysis. Long sensitive fingers attached to broad, equally sensitive, callused hands.

Hands that would see her if she let them, explore her secrets, relieve her unspoken, unknown aches.

Share with her his own.

She moistened her lips, let out a breath and swallowed.

As though that was exactly the clue he was waiting for, Nat's mouth curved, hand turned over and reached out to her.

She hesitated, looking at it, wary and expectant. Swallowed again.

They were married now, a union both sacred and secular—even though only the secular law had been physically represented at the ceremony. She'd meant the promises she'd made. And they'd left the "till death do us part" phrase in their vows on purpose—for Emma's benefit, for the kids' sense of security, for reasons they'd shied away from exploring, rationalizing instead that the future expiration of their commitments, the end of the children's need for them to be married to each other constituted "death" in every sense—symbolic or otherwise—that counted, no need to belabor the point.

No need to worry that Emma or anyone else could take the children away from them simply for setting a bad example, giving in to temptation and enjoying sex without the fetters and expenses of marriage.

Sex, she assured herself firmly, being the key word, the honest word, unadorned by the glossy euphemism of *making love.* Utilizing the marriage covenant and the marriage bed to sanction the marriage rite.

Funny how quick and easy it was to justify and accept doing the very thing you'd rationalized out of existence every day for a month.

Every night, whether she admitted it to herself before or not, since she'd first met Nat until this one.

"Helen." His voice was a warm, rough baritone issuing invitation, hesitating to turn request into command.

"Yes, Nat." Her voice was breathy, insubstantial, unlike her. Her hands trembled—also unlike her—when she turned to switch off the lamp on the bedside table. No reason she should be the only one able to take advantage of the light.

No reason he should be the only one allowed to depend on his hands to see.

He heard the flat snick of the light switch and his smile widened even as the heat surged and rose through him.

When he invited hoarsely, "Come help me with these damned buttons," there was a hitch in his breath.

"My pleasure," she heard herself respond softly, without hope of making any other choice and remaining rational, and crossed the room to him.

His hands stilled instantly where he'd moved them to ease out of his suspenders. The note of despair he wasn't supposed to hear—that she hadn't meant to strike—reached his ears, stuck there like a dart thrown carelessly at a target so as to intentionally miss its mark, but sticking in the scoreless outside circle nonetheless.

Of course, simply because they'd made the decision to enjoy the pleasures of the conjugal bed within the confines of their marriage was no reason that the path to it should be free of ruts. But this was one ravine he had no intention of floundering into. Not with Helen.

He'd been here with Amanda a time or two, ignored the signs—perhaps relying primarily on what his eyes could see did that to a man—and look where it had got them.

But that was different than this. Because he was not, he assured himself, in love with Helen as he'd been with Amanda—who'd had the time to fall there, given the insanity of the last month? In lust, yes. Passionately. Irrevocably. And time, the alleged tincture for all things, hadn't dulled the edge of that hunger at all, as it should have. Helen entered a room and his body recognized her before his mind knew she was anywhere near. She created a chaos in his bloodstream, a mayhem in his senses that Amanda, no matter how much he'd once thought he'd loved her, had never begun to approach.

He wanted Helen badly—more, he realized, than he'd ever wanted anything in his life. More than he'd wanted her even moments ago. But he didn't want her coming to him in despair of...compulsion. He would not have her regret anything that passed between them, ever.

He was witnessing, he suspected, a side of the woman she didn't let anyone else see: the vulnerable, normally granite-encased heart of her; the woman who dressed to meet each day by putting on an inner uniform along with the outer, defined a tough set of principles and lived by them no matter the personal cost. He didn't want her to take him between her legs only because she felt the same all-consuming, bestial passion for him that he felt for her, only because their mutual . . . obsession with an act of the flesh with each other made her feel she had no other choice because he didn't, either.

He didn't want to begin this marriage with Helen hating herself in the morning.

When they joined—and they would, he knew, whether tonight or eventually, have each other in bed—he wanted only passion and pleasure between them, laughter and enjoyment, friendship and caring. Those were the things that would see them through the tumult of the journey they'd elected to take, the things that would not fade the way love was wont to do.

He was as intimately familiar with the paling of love as was Helen.

He wanted the act as part of the whole, part of the . . . pledge they'd made, a natural extension of the . . . commitment and the . . . care and caring they needed to stay together for fifteen years, at least.

Beyond that was not his to say or speculate.

Beyond these children graduating high school was more than he had any intention of asking of anybody, including himself.

When she put her hands to his shirt studs, he caught her fingers and held them still, drew a breath.

"Helen."

"I'm here."

It was hard to remember what chivalrous and noble things he'd been thinking, with her so close he inhaled the sweetness of every breath she exhaled; nearly impossible to recall anything except her name when she brought her lips to either corner of his mouth and left butterfly kisses there, moved to feather them along his jaw, nuzzled his late-day stubble with her smile, her cheek, her nose.

Breath hissed between his teeth and he canted his head, pressing into her mouth. This sure didn't feel despairing or vulnerable. Instead it felt bold and brazen and—he groaned when she dipped her head to minister to the part of his throat available above his collar—and *good*. But not hopeless. Not defenseless.

Ah hell, maybe he hadn't heard what he'd thought he'd heard. Maybe his ears just needed tuning.

She moved back to his mouth, and he found himself responding, gently at first, a little at a time, kiss upon kiss, lengthening and deepening, building toward that instant when there'd be no looking back; found himself getting lost even as he made himself release her hands and take hold of her upper arms to ease her away. Told himself that despite the way it felt, he wouldn't die if he didn't have her tonight.

He hoped.

"Helen." Firmly.

"Come to bed, Nat."

"Helen, I—"

Out in the hallway there rose a sudden clatter: a dog's yelp, a child's *aauugh*, the thud of something—possibly a body—hitting the wall, a wet slosh and the rattle of an empty bucket.

"Toby!" Libby's stage whisper scolded. "Now look what you made me do."

"What do you suppose—" Helen began.

Nat snorted. "With this crew? You pick."

Setting Helen aside, he strode to the door, hoping as he went that there was nothing in his path to trip over. There wasn't. But there was water streaming under the door and puddling in the low spot in the hardwood floor just short of the rug. His socks—the same absorbent, cotton crew type that he wore everyday—cheerfully sponged up the wetness the moment he stepped into it. He swore, but at least he didn't slip—which Helen, wearing smooth-bottomed slippers, did.

With a startled "Oh," she skidded through the puddle, scrabbling the air for purchase, catching at Nat. He obliged by grasping her elbow and steadying her before she managed to slam into the door. Then he yanked it open.

"What gives?" he asked the hallway.

"Nothing," Libby said. Innocent to the grave.

Being her mother, Helen didn't believe her. "Then why am I standing in water?"

"Oh, Mom." Her greeting was less than enthusiastic. "Are you up, too? I thought it was just Nat."

"No," Helen said, "it's not."

"Trying to put something over on the sightless?" Nat queried mildly. "Because my feet are turning into prunes, soaking in this puddle."

"Oh, um," Libby hedged. "No?"

Nat shook his head. "Try again. 'No' isn't a question I can give you an answer to."

"Elizabeth Jane." From Helen. A warning.

"Well . . ." Libby hemmed, dodging an explanation she preferred not to give—not out of fear, but simply because, like her mother, she preferred not to explain herself, period. "I was trying not to—"

"Libby!" Cara's stage whisper reached the hall from the doorway of their room.

Libby made frantic no-no-no-go-back motions that Cara either didn't see or ignored.

"Did you fill the bucket yet? I got Jane out of her pajamas, but boy, is her bed a mess. You better bring sheets, too—"

Helen stepped into the hall.

"—And a clean mattress cover and a rubber sheet—oh!" Cara stopped, giggled nervously. "Colonel." Gulped when her father stepped out of the room, too. "Dad. What are you doing up? Libby..." Her tone was scolding. "You were supposed to be *quiet.*"

"Ahh..." Libby grimaced, gesturing. "Toby—"

The dog's tail banged the wall, his head dropped and he watched his humans guiltily, evidently certain he was the one in trouble here.

"—Got in my way," Libby finished severely, using the presented scapegoat. "Didn't you, dog?"

The furry, hanging head drooped another notch and the dog's eyes worked in the shine of the night-light, begging forgiveness of anyone who'd give it.

"What—is—going—on—here?" Helen asked in her softest, most ominous, velvet-toned, superior-officer, tell-me-or-die voice.

"Well..." Libby said again, and with a huge sigh, Cara stepped in.

"Jane's sick. She got up crying and threw up in her bed, and we didn't want to disturb you on your wedding night—"

"Zach said you'd get mad if we interrupted the orgy," Libby interjected.

"—So we—"

There was a strangled sound from Nat; Helen coughed, trying to maintain some composure, and pinched him.

"—Decided we'd better take care of her ourselves," Cara continued, "and tell you about it in the morning—"

"If you were available," Libby inserted. "Because Zach says sometimes people in the throes of sexual discovery stay in bed for days, which is why married people usually go on honeymoons, 'coz if they don't they get kind of nasty if they're interrupted in the middle of a, um, *crucial* moment—"

This time it was Helen strangling so hard on discomposure and disbelief that she couldn't stop Nat from slipping by her and stalking, soggy socks and all, toward the third-floor staircase roaring, "Zachary Nathaniel Crockett, get your butt out of bed and get down here right now!"

It would be funny, Helen decided, rubbing her fingers across her eyes, if it were somebody else's seven-year-old parroting her big brother's explanations and if she didn't have the unquiet feeling that there was something far deeper and more disturbing to this than a simple attempt by Zach to shock the grown-ups by getting Libby to spout things he, Libby and Cara shouldn't even be thinking about yet.

She cleared her throat. "Elizabeth," she said, "I think we're going to have to talk about this—"

"What?"

"This . . ." Helen shut her eyes, collected her patience and spread her hands. "All of this, but right now—"

"Why doesn't Cara have to have a talk, too?" Libby protested, hands on her hips. "She did as much as I did." Aggrievedly. "Whatever I did."

"Cara *does* have to have a talk," Helen agreed impatiently, mentally slandering her mother for cursing her with the old I-hope-you-have-a-daughter-just-like-you-someday routine, "but right *now* I'm speaking with you, got that?"

"Cara's right there," Libby sassed, pointing. "She can hear you, too."

"Elizabeth." It was no longer a warning, but a threat: baleful, forbidding, every letter of Libby's name enunciated clearly.

Libby sighed in disgust, unthreatened but put upon. "Okay, fine."

"Now—" Helen began firmly, but was interrupted again. This time by the rattle of someone gagging and retching, then by a pitiful child's wail.

"Tern'l," Jane sobbed. "I want Tern'l."

Helen headed instantly toward the sob, awash in guilt. Busy debating with Libby, she'd lost sight of what was truly important here: Jane, sick. How could she have done it? Oh, God, she made a horrible mother.

"I'm coming, baby," she called, even as she looked over her shoulder at Libby. "Mop, towels, Simple Green, read the instructions before you mix it up and bring me a bucket of it—*hot* water. Cara, start sopping up the water Libby spilled in my—your dad's and my—room. Libby, when you're done, help Cara, then bed, girls. Nat and I'll take it from here."

"But, Mom—"

"March, Lib."

"But your wedding night—"

"Libby."

"Oh, all right." Libby stamped over to pick up the tipped bucket, stomped off down the hall, muttering. "I'm going, but Zach said you'd be crabby if you guys didn't get sex tonight, and you better not be too crabby to take us to the mall tomorrow to watch Santa Claus come 'coz it's *tradition,* and every time I see you, you always tell me how important—"

Praying for the strength not to strangle her daughter and for the guidance to find the right words to deal with a situation that was getting way beyond her experience and expertise, Helen shut her ears to Libby's tirade and went to take care of Jane.

"Helen?" Nat's voice in the darkness was quiet and concerned.

"Here," Helen called softly. "Jane's room. Keep it down, I just got her to sleep." Carefully she eased deeper into the rocker-recliner and gently pushed back to extend the foot, then shifted Jane's uneasily sleeping body to a more-comfortable position atop her and hitched Jane's quilt over them both.

Nat appeared in the doorway. "Talk me in."

"Pile of dirty laundry just inside the doorway to your right. Throw rug in front of Jane's bed, sick-kid bucket on top of it near the head. Jane and I are in the chair in the middle of the room. Four paces, maybe. Come straight in and you can't miss us. Where's your cane?"

Cautiously, Nat made his way into the room. "I'm not sure. It disappeared somewhere between the hellos and goodbyes, and Toby hasn't found it yet."

Helen made a soft *tsk* of exasperation. "I swear, Nat, you're worse than the kids, losing their homework. I'm going to get you a Clapper beeper to put on that thing. If you wore glasses, you'd probably lose them, too."

He found the chair with his knee, hunkered down beside it, grinning. "Why do you think I never wear shades to cover my eyes?"

"Because you enjoy disconcerting people."

"Besides that?"

Helen refused to be baited. "Did you talk to Zach?"

"Not yet." Nat shook his head. "When I got up there, he and Max were taking turns puking their guts out in the bathroom, so I figured the other should wait."

"Oh, God, not the turkey, do you think?"

"No, I feel fine, you're okay, Cara and Libby—we all ate turkey, you didn't stuff it, it was cooked to perfection and Sam-and-Ella left with the rest of the uninvited guests. I think it's the flu that's going round."

"Aw, geez." Helen moaned. "That means it's only a matter of time before the rest of us . . . and if we're very unlucky the kids'll pass it back and forth to each other and we'll go round in circles with it . . . damn."

Nat nodded. "'Fraid so. I called a cab. I'm going down to Perry's for a case of anti-emetic, some Imodium-AD, 7-Up and soda crackers. Anything else?"

"Yeah. Ask the pharmacist if they've got any white canes in stock and if they do, buy a gross."

"Funny lady." He rose.

Helen caught his hand, tugged him down again. "Just so you know," she said softly, "I'm real sorry we didn't get to—"

Nat touched two fingers to her mouth, caressed her cheek with the back of his hand. "We can discuss that later, too."

There was the sound of a horn in the driveway.

He unfolded. "There's the cab. I better go."

"Do you have money? My purse is—"

"I've got money."

"Take the dog."

Nat grinned. They were Married, all right. For less than twenty-four hours to be sure, but nonetheless with a capital *M*. "What do you think I am, new at this?"

"You lost your cane," Helen pointed out. "Or forgot where you put it."

"Or you moved it and forgot to tell me," he suggested lightly. "Not to mention I had other things on my mind, and why is it women always remember the details instead of the reasons around them?"

"Just talented, I guess," Helen said modestly, and Nat chuckled.

Then, because it seemed like the best, most-natural thing in the world to do, he bent and kissed her goodbye before he left.

In the cab halfway down Huron to the twenty-four-hour drugstore at the Tel-Huron corner, with Toby lying on the floor in front of him, Nat made the decision to woo his bride.

He'd never thought about it before—who thought about things that simply existed, whether you wanted them to or not—but they had, he realized with some surprise, gone about their entire relationship backward. Out of necessity, to be certain, but backward all the same.

Their acknowledged and strictly physical desire for each other—"the hots," as Zach might put it, without knowing whereof he spoke—had been a thunderbolt striking them both before they'd ever been properly introduced: timing horrifying because of marriages that later failed without encouragement or infidelity from either of them. For the last month they'd been thrown together—again through necessity, living in close quarters, sharing children and nonphysical intimacies before they'd had a chance to know each other at all.

Today they'd married—this time necessity was born of convenience and vice versa, perhaps, but still the necessity remained—before they'd ever had time to date. And tonight they'd discovered that instead of dulling it, time and proximity had only served to turn their hankering for each other into an insidious, hungry thing that wouldn't go away.

The few private make-out moments they'd purloined in the weeks before the wedding hadn't blunted the edge of their appetite at all.

Even so, married or not, climbing into bed simply because they were now "legal" seemed like just one more instance of hitching the cart before the horse. And Zach's apparent comments, repeated by Cara and Libby, only served to illustrate the point: Nat and Helen had to do this marriage thing correctly from the start because impressionable kids were involved. Kids who had to be shown that there was more between Nat and Helen than desire; kids who needed to know that the adults who loved them could be counted on to care for each other come hell and a hurricane, too.

It was an odd equation, when he examined it, and no matter how he sliced it, the damned thing always came out just about as clearly as the old math story problem: if a train leaves New York for Chicago at 8:45 a.m. traveling sixty miles an hour and passes through X at 10:30, and another train leaves Chicago for New York at 9:05 a.m. traveling seventy-two miles an hour and passes through Y at 11:45, where and at what time will they meet?

The logical, adult side of his brain said that if the Amtrak people programmed their computers properly, the two trains would never meet, because if they met on the same track they'd crash.

The illogical side, however, the part of him that never seemed to grow up beyond age fifteen or thereabouts, had never been able to solve that particular riddle when he was eleven or fifteen or twenty-three, or indeed, now. That part of his brain told him that the meeting was coming, no way to avoid the crash without both trains being in constant communication so they could stop or switch tracks before the disaster occurred. And since they couldn't switch tracks...

Since they couldn't switch tracks, what? He'd been headed somewhere with this thought when he'd commenced thinking it, but now—as had always happened back in math class—he merely had a headache.

A bad one.

"Meijers still have a twenty-four-hour flower shop, d'you know?" he asked the cabby.

"My wife does the grocery shopping and I ain't been there in a while, but far's I remember, they do. Got those fancy silver helium balloons, too. You need somethin' like that?"

Nat pursed his lips, puffed out a breath. "Yeah," he said, "I do. Listen, let's skip the drugstore and just take me to Meijers."

The hell with the train problem, he told himself. If you want to do it, just do it.

Since when did a man need an excuse to court his wife?

Chapter 8

First Sunday of Advent

The wooing commenced at breakfast—which Nat fixed—with a rose on Helen's tray and brought to her by him in Jane's room, where she'd set up the "infirmary" for the sake of convenience, dosed everyone who'd needed it with the anti-emetic and had Max and Zach sleeping on a couple of the household's fold-out mattress cubes on the floor.

She barely noticed the flower or Nat's infamous toasted cinnamon bagel or the English Breakfast tea sweetened the way she liked it, because at the moment Nat, guided by Cara, set down the tray on the Fisher-Price table, Helen was busy mopping up after Libby, who'd suddenly joined the sickies. And when she finally did get to sit down opposite Nat to eat at the too-short table in its accompanyingly too-short chairs, it was only to notice that Nat appeared distinctly pale and feverish—a truth borne out in the next moment when he all at once excused himself and groped his way down the hall to the bathroom.

Fortunately, Helen was faster than he and cleared the obstacles out of his path before he could trip and add injury to his nausea.

By Sunday she was the only one of the seven of them who wasn't recovering from the flu, and who hadn't been sick at all.

"Flu shots," she told Nat cheerfully when he, feeling better enough to be cranky but not well enough to hold his tongue, asked why she was still healthy.

"And you didn't share the preventative with the rest of us? Why?"

"Got 'em in October before I knew there'd *be* a rest of you," she retorted tartly. "That's why. Not my fault you didn't pay attention to the health news and follow the experts' advice and get your own shots before the season started."

To which Nat responded with something unprintable but forgivable, given the aches and pains his *aging* body was suffering due to the flu that neither anti-emetics nor the Imodium—nor even a dose of an extra-strength analgesic—could fix. Which is exactly what Helen told him before she gave him a let's-humor-the-poor-thing pat on the cheek and went off to fix him a turkey sandwich for lunch.

The sandwich did him a world of good, but it was the pat on his cheek and the cheery sarcasm that cured him.

By midafternoon he was parked in front of a football game with Max, Zach and Libby—the seven-year-old continually competing with the sportscasters to give Nat the blow-by-blow, while Max described all the colors and uniforms and Zach maintained an expressionless silence.

Jane and Cara played tea party behind the couch, offering Nat tiny cups of something that tasted suspiciously like—and was—Hi-C Ecto Cooler. Green, Cara informed him, because it wouldn't stain the carpet like grape juice if they spilled it.

And Helen thought she didn't have what it took to be a mother.

Smiling, Nat listened to her bustle about the house, imagined her as she came to him in his dreams: visually ageless, indomitably beautiful. Saw her naturally curly hair deceptively short so that only if a man had his hands in it would he understand how much of it there was. Got drunk on the remembered depth of her sea green eyes, the creamy paleness of her black-Irish skin. Added to the conjured imagery the portrait his mind had created of her with Jane sleeping atop her, Madonna and Child, the crux of the most-anticipated season of the year in a modern-day, well-used, velour rocking-reclining chair.

Visualized the gentle sway of her breasts beneath the loosely wrapped terry robe she wore when she got up in the middle of the night to take care of the children; felt the strength in the arms she'd slipped around him trying to help warm him through his fevered chills, the gentle press of her length along his back.

The longing ache that had coursed through him even in the midst of his flu sufferings and fretful sleep. The want elicited by every drift of her fingers across his brow, the back of his neck, his shoulders, his chest.

The volcanic, nerves-to-instant-attention jolt his system had experienced when she'd slid her fingers down his arm and into his palm. She'd only been handing him acetaminophen at the time, but the resulting shock was no less intense for all that.

He wanted her.

After a month in her company, he'd grown accustomed to having her around.

After three nights of marriage, sharing her bed with only pajamas and his flu between them, he was starving for her, hungry beyond anything even his dreams were capable of creating.

He needed her.

Urgently.

With every passing moment he grew more aware of her, who she was. Became manifestly more disturbed by what she was beginning to mean to him, more mindful of the intolerable burn thirty-two days of touch-but-don't-feel proximity had created.

Perhaps it was the simple adrenaline surge of feeling well after spending days in a hell where he knew he wasn't about to die but had occasionally felt bad enough to wish he might do so just to get the torture over with, but for the first time in a month of wanting-Helen insanity diluted by wanting-to-make-sure-they-wouldn't-lose-the-kids lunacy, he truly itched for time alone with his wife—without their children interfering.

Without having to even remember they had children.

Judas Priest, he thought, guilty because the wish wouldn't go away no matter how hard he tried to make it, what kind of a parent didn't want to remember he had children?

And the joker who lived in his mind rejoined promptly, *A real one. The same way real kids don't always want to recall they've got parents.*

Everybody—kid, parent, bus driver, naval commander, priest—needed time out now and again. That's why the military invented "leaves," universities offered sabbaticals and God created vacations. And today, right now, this minute, Nat wanted an immediate vacation with his bride, a chance to explore and broaden the boundaries of their . . . marriage.

Provided she was willing.

Shifting Max out of his lap and onto the couch, Nat collected his cane and followed the sound of Helen's sotto voce, off-key humming into the laundry room.

And shut the door behind him.

And leaned against it, waiting for her to say something so he'd know exactly where she was. He could hardly ravish her if all he wound up doing was clutching at air. Not to mention that tripping over piles of laundry and knocking himself out could prove a real mood killer.

"Hey," Helen said. Her voice sounded hollow and metallic, as though she might be peering down into the washer or maybe stooped in front of the dryer. "What's up?"

Ah, good, higher up. She was standing in front of the washer.

"Me."

He put out a hand and felt his way carefully toward her, allowed his palm to glide familiarly over her hip, slid his arms around her waist and pulled her back against him to nuzzle her neck.

She stilled at his touch, stiffened briefly, then fitted herself into his caress.

The way he'd known she would.

The way she had from the first time he'd given in to the urge to kiss her, on Guy Fawkes Day.

"Nat." Her neck arched into his mouth, belying the scolding even as she gave it. "You're sick."

"I was sick." His hands molded her stomach, strayed restlessly down across her belly and along the front of her thighs. His mouth dragged across the nape of her neck, teeth and tongue laid waste to the other side. "Now I'm better."

Helen's breath caught and she sighed. "You won't be if you overdo it. If I let you."

"I trust you. You won't let me overdo anything."

"Don't tempt me. I might." She was turning to him, twisting in his arms to get her own taste of him, to get closer to his mouth. "I'm not very trustworthy when I want something. I go all out for it, no holds barred, damn the torpedoes, full speed and all's fair. Ask anybody who graduated in my class from the Point."

"Consider me warned." He found her mouth, supped briefly, lifted his head. "Now, one for you. I want you, Helen—"

"Big surprise," she interrupted mildly, tucking her arms underneath his to link them around his waist. "It had to either be that or you're outgrowing your sweatpants in a major wa—"

He bent his head and stole the rest of the observation with her breath in a mind-numbing, devastating kiss that reached inside her and plunged something sharp and searing, uniquely... unexpected into her soul.

She'd had a month to learn to accept the desire between them, a fortnight to reconcile herself to the choice they'd made to make a marriage in name only, and four days to understand that their choice to remain celibate was unrealistic at best, absolute denial of the truth at worst. She had no time at all to comprehend the warning he gave her in this kiss, only a heartbeat to grasp an iota of the danger before she was engulfed in the whirlpool and sucked under.

She opened to him and demanded what he gave: hard hands laced in her hair, hard body taut against hers, hard tongue claiming her mouth in quick, brutal lashes that wouldn't be denied.

She was the fountain to be drunk from, the field to be harvested and hoarded without sharing... then suddenly she was the repository to be filled, the starving stranger to be shared with... the feast and a partaker of the feast... greedy... gluttonous... selfless—a human rainbow colored with sin and sainthood in the breadth of a kiss.

He'd begun the kiss to shut her up, to illustrate a warning he knew he should give her, punish her for making a joke out of something that was more deadly serious to him than he'd known. But that had been the beginning, and they were way beyond the beginning now, well out in a rough surf without a life preserver to share between them.

He'd begun and now he couldn't stop; at the crest of every small wave a bigger wave rose up, crashed down and drove him deeper; rose, crashed, drove until there was only a roaring in his ears and the darkness caved in and his mind went blank—and he didn't care that he was drowning because living had never felt anything like this. Living had never been this insanely risky nor this absurdly safe. And not even when he'd held a camera in his hands, focused on the single, instinctive instant when he and it seemed to fuse to capture moments rarer than any gem—not even then had he felt this... intensity of purpose, this singleness of direction, the absolute obsession to complete what he'd begun.

He couldn't breathe, yet he couldn't come up for air. His pulse was off the charts, yet he couldn't stop and slow down.

And this was what he'd needed to tell her, the caution he had to give.

But it was too late for cautions now.

Too late for anything.

His knees gave, her knees gave; it didn't matter, they were down. Something hard and angular was sticking in his back—a carved door panel, the sharp edge of a wicker laundry basket; he didn't care, it didn't matter. Helen's blouse was open, her bra was undone; the scent of her was in his nostrils, filling his lungs; her taste was on his tongue, in his mouth, swallowed to nourish his famished system; the sound of her breath, the thud of her heart were in his ears, tattooed in his brain, making and matching the rhythm of his; the feel of her skin was on his hands, under his fingers, a part of him. Her fatigue pants were gone, his sweats were bunched down around his thighs, her knees splayed to either side of his lap. The elastic leg of her

French-cut briefs was stretched aside; her fingers were on him, around him, guiding him in.

And then he was in, hot, wet and deep.

The pleasure was sharp, a minefield of sensation, and madness surrounded by delirium. Her body stiffened and relaxed, rose and fell, riding him. He clamped one arm about her hips and speared up into her, hard and harder, correcting the pace, setting it; his other hand twisted in her hair, brought her gasping mouth down to his, tongue thrust violently in. She was the earth and he was both rain and seed, planted and driving in.

And greedy as fresh-turned soil, she accepted the one and drank the other dry.

When it came, the earthquake rocked them both, leveled them, sent aftershocks rumbling through in long, sustained tremors that shattered whatever pieces of them might have remained intact.

Lost and abandoned but not alone, they held on to each other, unaware of anything but that glowing, stormy place where lovers went to leap while the shudders that joined their bodies gradually subsided, released them slowly back to where they'd begun: linoleum floor, wooden door, clothing in sorted mounds, the scent of laundry detergent, fabric softener and bleach.

The sound of the telephone ringing and children rushing to answer it.

The slap of basketball shoes outside the laundry-room door, the rattle of the knob when a child tried to push the door open, looking for Helen to come to the phone.

Zach's voice demanding to be let in, to know if everything was okay, if the Colonel needed any help, was all right, if she'd gotten sick.

Zach's voice concerned when he didn't get a prompt answer, then afraid.

It took all of Nat's remaining willpower to stay quiet, every bit of Helen's strength to collect her wits and make her voice sound normal when she said, "What? Oh, sorry, Zach, you caught me wool-gathering. Don't come in, I spilled the laundry soap all over the floor and I don't want anyone to slip. What do you need?"

"Phone," Zach responded. Toneless. Denying the moment of fear. "It's..." He hesitated, weighing relationships. Decided to conditionally accept this one. "It's Aunt Alice. Something about all us kids not drawing names on Thanksgiving as usual so she and Aunt Twink went ahead and did it for everybody and now she wants to give you ours."

"Oh, ah, okay." Draw names? Thanksgiving? She couldn't think straight enough to remember what either might be. "Umm, will you ask her to give the names to you, or, ah, tell her I'll call her back after I get this mess cleaned up or something?"

"Yeah." Laconic. The slap of rubber soles retreating back toward the other phone.

Helen's attention reverted to her and Nat still united intimately—on the laundry-room floor.

Nat's ragged breath still warm on her bare chest, the pounding of his heart keeping concert tempo with hers.

The milky evidence of passion beginning to leak around their joining, soak into the cotton of her underpants and cool.

Nat's silence and the tremble of his arms as they went around her, gathering her tight while he pressed his forehead hard into her breast.

The beast of shame and guilt rearing back to bare its teeth and snarl its laughter at her. How could they here and now with the children awake and able to walk in on them at any moment, and never mind that Nat was pressed so hard against the door that it would have taken a Mack truck to move him before he was ready to go, how could they simply step so far outside themselves and forget who they were and what their priorities were here, and Nat was sick, damn it, just getting well, and overexertion could give him a relapse and how could she, damn it all to hell, how *could* she?

The sensation of dampness running down the valley between her breasts and the muffled, inarticulate sound of Nat's voice, his groan stinging her ears.

His face raised to hers, tracked with tears.

His hand shaky at the back of her neck, hauling her into his kiss.

His sex already hard inside her again, eliciting tension and constriction in her corresponding muscles before they'd even had time to relax.

The scratchy, gravelly texture of his beard along her cheek, the harshness of his remorse beside her ear.

"God forgive me, I need you, Helen. Be my lover, be my lover, you are my wife...."

They should have realized that if they didn't deal with it in a more appropriate time and place it would get away from them—had realized it, in fact, and still managed to let it get away from them.

And because they'd let it get away, get *in* the way, in the end it didn't bring them closer the way it should have. It manufactured a distance, fostered an awkwardness that hadn't separated them since their first night under the same roof.

They were both passionate people, individuals who rarely let common sense stand in the path of a goal.

Which meant that chaos stood there now in the center of a bramble thicket, with them on opposite sides, and the only boulevards through it were a thousand miles to either side or straight through the roughest and thorniest part directly in front of them.

They avoided the thorns as best they could.

"Where'd you go, Dad?" Libby complained over a light dinner of Campbell's chicken soup with rice. "You missed the best play of the game. Barry Sanders caught the ball and made this run—you should have seen it! Bodies flying everywhere..."

Dad.

Why'd she have to pick now to call him that when at least three-quarters of the rest of the time she called him simply "Nat?"

He didn't feel the need to be quite so...superhuman when all she called him was Nat.

"Bathroom, Lib," he lied, glad he didn't have to think about meeting her eyes. "Guess this flu wasn't as out of my system as I thought."

"That's too bad, it was some game and the Lions *won* for a change and—"

"Daddo..."

Daddo. Max at his elbow with the calendar, tapping his arm.

"...Tomorrow you hafta bemember to be at school at quarter after nine to go on Cara's field trip to Greenfield Village and call your eye doctor and Kern'l's taking us all to the dentist after school, even Jane, and you have a class tomorrow night at six—"

"Tern'l." Jane leaned over in her high youth chair, earnestly patting Helen's arm.

"Whatcha need, sweet pea?"

"D'zert."

"Dessert?" Helen's glance drifted across the kitchen table to Nat, slunk away, a voyeur with nothing to look at. Not sure what she needed to see. "Already? Did you finish your soup?"

Jane waggled her head regretfully. "Tan't."

"Full?" Helen asked.

"No." Emphatic. Illustrated by Jane picking up her bowl and sloshing it forward to show Helen what was left in the bottom. "Tan't stoop it up."

"Slurp it," Helen suggested.

Jane eyed her a moment, reflecting, then grinned and picked up her bowl and slurped the contents into her mouth, spilling half of what was left down her bib in the process. Expression serious, she pulled the dish away from her mouth, peered into it for several seconds, then swung it at Helen, beaming.

"Gone," she crowed.

"So I see," Helen agreed dryly.

She caught the bib before Jane could whip it off and scatter spilled dinner into her hair and to the four winds, folded crumbs to the inside and mopped the tyke's face with it after she took it off. The she released Jane from her chair and handed her two cookies; Jane promptly climbed into her lap and wiggled into a comfortable position, using Helen like an easy chair.

"My Tern'l," Jane announced, munching happily, waving her arms in the air and offering a mushy bite of cookie that Helen wisely declined. "My fern-cher."

"Furniture," Helen concurred. "That's certainly what I feel like sometimes."

Again her gaze slipped to Nat, studying the mobile features, remarkable in stillness. What was she looking for? What did she want to see?

Reassurance, familiarity, ease . . . mobility. Expression. Not this . . . blankness. Not guilt.

Not regret.

Family life, routine, filtered back in.

". . . It's part of social studies, so when we go tomorrow I have to dress like people who lived in the 1870s," Cara was explaining to Nat. "Grammy Sanders made me a dress and a pinafore, with a bonnet and a pair of bloomers. The dress is kind of minty-green-and-white striped and the pinafore and bonnet are kind of a stripy-plaid-patchwork sort of stuff—she says it's calico—that match the dress pretty good, and the bloomers are white." Softly, wistfully, she added, "I wish you could see me."

"Oh, darlin'."

Nat reached for her and she came to him, pressing in for a hug, and Helen, watching, felt a stab of pain for them both.

Nat squeezed his daughter hard, held her away, touched her face, outlining her cheeks and nose, around her mouth. "I can see you, you know, very clearly—in my imagination. It's not quite the same as seeing you with my eyes, but it's pretty good. Because you described them to me, I can imagine your dress and the colors and what you'll look like in it. You're beautiful. You look like your mother—"

From beside Nat came the harsh, deliberate squeal of wooden chair legs scarring linoleum, the crash of the same chair falling backward to the floor, the clatter of flatware and Corel dishes following it.

"Zach?" Nat asked. "What happened? Are you all right?"

"Fine," Zach snapped, "just fine, except this is all bull and I hate it and I don't want to be here anymore. I don't want any of you here anymore." He kicked his silverware aside, pushed around the table to snatch his jacket off its peg beside the basement door. "I'm goin' out to shoot baskets."

"Zach, it's dark, you've been sick—"

"So I'll turn on the stinkin' lights, okay, *Colonel?* Not that you have anything to say about it anyway, 'coz you're not my mother and you never will be so stop tryin' to take her place and just keep the hell away from me."

"Zach." Nat's voice was puzzled. Cool and firm. "You don't talk to anyone like that, but especially not Helen. Come back here and apologize."

"Apologize for me, *Dad*," Zach snapped. "Same way I'm always apologizing for you."

The window in the door rattled behind him with the slam.

"Zach!" Nat's chair hit the floor with the force of his rising. "Toby, cane," he commanded sharply.

Hands out, he felt his way around the table, headed after his son.

"Nat, don't." Helen rose with him, hoisting Jane out of her lap and depositing her on the floor.

"Helen, he can't do this. I can't let him."

"Nat, he hurts, he's got to work it out."

"You think I don't know that, Helen? You think I don't know how he feels? His mother abandoned me once, too, remember?"

A sock in the jaw would have hurt less. Especially after what she'd shared—done—with him this afternoon in the laundry room.

Helen drew herself up, worked her jaw metaphorically back into place. She had to believe he didn't mean it the way he said it. She would not let this affect her. She was tougher, she told herself, than a comment made in the heat of a moment. She was tougher than anything any mere man had ever done or said to her in her life.

"Nat," she said, keeping her voice even, aware of the fearful intensity with which Max, Libby, Cara and Jane watched them. "Whatever this is about, he needs space. You have to allow him time."

Nat's jaw squared, face hardened. He took the collapsed cane Toby nudged into his hand, unfolded it and snapped it together. "Don't," he suggested softly, "try to tell me how to handle my son."

The window in the door rattled almost as hard when he slammed out as it had for Zach.

Angry voices sounded in the driveway, the *slap-slap* on concrete of a basketball in need of air, the bang and rattle of a well-used backboard every time the ball hit it.

Reaching for something normal, Helen settled Zach's far too wary siblings in front of a Disney movie in the playroom and retreated to the sun porch off her bedroom to stand in the dark, looking down on Nat and his son. There wasn't a lot to see. Zach played basketball by himself, ignoring Nat, and Nat talked himself blue, then simply stood silent, listening to the sounds defiance made in a city driveway: *bonk-bonk-bonk, slap, bang, rattle,* the occasional loud crash when the ball hit the aluminum garage door. Not much to communicate with there.

Thoughtfully Helen left the porch, went to rummage in Nat's side of the master closet. She thought she'd seen one of the kids bring in...ah! There it was—Nat's athletic bag. She wrinkled her nose at the contents—two smelly, cutoff sweatshirts, *sweat* being the key word there; a pair of worn, formerly white high-top basketball shoes; a clean jock strap without the cup; a pair of University of Michigan gym shorts of indeterminate age; and what she was looking for: one Visually Impaired Association Air Attack audible basketball and a goal locator—sans battery, of course.

Carrying shoes, ball and locator, she headed for the driveway, stopping long enough in the playroom to let Cara and Libby know where she'd be. Then she took the long way to the driveway, stopping in the kitchen to find a nine-volt battery and detouring through the basement to collect the tall stepladder before she went outside.

The silence of a father and son at odds with each other was loud even by city standards—and they were barely a block and a half around the corner from one of three local hospitals and its emergency room. Ignoring Nat and Zach both, Helen dropped the ladder and the ball, *oofed* Nat's shoes into his midriff without announcing herself first, intercepted Zach's ball out from under his nose in mid-dribble and tossed it into the bushes along the side of the house.

"That will be enough of this," she announced to the world in general.

Then, before the two sap-skulled, dumfounded males of her household could react, she set up the ladder, climbed up and attached the goal locator to the basket rim, climbed down and set the ladder carefully aside. Picked up Nat's audible basketball, backed up, bounced the jingling thing twice and swished a three pointer from the foot of the driveway. The goal locator did its job to perfection, but just to make sure, Helen took the ball in for a lay-up, then dribbled it back down the driveway, feinted around Zach and sank a hook shot—catching nothing but net, thank you very much.

No one had ever had the nerve to say of her that she was content to leave well enough alone. Nor that she didn't enjoy showing off from time to time—as long as it was for a good cause. Nat might not be able to see what she was capable of, but Zach could.

Satisfied, she slapped the ball into Nat's chest as she had his shoes, repossessed the ladder and Zach's ball, and headed for the house.

"Play nice, boys," she suggested gently from the steps.

Not even the knob rattled when she shut the door behind her.

She was back upstairs bathing Jane and supervising Max while he bathed himself when she heard the back door open and slam, open and close, heard the stomp of angry-boy feet on the stairs, the quieter tread of his father following. Listened to the father sigh when the angry son slammed yet another door in his face. Caught the faint sound of Nat's basketball being dropped back into his closet with his shoes.

Remembered the illusions of her childhood, where it seemed that her parents, no matter what the situation, always appeared to have all the answers.

Another good story shot full of the holes of experience.

She felt Nat before she heard him enter the bathroom behind her.

"Helen, I—"

She stood, handed him a towel. "Why don't you help Max finish up while I pajama Jane. Cara and Libby already showered and brushed their teeth. They're waiting for their story."

There was no tightness in her voice, no "you supreme jerk," no "we'll talk about it later," merely the continuation of life, the application of routine, the same bedtime ritual the children had expected from them from the first.

He wasn't sure whether he was grateful for the consideration or not. Of course, maybe she just didn't want to get into it in front of the kids. That was the trouble with having the family first and marrying someone you didn't know second; the rules of war were usually the last ones to be established.

Helen's, he discovered the minute all the children were tucked in, had to do with a basketball game called "Horse."

"Helen..." He followed her into the bedroom, once again trying to get her attention.

"Save it and put your shoes on, stud," she said crisply, collecting the basketball from where he'd dropped it. "I'll be in the driveway."

"Pardon?"

"Five minutes," she informed him, "then I spot you two points and start without you."

Leaving him openmouthed, head canted, listening hard after her, she left.

It took him less than three minutes to follow her.

"Okay, Helen, what's goin' on?"

"B-ball. You got your shoes on?"

"Yeah."

"Great." She bounced the ball twice. "Then let's do it."

Nat puffed out a barely patient breath, felt his way down the back steps. "Do what, Helen? Pretend I'm slow. Spell it out for me."

She crossed to stand in front of him, excruciatingly indulgent. "We play," she explained carefully, "one game, twenty-one points, one-on-one. I'm handicapped by having the lights out and spotting you two points. If I win, you explain what happened over dinner and in the laundry room to me. If I lose, you explain what happened over dinner and in the laundry room to me. Simple."

"Let me get this straight." Nat reached out, found the ball and took it out of her hands. Set it on his hip and draped an arm over it. "You win, I explain myself to you. I win, I explain myself to you. That it?"

"Pretty much."

"And there's no way you're going to let me just skip to the explanation and forget the exercise."

"Nope. If you're well enough to baptize me and the laundry room twice, then do battle with an eleven-year-old, you're well enough to help me get rid of your excess aggression out here first."

"My excess aggression, not yours?"

"That, too."

"Hmm." Thoughtful, Nat worked his jaw. "How do I know the lights are out and you won't try to cheat?"

"You don't. Or you trust me. Or you go next door and ask the judge to ref."

"Hmm." He rolled the ball off his hip and spun it between his palms a couple of times, getting the feel of it before twirling it up to balance on the tip of one finger. "I'm pretty good, you know—All State in high school, scouted by the pros in college, my team finaled in the Gus Macker three-on-three out at Oakland last year. With the lights out and you trying to see through the shadows instead of playing blind...maybe I ought to spot you six points and give you first outs."

"West Point intramurals," Helen retorted. "Captain of the championship team four years running. Voted army pick-up league MVP last year."

"Oh, right." Nat snorted. "And probably by a bunch of suck-up junior officers and enlisted personnel, too."

"No ranks on the court," Helen said frostily, causing him to grin. "Merit only."

"Anybody ever tell you you've got a nasty competitive streak in you?"

"All the time," Helen confirmed.

Nat's grin broadened. "Show me the court," he suggested.

If anyone had told Nat that three days after his Thanksgiving wedding he'd be out in his driveway while it snowed going all out to beat his bride at a game of Horse, he'd have told them they were nuts. Even now, while it was happening, he could barely believe it.

It was a hard, fast, physical game, played by street rules with a lot of body contact. After she'd fouled him onto his keester for the second time in five minutes, he quit trying to play any kind of chivalrous game, stole the ball from her and concentrated on playing to win.

The fact that after twenty minutes the score was only eight to six and he was ahead by a scant two points and was breathing a lot harder than she was floored him.

"Maybe we ought to call time," Helen offered kindly. "Let you catch your breath. You have been sick, after all."

Grimly Nat swiped sweat and snowflakes out of his face, pitched the ball to her and stripped off his shirt. "Shut up and take it out."

"*Tsk, tsk, tsk.*" Helen dribbled the ball slowly, calculating her attack. "You're starting to sound crabby. This is a friendly game, remember? Better be careful, your temper'll screw up your judgment."

"Friendly game, my eye." He lunged for the ball, felt Helen dodge around him, heard the ball hit the basket and knew she'd racked up another two. "If this is what you call friendly, I'd hate to see you when you're not. Where'd you learn to play, anyway?"

"The Point. Played a little in high school, but you know how it was then. Pretty backward as far as women's sports were concerned, unless I wanted to play tennis, which I didn't. Found out I've got kind of a knack for games men play. Not to mention I discovered that if, as a plebe and a woman to boot, I took the court and mopped the floor with upperclassmen, my credibility went up, not to mention the respect. Got called a lot of names for a while, but the sexual harassment stopped. A few morons questioned my, um, orientation, I guess you might say, but I survived and a lot of them didn't, and I guess that's the best revenge."

"Sounds like a tough crowd."

Helen shrugged; Nat could almost hear it in her voice. "Can't beat it for life prep," she said. "Never have been good at girl stuff, but I never felt like a tomboy, either. Had to learn how to handle the fact that a lot of men don't like competing with women. Especially women who can dress and feel like women and still play on their courts and win. And I can."

He stopped short, arrested by something in her voice. "That what this game's about? You feel you got something to prove to me? Or maybe yourself? I'm not other men, Helen. I believe in letting people—men, women or green things from Mars—do what they're capable of doing."

"No." Helen paused in front of him, mopped her face on her forearm. "Not to you. At least . . ." She hesitated. "Not anymore. I think this is just blowing off steam because I need to. Spending time with you because I want to.

Maybe letting you see a side of me some people don't like. And maybe because I think you—we—need to understand that the same rules that apply out here apply in the house.''

"I play fair with you, you'll play fair with me?"

"Basically."

"But out here we're one-on-one," Nat said quietly. "Opponents. In there we're on the same side.'

"We weren't tonight and it scared the kids. They've been through a lot, Nat. They need to know they can count on us."

"They also need to understand we're not always going to agree about everything, Helen, and that's okay."

"Is it, Nat? I don't even know that, so how can they?"

Nat turned to her, face carefully blank. "You don't even know what?"

"You." Passionate. "What you expect from me."

"Helen, I don't..." He tried to catch her arm, but she yanked away, spun to face him.

"I don't know that disagreeing with you is okay, I don't know what your temper's like, I don't know how easy it might be to push you too far, I don't know where all your buttons are and I'm not even sure where all mine are anymore."

She took his hands, laced her fingers through his, linking them physically the way she'd begun to need them to be linked emotionally. "They're lookin' to us for their cues, Nat. They need us to be like an old married couple that's been together for years, need us to know where we stand with each other all the time, what we expect from them and ourselves, and I *don't,* Nat. I don't."

"Helen, I—"

"You may take yourself and this entire situation for granted, but where you're concerned, I can't, because where you're concerned..." She touched his hand, his cheek in a gesture of futility.

"When it comes to you," she finished softly, "I'm not even sure where I stand with me."

Chapter 9

How did that old song go? *You shake my nerves and you rattle my brain....*

Well, his nerves were pretty jangled, all right, and his brain felt like a pair of broken maracas. Had been all day, all week, the last month, most of his life since he'd first run into Helen.

She was supposed to be the one who understood what was happening to them. She was the one with the serenity in her genes, housed within her body, where she'd taken him in without question, without an ounce of caution or prevention.

Where she'd made him feel whole within himself for the first time in years, then left him wary, afraid that where he'd gone—where he'd taken her—this afternoon from instinct would be withdrawn from him—from them—again because he didn't know where he stood here, either.

With her or with himself. And if she wasn't sure in turn...

He swallowed the taste of something that disagreed with his stomach. All he knew right now was that there was a hollow place inside him that simply having his kids back didn't fill the way he'd assumed it would. A space that needed not only a woman's touch, but required *this* woman's touch.

But whether that vacancy merely needed redecorating so she could rent it, or if it was in search of a permanent resident, he didn't know.

Didn't want to know at the moment, truth be told.

"I mean..." She squeezed his hands hard, her voice was wistful. "Nat, you gotta tell me. What am I gonna do about you? I want to know, I need to know...do I kiss you hello and goodbye, do I kiss you in front of the children, do I come to you when I need a hug? Can I crawl into your arms, sleep on your side of the bed, expect to snuggle without having sex? Can I relax with you, or do I need to worry whether or not I brushed my teeth three times a day or put on deodorant, instead of paying attention to some kid who's gotta have this or that for school this morning and forgot to tell me the night before, or if I smell after a game of Horse, or put on makeup when I'd rather not?"

She withdrew her hands, turned away, arms about herself. "Do I talk to you about Zach or talk to him myself and hope that what I tell him isn't diametrically opposed to what you'd tell him? Do I discipline Cara the same way I do Libby, or do I worry about crossing into your territory and stepping on your toes? I mean, we have to have some consistency here. When I refer to you when I'm talking to them, do I call you Nat, Dad or something else, or do I pretend that it's okay not to call you anything and hope they'll come up with something that makes them comfortable even when I'm not? And do you think it really was an omen when Max threw up on the rings?"

She looked over her shoulder at him, confusion plain in her voice. "Is it okay to come to you when I want you so bad that not having you hurts? How do I respond to the kids when they make the comments they've been making lately about sex and orgies and the expectations of wedding nights? Do we go back to separate bedrooms and let them wonder where we stand with each other? Do I talk to them about us, or do I pretend not to hear when they're wondering and hope that ignoring it all is the best solution?

"And what about love? Will they accept it if we say it to them but not each other, or does it really matter if we say it at all? Can I assume where I stand with you, or do I have to worry that the minute I say something to the kids, you'll come along and say the opposite? How do we handle the finances—split everything down the middle, each pay for our own kids and divide Max and Jane between us? It's damned dark in here where I am right now, Nat." She came back to him, placed a hand on his chest to make sure she had his attention, asked softly, "How 'bout it, Nat? Can you reach the lights or aren't there any?"

"God, Helen, I don't know."

His hands clenched; her hand was warm on his cooling skin and he wanted to feel that warmth elsewhere on him, all over him, the way... earlier.

He knew he should move away from her then, wanted to and couldn't. Wanted to reach for her and couldn't do that, either.

Instead he tipped his face to the sky, felt the drift of snowflakes on his cheeks, beneath the tangle of damp hair on his brow. They were clean and cold and known. "It's pretty damned dark where I am, too, and huge, and nobody's bothered to show me where the walls are so I can feel my way along 'em, let alone find out if there's a light switch so you can see where you're going, too."

"So what do we do, Nat? You were so sure about this from the beginning. I had to trust you because I was afraid of all of it and I knew I couldn't be, or at least couldn't let it show, and I figured that if maybe you knew where we were going, I could just climb on for the ride and pray. But then Zach..." Her voice trailed away, not sure how much farther to go.

Nat turned away from her, wrapped himself inside himself, knowing he was probably about to hurt her. Not wanting to.

"Zach asked me if I..." He rocked his head, still disbelieving; laughed without humor. "...Asked me if I *bonked* you in the laundry room this afternoon."

A sharp pain in the vicinity of her heart made her suck in her breath. "Excuse me?"

Nat turned back to her, nodding. "That's what I said, so he repeated the question, then translated it into cruder...euphemisms, figuring he'd either shock the hell out of me or finally come up with ones I understood. I don't know, he must have seen me go in and not come out or something...."

"God, Nat."

"Yeah. He shocked the hell out of me and I understood every single damned one of 'em, but he shouldn't. I'm not sure he really does, but he's got the words and he's got the act and I didn't know how to respond. I still don't. I told him that what happens between married people— between you and me—is between *us* and none of his business unless it involves him directly, so he proceeded to tell me what he'd observed between John and Amanda and he shocked me all over again, as I'm sure he intended. I can't imagine—hell, I don't want to imagine—where he learned this stuff. Psychologist I went to after my accident told me kids from bitter divorces sometimes have real problems with their emotions—real confusion. That they have a tendency to act out when it comes to changes in their routines or their parents finding new partners and a lot of other things, but I didn't realize..."

"He still wants to go live with Emma and Jake, doesn't he?" Helen asked. It cost a lot to keep the tremble out of her voice, to keep it neutral.

To not turn tail and run away.

Nothing anyone had ever done to try to keep from winning her place in the army had ever hurt like this.

"Yeah," Nat said, "he does. Jake told him they've got a room for him anytime he needs it, but Emma told him he couldn't come, that they stood a better chance of getting custody of him and the rest of the kids if they could show the courts what a bad environment the children had been forced to live in, how... confusing our sudden marriage and our resulting sex life and I don't know what all else is for them. I don't know, I think that's the gist. He was ranting at the time."

Helen stared at him, astounded. "She can't have told him all that."

"Who?"

"Emma. Why would she say those things to her own grandson?"

"I don't know, Helen. People say and do stupid things when they're in pain, and Emma's been in pain for years."

"She's not in pain, she's ill, Nat, if she's trying to use a little boy in that way. Did you tell him that?"

"What was I going to say to him, Helen?" He threw out his hands, frustrated. "Your Grammy's a cruel and vicious woman who shouldn't be allowed anywhere near you if she's going to say things like that? He loves her. You and I are the virtual strangers in his life, not Emma. If I tried to tell him something like that we'd lose him for sure. Not to mention that the way he overreacts to everything these days, it's hard to distinguish between what Emma or anyone else might have actually said or what he *thinks* he heard. Eleven is not the most rational age for boys, if my memories of Jed and me at Zach's age are anything to go by."

"But can't we—shouldn't we..." Helen floundered, helpless. "We have to do something...don't we?"

Nat released a painful laugh. "Hell, Helen, how do I know? What can we do tonight, anyway? It's getting late, I'm getting cold and I've got a field trip in the morning with thirty-three fourth-graders. For now I want to go to bed and forget about it. Maybe the answer'll come in my sleep."

Helen found his shirt where he'd tossed it, brought it to him. "Share it with me if it does?" she asked.

He caught the hand that handed him his shirt, squeezed it hard. "You got it," he promised, and let her lead him inside.

They checked on the children, rearranged kicked-off covers, went to their room and undressed in darkness in separate corners, listening to the quiet rustle of clothing tossed aside, the house settled for the night, the sounds of the city outside.

Helen used the bathroom first, washed up, brushed her teeth and crawled into bed, leaving it free for Nat. She listened to the water run, the sound of the brush on his teeth, the toilet's flush, and tried to imagine what it must be like to inhabit the world Nat inhabited, how inconvenient it must sometimes be to have to get about in a five-sense world with only four senses, depending on other people to match his clothes, set up other aspects of his life so he could live it.

Having to trust people he barely knew to play fair with his questions.

Be my lover, be my lover...

When she and John had gotten married, she'd kept her Brannigan surname for a variety of reasons that had seemed relevant at the time: pride, no male Brannigans to carry down the name to the next generation, her sense of her own identity, principle, career identification and other reasons she couldn't even remember anymore.

Later, when things between her and John had begun to be...less than satisfactory, she'd wondered whether if she had taken—or at least used with a hyphen—his family name, cemented their unity with more than a piece of paper and Libby, things would have been different, if they'd have felt more like a family....

Well, the ifs were a little murky by now, but nonetheless potent for all of that. Were part of why she'd chosen to change her name to Crockett both on the marriage license and everywhere else this time. Because the reasons not to had ceased to matter with the passage of time.

The other part—as everything else—was for the children. There were enough surnames floating around in this household, enough confusion of identity between the Crocketts and the Maximoviches and the Crockett-Maximoviches without adding Brannigan to the mix. And so she was, for the duration, Colonel Mrs. Crockett. Not Brannigan hyphen Crockett nor any other variation on the theme. No other ambiguities, simply Helen Marie Crockett, Colonel, U.S. Army, Active.

It didn't change who she was in the least and it simplified life considerably from the children's standpoint. But she hadn't spelled her decision out to Nat, he hadn't asked and maybe assumed...what so many people assumed: that a woman automatically took her intended's name without any thought whatever going into the process.

But Helen had thought about it a lot, and maybe he needed to know what he was unable to see.

Be my lover, be my lover...

She'd asked Nat a lot of questions tonight that only time could possibly answer; he'd asked her only one: where do I stand with you, what do you expect of me? And suddenly she knew it was the one question she could—and wanted to—answer before any more time passed.

She got out of bed and went to lock the bedroom door.

Everything about their...relationship was already backward, anyway, so maybe that was the way it was supposed to work for them: back to front, inside out and sideways instead of the old-fashioned, linear start from *A* and wind up at *Z*. It was only a middle-of-the-night theory, mind you, but she sort of liked its lack of logic in the midst of all this chaos. The simplest principle she knew of to describe the science of chaos, after all, was the one she'd learned from *Jurassic Park:* that no matter what you did to it, no matter how illogical it seemed, in the long run somehow life would find a way.

She grinned. Life lessons from the movies—"life will find a way." Gumpisms such as "life is like a box of chocolates" and "stupid is as stupid does"—homilies from fictional lives to describe a reality that had begun to read like fiction. Maybe eventually they could get their real lives to mesh like fiction did, too; work out—at least a few days at a stretch—to happy ever after.

Or as reasonable a facsimile thereof as they could manage with chaos as their guideline.

She was glad when Nat came out of the bathroom and the distraction allowed her to discard her thoughts.

He dropped his watch, pocket change, wallet and comb on the nightstand, paused at the rustle she made drawing back the covers for him.

"Helen?"

"Can I...say something to you?" she asked quietly.

He sat on the edge of the bed, rubbing his neck, hesitated a tick over his answer. "Sure," he agreed finally, guardedly.

She didn't blame him.

She slid up on her knees behind him, slipped her fingers under his on his neck. "Stiff?" she guessed.

He nodded, still wary. "You play a rough game."

"You're no slouch in that department yourself." She worked her thumbs and fingers into his tight muscles, felt them begin to relax—barely. For a few moments longer she worked his muscles in silence, deciding what she wanted to say. "We asked each other a lot of questions tonight."

"One or two," he agreed wryly. "Is this going someplace? Because, I'm sorry, but your hands on me aren't the most relaxing things in the world. In fact, I'm starting to feel just a little more tense than I did before. And warm."

"Yeah, well..." Helen spread her knees along the back of his hips, pressed closer along his back. "That's kind of what I wanted to say to you."

Again she paused, adjusted her position.

He turned his face toward her. "What is?"

She moistened her lips, gathered a breath of courage. She didn't think he'd reject what was on her mind, but the risk existed nevertheless. "I can tell you where you stand with me—at least in this room with the door locked."

He kept his voice neutral, even while the heat began to flow and a current seemed to electrify his bloodstream. "You can."

"Yes."

He shifted further around, hooked a knee onto the bed. "And is the door locked?"

"Yes."

He leaned back against her slightly, felt her bare breast on his upper arm. His pulse chugged faster. "And?"

"And I'm naked."

"Ah." He kept his breathing steady, but it was work.

"Yes." Her hand brushed his forearm, up under the cutoff sleeve of his sweatshirt, over his chest. "And I wish you were, too."

His breath snagged in his throat. "You do."

She leaned in closer, brought her lips to his ear. "Very much."

He groaned. "Helen, I... you're sure?"

"You are my husband," she whispered. "I am your wife. This afternoon we became lovers. I don't understand most of what's going on outside this door, but I understand what happens when you come near me, what belongs to us in here. Physical attraction and five kids is what we have to share, so let's. While we learn the rest of whatever we've got to learn, make whatever adjustments we've got to make for the kids, in here at least, I want neutral territory, something for you and me and nobody else. We need something between us that doesn't belong to anyone else, something we can count on."

She swallowed, touched his face, let her hand drift down until it rested on his. "I want to be your lover, Nat. I want you for mine. Be my lover, Nat. Be my—"

He hushed her with a hand over her mouth, an arm wrapped around her waist, hauling her naked body into his lap. "In here, Helen? Only in here? What about out there? What about in the laundry room? What about any damned place it gets away from us again? What do I say to my son when he makes crude remarks about my wife? Tough luck, kid, we've got a piece of paper and it makes it okay? I always kind of thought I'd tell him that the key word in the phrase making love is *love,* Helen, not *bonking.*"

"You're right," she said calmly, but there was steel in her tone, "*love* is the key word in the phrase. And no, a piece of paper is not all that makes it okay because a piece of paper is just...mushed up tree fiber until two people make it mean something more. And since we're the two people in question and we haven't had time to even consider love as part of the equation, we start with what we've got—five scared kids and two frightened adults entrusted with their keeping and the awesome responsibility of turning us, *you and me* and them—into a family."

Earnestly, she took his face in her hands. "Nobody said it would be easy. Hell, you probably know better than I that nothing worthwhile ever is, so there we are. And damn it, Nat, sex is part of a marital relationship, part of the way the bonds are formed. Lust, then kids, then marriage, then sex, then shocking questions we can't answer from hormonal preadolescents may be the backwards way to go about...everything, but the mark of people who...people who... Hell, I lost the damned word, but it's got something to do with winners.

"And that's us, Nat. If we want to win not only this battle but the whole blasted war, we need to be creative, work with what we've got, and this is what we've got, damn it. This room, this bed, a few minutes of privacy a day, and if we're lucky and give ourselves permission to lust after each other as spouses, we've got a lot of little seconds throughout the day to create anticipation, show Zach that marriage is more than a bonk in the middle of the afternoon. It's us, you and me, workin' at it even if we don't say I love you to each other. We say it to them and we mean it where they're concerned and—"

"And maybe our actions will speak loudly enough to let them believe in the fairy tale until they don't need the fairy tale any longer," Nat finished for her.

"Yes." Helen dropped her hands from his face. "Sometimes I think we all need a fairy tale to believe in."

"Okay." Nat stroked her face. It was an apology. "I can buy that. You speech real well when you throw your heart into it. Ever consider selling used cars?"

"Nah." Helen shook her head. "I got asked once if I'd be willing to sell used tanks in the third world, but I turned that down. No challenge."

"Not to mention you're a terrible liar and if you had to appear in front of a senate subcommittee, nobody'd be safe from the truth as you see it."

"Well . . ." Helen agreed modestly.

He traced her lips, outlining her mouth, taking stock of details he hadn't paid attention to before. The fullness of her mouth, smoothness of her cheeks, the fact that her nose turned up just a little at its tip. How long her neck was, how sensitive the path along her collarbone was, and how incredibly fragrant and silky the skin of her chest was. How impossibly, tantalizingly full her breasts.

"I think I'm going to enjoy making love with you," he muttered. "A lot."

"A lot as in very much?" Helen wondered, arching to him. "Or a lot as in often?"

"Mmm-hmm," Nat said, and tumbled her onto the bed.

"One other thing maybe you should know..." she murmured before he had a chance to kiss her.

"Oh, God." He flopped onto his back, laughing and groaning at once. "Do I have to? Every time you decide to reveal something to me it seems like hell comes to call."

"I'm just...so enamored of your revelations, too," she responded tartly. "I mean, please...'did you *bonk* me?' Couldn't you at least have translated that into something like 'did we *do* it?' and spare my feelings that much?"

Nat rolled onto his side, slid his hand across her belly, hiked her closer. "Yeah, well, you're the one wondering if Max throwing up on the rings is some kind of omen. Where'd that come from, anyway? Ida?"

"No," Helen admitted. "She said the idea was hogwash, that kids throw up on wedding rings all the time—especially once they're on your finger. No, I'm afraid it was Edith. She loves a good disaster almost better than anything—except planting ideas where they do the least good."

"Your entire family seems to enjoy doing that."

"I know. We can't help it. We were raised to be interesting, or barring that, controversial. Or at least," she amended, finding Nat's left hand and linking hers with it so their rings touched, "I used to think it was nurture and not nature until this last month with Libby. Now I just think it's a dominant trait passed along with the rest of the genes. Which is pretty scary when I look at Grandma Josephine and realize I'm descended from that."

Nat rubbed his thumb across her palm, smiled when Helen's skin quivered in response. "Grandma Josephine? Was she at the wedding? I didn't meet her."

"No." Helen withdrew her hand from his, let it glide up his hip to the ragged hem of his sweatshirt. "She turned ninety-eight this year and isn't going out as much as she used to. I imagine she'll jet in from Phoenix for Christmas though, so be warned."

"Jet?"

"Yeah. It's private, but it belongs to a friend of hers, who flies it. Gram just goes along for the ride."

"Oh, good." His tone was dry. "Is this the other little thing you had to tell me?"

"No." She took a breath, scooted away from him and sat up. "No. I just... I want you to know that it's not an accident that I took your name during the ceremony, that I'm a—a Crockett now."

"No?" Soft, curious. "So simply assuming you'd change your name makes me an ass? The way I assumed you changed it back to Brannigan after you and John divorced?"

She laughed, fiddling with the ring on his left hand. "I didn't say that. Implied it, maybe, but the words are yours."

"So, Mrs. Crockett, what should this ass know?"

"I'm Colonel Crockett now, too, Nat," she said.

He felt something in his heart clutch. As long as he'd known her she'd been Captain-Major-Lieutenant Colonel-Colonel Brannigan.

"I filed the paperwork last week," she continued, as though she weren't exploding a bomb underneath him. "Before the wedding. I never did that for John. I was never Mrs. Maximovich, for him either. I was whatever-my-rank-at-the-time Brannigan or Ms. Brannigan. No

Maximovich added to my name. No convention. Ever. Not even for Libby.''

He couldn't breathe. Damned woman. What the hell was she trying to do to him?

"I hardly ever wore my wedding ring, either—figured I didn't need all the trappings to feel married. But maybe John needed me to have them. You and I didn't marry for love, but we did get married, and I want you to know that I take this...commitment seriously, and that this family is the top of my priority list...."

His pulse wouldn't cooperate and his lungs were starving for air. Damned, insane, lunatic woman. Whatever he was feeling, whatever was tearing little pieces out of him and stapling them back in some chaotic, gee-hawed order he couldn't recognize, he hadn't expected to feel this. He expected her to make him hotter for her than a heat-seeking missile, that was a given. But this was not heat of that nature. This was something fuller...something rarer.

Scarier, too.

"I don't know how much longer I can stay on this leave, or if there's a post in need of my...specialty...around here, but I want you to know I consider myself really married—your wife, my husband—and I'll do whatever I can to make this work...Nat?"

He was on his knees in front of her; his hands were on her arms, holding on to her so hard he could almost feel the bruises forming beneath his fingers. He couldn't let go.

"Nat, what's wrong?"

"I don't know." He swallowed, trying to get hold of himself, but the only thing he managed to get hold of was the thought that the one consistency available to him where Helen *Crockett* was concerned was completely uncivilized and more than a little depraved.

Want. Need. Avarice.

Craving.

Take the laundry room, for instance. Helen had accepted him—hell, taken him as much as he'd taken her—there for their maiden voyage, as it were, without thought or protest or anything. Amanda would have demanded a bed in a fancy hotel with satin sheets and all the trimmings—and then the act itself would have been satisfying but strictly conventional: baby-doll nightgown, bathroom primping, champagne, darkness and traditional position.

He wasn't used to feeling insecure with a woman and despised himself for giving in to ye-olde-immature-jealousy cliché, but he suddenly couldn't stop from wondering if Helen had been as generous with herself with John, and he found himself wanting to leave his mark on her the way John had imprinted himself upon Amanda.

God, did people who'd been married to other people who'd divorced them and married each other ever get over the urge to compare notes?

Maybe with maturity.

"Helen..."

He was floundering in deep water, and she was the lifeline he'd never intended to need to depend on.

"Nat." Her voice was soft and sure, and she seemed to understand something he didn't. "Nathaniel."

No one had ever said his baptismal name quite that way before, with quite so much loving or proprietorship.

No one had ever said it so it sounded quite so...

Right.

You are my husband, I am your wife....

"Nathaniel."

His hands were still clenched around her arms; she couldn't shake him loose without losing him, so she simply turned her hands palm up and hooked his elbows, drew him with her when she eased herself back onto the bed.

"Nathaniel, be my lover," she whispered, untangling her legs to wrap them around him. "Be my lover, be my lover, be my husband—"

He didn't let her say any more, was afraid to let her, so in self-defense he released her arms and moored her face between his hands and pillaged her mouth.

Instead of being silenced and ravaged, she moaned. "*Yes . . .*"

Instead of laying siege to her to protect himself, he surrendered to her. His mouth grew tender, his hands gentled and he let himself get lost, exploring her without caring that the trail back had collapsed behind him.

Not just sex.

She knew that before his hands strayed off her shoulders and over her breasts; felt it in his kiss and her response to him; hid the knowledge deep, where her heart wouldn't find it at the same time that she found him; skimmed her hands beneath his shirt to cover territory there'd been no time to explore this afternoon.

Touched him and felt the burn begin in her, rising like fever when he groaned and hiked off his sweatshirt fast.

Kissed and tasted him, familiarizing herself with his flavor, heady and drugging.

Addictive.

More than sex. And more and more.

He'd known this afternoon that it was, known it from the first time he'd kissed her, first time he'd seen her—forgotten it in the practicality of their practical marriage; lost sight of it with his vision and Amanda's desertion and his anger at Helen for not keeping better track of her husband.

And now *he* was her husband.

Be my lover, you are my husband . . .

Yes, he thought. I am.

Yours.

Sliding away from her face, he found her breasts, treasured them with palms and fingers, mouth and tongue; moved without haste to sample the flavor of her belly, learn the fabric of the inside of her thighs with his fingertips—with all his senses extended to absorb the essences and nuances of Helen.

While she absorbed his.

He felt the wetness of her open mouth on his shoulders, his neck, felt her tongue with her ragged breath in his ear, and laughter, wild and reckless, surged through him.

In here, this is where you stand with me... this belongs to us in here....

"Nathaniel, please...."

He shed his gym shorts and caught her hands, linked them with his as he rose over her. And this, he thought fiercely, driving into her, is mine.

Not just here, but out there, too, among the children, in the midst of the relatives, amid strangers in the street.

Mine.

"Mine," she sighed aloud. The echo of his thoughts. And repeated it in a gasp when he withdrew and thrust into her again. "Mine...yes...please..."

He tore the words from her mouth with his tongue, swallowed them along with her startled, pleasure-filled "Ahh...Nat..." when he brought her suddenly to the ledge and sent her sailing off.

He didn't expect her to make sure he went flying with her, expected to take his time, stoke the fires and feel her burn again, but she had other ideas, twisting against him and locking her heels at the small of his back and pulling him in and in—to the heavy contractions coursing through her, to the shattering swirl and eddy of recognition, to the heat of a place he'd never imagined or felt.

A place where the only name he knew was hers, where the light was so intense he would have been afraid that it would blind him—if he'd been able to think enough to be afraid at all, and if he wasn't blind already.

A place of no tomorrows and no todays, no yesterdays, but where all three of them were bound inextricably together in a soul-devastating *now*.

It took him a long time to come back from the place she'd brought him to, longer still to understand that the salt taste he kissed from her cheeks and temples was tears—hers.

To comprehend that the clogged and shaky whisper he heard was his own voice proclaiming through the rain of kisses, "Mine."

Mine.

And he meant it.

Chapter 10

First Monday of Advent

He slept sprawled across her, with one hand tucked beneath her right shoulder, the other beneath her neck, his head pillowed on her chest. She slept with her arms wrapped around him and her fingers sifted into his hair.

There was a lot of wasted king-size bed to either side of them.

It was a good thing neither of them had remembered to unlock the door, unclothed as they were, because the children were up before them, pounding on it.

"Mom!" Libby shouted. "Get up! The door's locked and it's a quarter to eight. We're going to be late!"

"Huh? What?" Groggy, foggy. Wishing to still be asleep.

"Dad, come on!" It was Cara this time, pleading. "We *have* to be to school *on time* or we'll be late for the buses. Colonel, I have to take an 1870s lunch today to eat on the field trip, no juice boxes or plastic bottles or thermoses. What can I take? Do we have any big pickles or apple butter or homemade bread?''

"Tern'l!" Jane was cranky and demanding. "In!"

"Daddo, don't forget to call your eye doctor today." Max-the-calendar was putting in his two cents. "Kern'l, we have to go to the dentist after everybody gets out of school, bemember."

"Come on guys." Zach's voice sounded disgusted. "Door's locked, you know what that means—leave 'em alone, they're probably naked. Come on, let's just get dressed. They'll be up."

"Well, okay." Libby was rebellious. "But if they're not out of bed by the time I get dressed, I'm findin' the screwdriver that unlocks this door."

"We're up," Nat groaned, without lifting his head. "Geez-oh-pete, we're up!"

"No, we're not," Helen assured him sleepily. But she made certain Libby didn't hear her.

Nat turned his head, dragging his mouth and beard across the breast that had pillowed them, leaving a trail of damp kisses in his wake. "I'm pretty sure I didn't leave a wake-up call for this morning, did you?"

"Absolutely not. Would I do that to us? Not to mention I don't know if I can move, and you feel too damned good for me to want to even think about getting out of bed yet."

"Mmm." Nat used the hand cradling her head to lift it for his seeking mouth. "That's definitely mutual."

Their good-morning was warm and a tad too erotic to ignore.

With an effort, Nat raised his head. "How long do you think we've got?" he asked thickly.

Her response was breathy. "Fifteen minutes, max."

He made an unprintable comment. "I need a shower."

"Me, too. We could lock the door and take one together. I could scrub your front...."

He pulled her in for a scorching kiss, hauled her across the bed with him. "What about your daughter and her screwdriver?"

Helen caught his hand and tugged him to her, into the bathroom. "She needs a different screwdriver for this door," she murmured against his mouth.

"Ah," Nat said, enlightened, and he bent to her without further encouragement.

When he hooked his foot around it to shove it closed, the bathroom door clicked tight behind them.

The reality check came in the form of a phone call, after she'd dropped the kids and Nat off at school and returned home to a day of organizing what promised to become a busy week, planning the meals and making phone calls to line up workers for the Santa's Secret Shop opening at school next week.

"Colonel Crockett?" the diffident voice asked when Helen caught up the receiver.

Grimacing as she swallowed a single, heartfelt oath, she acknowledged her identity.

"Hold for General Greene," the voice said.

Muttering epithets that should have scorched her adjutant general's office boss's ears, Helen did as instructed. It took two-star general Caroline T. Greene exactly one hundred thirty-five seconds to pick up on her end—by which time Helen was both antsy and frothing.

"Colonel—"

"Look, General, I don't know what this is about, but I requested two months and you signed my paperwork and it's only been five weeks. I just got married Thursday, the kids are insane—"

"Whoa! Hey, Helen," the thick Arkansas accent drawled. "Start out with 'Hey, how ya doin', ma'am?' before you jump my throat would you? Shoot, 's a damn good thing we been friends a long time or I might decide you're spoutin' insubordination 'n have to come down on you for it.''

"I won't go down alone, Caro," Helen said frankly.

The general laughed. "Didn't think you would, now did I?"

"Not since that night in Cairo, anyway." Helen grinned. "So, hey, how ya doin', ma'am? This a social call or do I jump down your throat now?"

"Stow it for later. Right now the AG's got a problem in your neck o' the woods. Grayling's got a reservist jailed on charges of serial rape. You're senior in the area and this one needs your...expertise."

"Find the facts, expedite the situation and damage control with the media?"

"In one."

"Whose kid is it?" Helen asked bluntly.

Another short laugh. "'S what I like about you, Colonel, no flies. You're quick."

"I know," Helen acknowledged. "Hence my reputation and the reason you let me get away with half the stuff I do. Whose kid?"

"Representative—" She mentioned the name of a female out-of-state politico Helen wasn't familiar with. "Friend of a friend of a lobbyist with clout out here."

"And sonny boy's innocent."

"She hopes so." Regret was evident. "But she's not countin' on it."

Helen felt sick with the knowledge that this mother must have been here with her grown child before. Reaction was swift. "Cripe, Caro, dump it on somebody else, can't you? I've got my hands full—"

"Stuff it, Colonel." The laid-back Arkansas drawl was gone. The voice in Helen's ear now was crisp and commanding, the boss, not the friend. "I understand your sit-

uation, but this has to take precedence for the moment."
Her tone softened. "Heck, Helen, if I could dump it elsewhere, I would, but I got my orders, too. This wants your
rank, but mostly it wants your reputation. Clean it up, put
it to bed, go home and stay there. I'll make sure you're
comped."

Helen articulated her frustration with a well-chosen
word. "Yeah, till the next time."

The general was silent.

Helen dug at a molar with her tongue, blew out a sigh.
Sorry, Nat. "When?"

"I dispatched a helo out of Grayling. Should be at
Oakland-Pontiac within the hour. You oughta be able to
put this one down in three days, tops. Two if you're as
good as you think you are. Just make sure that if the kid
did it, he goes quiet and does his time."

"Three days?"

"Maximum."

Helen pinched her nose, rubbed finger and thumb across
her eyes. "I got a husband out of touch on a field trip, a
three-year-old comin' home from preschool in ninety
minutes, a kindergartner out in two and a half hours and
five kids to take to the dentist this afternoon. You sendin'
me a baby-sitter and a marriage counselor with this helo?"

The general chuckled. "What was it you always used to
say about women in the military balancing family with
career while they tried to get ahead?"

"With all due respect, General," Helen said mildly,
"stuff it, ma'am."

Then she hung up and called Sam.

Samantha was, Helen was disturbed and suspicious to
discover, a little too enthusiastic about being asked to pick
up Jane and Max at their required times, baby-sit for the
afternoon, then go back later to collect Nat and the rest of
the kids. And she was downright thrilled to be asked to
deliver the message of Helen's whereabouts to Nat, along

with Helen's assurances that she would call about dinnertime to talk to everybody.

But Helen didn't have time to worry about what Aunt
Sam might be cooking up—or merely setting up for the rest
of the plotters. Instead she packed her bag, put on her
uniform, polished her brass and headed for the airport.

Ex-navy officer though he was, Nat was hard put to accept Helen's absence after the day he'd put in with Cara's
class.

While not wanting to appear ungrateful for his willing-
ness—particularly as a father who could take young men
to the bathroom—to help chaperon the field trip, Cara's
teacher was more than a little nervous about leaving four
students plus Cara in his keeping. She'd hovered near him
most of the day, continually counting heads, until Cara
and her friends convinced her that they liked dragging Nat
around, showing him everything.

A blind man was a novelty to them and far too interesting a phenomenon for them to stray beyond his reach. He
had a smart dog. He needed things described to him. He
listened to everything they said no matter how outrageous. He knew things about Greenfield Village and its
history their teacher didn't, and when he talked about it,
he spoke from a different perspective and was interesting.
And he appealed to their baser kid-instincts by talking out
of turn in the mock 1870s classroom session, correcting the
teacher. When she made him sit in the corner wearing the
dunce cap, he laughed, then made faces behind her back
until he got caught when his charges forgot to signal him
that she was watching.

Cara thought he was wonderful.

Her teacher signed him up for the next field trip immediately.

Still, he was exhausted by the end of the day and looking forward to Helen's promised private time—a little

clandestine foreplay while the kids did their homework or watched TV after dinner—and an early night.

He was definitely not thrilled to find one of her more peripatetic sisters waiting to take him and the kids home, then discover a second one—Twink—at the house "doing something about dinner."

Like Helen—or perhaps from Helen—he got the distinct impression that plots were in progress, and he was pretty sure that whatever they involved, he wasn't going to like them when they hatched. There was a lot too much innocence and Christian charity going on with Helen's sisters to be believed.

When he found one of them counting rooms and musing over the number of beds available, he was certain of it.

"What's up?" he'd asked darkly.

"Nothing," Twink had answered guilelessly—much the way Libby had a tendency to do. Except Twink was a grown-up and Nat's implied threats didn't work to get her to reveal what "nothing" was.

When Nat spoke with Twink's husband, Rob, that man was of no more help than his wife—but for different reasons. He wasn't, he assured Nat, positive about what the Brannigans were up to, and the parts he had an inkling of... well, Nat would have to understand. Rob had to live with the woman, and preparing her brother-in-law for the worst was not allowed, according to his marriage vows.

Although he did suggest that Nat really should prepare for the worst—and then pray that Rob was wrong.

"Thanks, bro," Nat muttered moodily. He wondered what Helen had ever done to her sisters that deserved this—whatever this turned out to be—then figured it'd probably be better if he didn't know. Ever.

When Helen called, she sounded tired and anxious, concerned about how he viewed her desertion so soon after "well, you know." They couldn't say much: he had kids wanting to tell her about their day, she had subordinates

who weren't happy she'd been called in to do their jobs for
them impatient to get rid of her and so get her off the
phone and back to work. She would, she told Nat, call him
later, after his class. How late was too late?

Whatever time she could call wouldn't be too late, he
replied. Then, afraid he'd betray himself with some emotion he wasn't ready to feel, he handed the receiver to Jane,
who was bouncing up and down in her high chair at the
table, wearing a spaghetti-sauce face and insisting, "Me
talk! Me talk Tern'l."

Which she did with tremendous excitement and anima-
tion, and Helen didn't understand a word, but that hardly
mattered. It was the laughter and the tone of voice and
Helen's exclamations that counted for Jane. For Helen it
was listening to her baby share the wonders of life and the
revelations of preschool with her Tern'l.

Details were merely unimportant window dressing that
had nothing to do with anything. Love was all that Jane—
and Helen—needed to hear.

When Jane was finally coerced into giving up the phone,
Helen spoke with Max, Libby and Cara in backward order. Max had grave questions regarding rescheduling her
part of the calendar for the rest of the week and a lot of
enthusiasm for a project he was working on at school but
couldn't tell her about because it was for Christmas. Libby
wanted the details of Helen's assignment and volunteered
to come north and help her mother expedite the investigation. Cara was full of the field trip and how Toby had
behaved and how everyone had liked her outfit and how
dad had to sit in the corner and wear the dunce cap 'coz
he'd been mouthy in class.

Zach didn't want to talk to her at all. When Nat handed
him the phone, he managed a moody "Hello" and a few
terse responses to the questions Helen asked, then shoved
the receiver back. Nat and Helen exchanged brief good-

byes without the chance to speak their minds and hung up, not exactly the better for the contact.

Certainly they weren't the worse for it, either, but it did create a rather gnawing ache that felt suspiciously like loneliness and quite possibly something else mixed in for spice.

Just randy, Nat assured himself, disgusted. It's not like you've never had a wife or a lover before. She'll be home in a few days. Get over it.

But he couldn't get the taste of her out of his mouth or the feel of her off his skin, or the voice, low and deep and sexy in the shower, out of his mind. And when he went upstairs to collect his briefcase and a jacket before leaving the kids with his mother—Grama Kat—and heading off to class, the scent of Helen lingering in their bedroom, in their shower, nearly drove him crazy.

He was worthless in class, but fortunately he was the only one who noticed.

He arrived home late to find his mother answering the phone in the hall.

"Helen," she said briefly, and handed him the receiver as she went to get her coat.

"Hey," Helen said in his ear, and he knew from the wash of heat, peace and energy through him that what she said wouldn't have mattered in the least, it was as though he'd been waiting all his life solely to hear her voice.

"Hey," he said back. "Where are you?"

"My room." Sultry steam creating a geyser of tension simmered up through his body from his toes. "Alone."

"I'm not. I just walked in, my mother's still here. Give me five minutes and call me back? I want to take this upstairs."

Helen laughed—nervously. Indecently. "Make sure Toby doesn't let you fall on anything on the steps. I want all of you in working order."

He was glad he couldn't see his mother. It saved him the embarrassment of watching her understand from the heat climbing his neck where this conversation with his wife was headed. "Yeah?" The flush had nothing actually to do with his feeling embarrassed, everything to do with imagination, anticipation and roaring desire.

"Yeah," Helen said. Nothing about her voice was steady.

Good, he wasn't the only one.

"Five minutes," he told her, and the geyser was there, steaming through the phone wires before he hung up.

From somewhere in the vicinity of the kitchen doorway his mother cleared her throat.

"So," she said, "you'll need me again Wednesday night?"

He nodded. "Appears so. Thanks, Mom, I appreciate it."

"What about getting the kids to and from school?"

"Couple of Helen's sisters have kids in school over there, too." He was uncomfortable. Seemed he was often uncomfortable with his mother anymore. "They'll help out with Jane and Max, and there's the neighborhood car pool."

"Did you talk to your eye doctor?"

She was lingering, working up to whatever she wanted to say to him with small talk. Gathering information for a conclusion she seemed about to draw.

"Yes." Another nod. He wanted to head upstairs. *Get to it, Mom.* "Got an appointment Friday morning at the VA in Ann Arbor. They want to take another look."

"You going to have the surgery?"

"I don't know yet, Mom." He was becoming impatient. "Far as I know the prognosis hasn't changed, so I'm going to guess no."

"Will she take you?"

Ah, they were at it now. *She.* Helen.

"Her name's Helen, Mom, and I imagine she will if she's here."

He heard the rustle of a ski parka being put on and zipped, the foot shuffle of hesitation. She was no more at ease with him than he was with her. "You'll let your father and I know if you need us to drive you?"

"I'll let you know, Mom. Here." He moved toward the sound of her, Toby's harness under his hand, dog at his knee. "Toby and I'll watch you out to your car."

"You don't have to do that, Nathaniel."

"Yes, we do." He tucked a hand beneath her elbow, urged Toby forward. "Come on, Mom. Dad'll be worried about you."

He got her as far as the driver's-side door of her LeBaron before she finished what was on her mind.

"Are you sure you're all right with this...marriage? Her? You're sure—"

"As sure as I can be of anything, Mom. They're Helen's kids, too. She wants 'em as much as I do." He planted a brusque kiss on her cheek. "Go home, Mom. Stop worrying. We're fine."

"She's got ambitions, Nat. The Colonel. Helen." She was imitating him. Making a point of the name.

And the rank.

"She won't quit the military for you or those children."

Nat nodded. "I think she'd like to make general before she's fifty. I didn't ask her to quit and I won't. For me or them. Especially for them. They need to see somebody with a dream reaching for it. That's Helen."

"If she wants to be a general, it'll always have to come first for her, the same as it did for you when you were still in the navy."

"Mom—"

"I just remember reading during Desert Storm about all those military women who lost their marriages and families to their careers and, I just wonder if something doesn't have to give in these situations, if you haven't been too hasty to accept—"

Irritation hissed between his teeth. "Go home, Mom. If a problem develops, Helen and I will handle it the best we can."

"Yes, but, Nat, isn't her career the reason—"

Through the open, back-porch door he could hear the phone begin to ring.

"—She lost her ex-husband to your Amanda—"

He didn't want to think about this, examine it too closely. There were a whole lot of reasons why he'd lost Amanda, and Helen had lost John—

"—And they took custody of all the children?"

—And a million other reasons that the children had gone with them.

"Go home, Mom. Now."

He would apologize for his shortness with her late, perhaps, but not tonight. Besides, the things she was saying to him about his marriage and his wife—life—were none of her damned business. Were nobody's business but his.

And Helen's.

The phone trilled again. His heart pumped and he turned toward the house, anxious not to miss her call.

"Phone, Mom. I can't talk anymore, I have to go. Drive safe. Helen's waiting for me."

"Helen?"

She shut her eyes and gladness washed through her at the sound of his baritone in her ear. "You sound like you've been running."

"Damn near killed myself gettin' here. Wait a minute, I've got the cordless. Let me switch phones." He was back in a moment. "How'd everything go today? How close are you on this investigation?"

"I don't know, Nat." She sighed, swung her legs up onto the bed in Camp Grayling's visiting-officers quarters, stretched her back to unkink it. "Kid's guilty of something, but I don't think it's what he's accused of. He won't talk to me, of course, but that'll change as we go on. Always does. Doesn't appear as cut-and-dried as the general painted it, but I should be able to get home at least for the weekend."

"Good." He hid his relief in playfulness. "I need a ride to the VA on Friday for an eye exam."

"Oh sure." Her response was dry, derisive, mock-wounded. "Puncture my balloon. Here I thought maybe it'd be my body you'd miss and all you want are my chauffeuring skills."

"Be nice to have the body here, too. And the hands." She heard his grin in the appreciative, under-his-breath "oh, yeah" that followed. "Don't believe anybody's ever scrubbed my front quite the way you and those hands of yours did this morning."

"Nobody else better be scrubbing your front for you, period," Helen told him severely. Lord, it felt good to talk to him, hear him. His nonsense, his desire, even that undercoating of... restraint. She shut her eyes and hoped it meant Nat didn't care for phones instead of what it had meant when she'd started hearing the reserve in John's voice, even while he was still telling her *I love you* every time she called. "I can be real hard on trespassers."

"Likewise," he assured her flatly. "Trespassers will be knocked senseless, trussed up and pitched into the nearest lake, if I have to drive 'em there myself."

"Nat." She was laughing. "And here I thought you were civilized."

"Not about this." He didn't say *not about you*, but that's what he meant. That's what he felt, and it scared him. "Anyway," he added, looking to lighten the moment, "this sounds an awful lot like, 'Ring, ring. Pot, this is Kettle, you're black.'"

She gave him mischievous. "That's not what you said this morning."

He snorted. "I was out of my mind this morning. And you didn't seem to mind at all the things I was telling you this morning."

"I was out of my mind, too. Delirious." Her voice was teasing. "You have one talented tongue, my inventive husband, anyone ever told you that? No..." She reversed course quickly. "On second thought, I don't think I want to know and they'd better not have."

He relaxed, chuckling. "Jealous?"

"I don't know." She felt and sounded tentative. "Maybe."

He let that one go without comment. Saying anything would have given him away. Remaining silent was his only defense. He didn't want this to end like—

"Nat?"

There was something in her voice: apprehension, wariness, doubt. He knew that tone. He'd sounded that way himself, once upon a time. "I'm here, Helen."

"Are you all right with this...today?" She swallowed. "Is there anything we need to—to discuss? I—I don't like to sound like this—suspicious, afraid—but well, we've only begun a few things and my nagging insecurity makes me ask."

"Ah, Helen." He laughed uncomfortably.

He didn't want to talk about this right now, but barely four and a half days ago he'd let her put her ring on his finger and promised her honesty, given her his ring with the same conditions. Yesterday they'd become lovers, and that shed a whole new light on honesty, complicated the convenient and practical vows they'd exchanged immeasurably.

Well, they would have to talk about this sometime; now was as bad a time as any.

He sighed. "I was a little ticked not to know anything about anything until I got back to school and found your sister picking us up, but it goes with the territory, doesn't it? Uncle Sam never did give his finest much room to maneuver in their personal lives." He shrugged. "I'll get over it. Mostly, I was angry because I was looking forward to tonight. With you. I wanted to, um, court you a little. Maybe. Ask you for a date."

"That's all?" Helen asked. "You don't need to...I don't know...get into it more?"

John had needed to get into it all the time. Had analyzed her "craving," as he'd put it, to be the best she could be in the army as a need to emasculate all men by outranking them. To be powerful and less than feminine. This was not an easy place to return to so soon into her second marriage.

Any marriage.

"No," Nat said quietly, guessing what was on her mind. He hadn't been able to avoid hearing what other officers—naval and otherwise—used to say about women officers who weren't nurses in the military. It had bugged the hell out of him then; it bugged him double now, knowing that she badly needed to hear him say that any guilt she felt over her career was her own. He didn't think she had anything to feel guilty for—no matter what John might have once told her. "I don't. I don't think you're trying to geld anybody—especially me—by being who you are, and I don't think it makes you less a woman to want to punch a hole in the military's glass ceiling, either.

"No, darlin'..." His voice was soft, caressing, tender. Passionate. "The only way you're likely to unman me is when I want you so badly I can't think straight. Now, for instance. I want you under me, above me, in the kitchen, in the laundry room, in a desert or in a general's office— any damn place I can have you. You devastate me. You leave me breathless. You always have. How 'bout a date

when you get home? Dinner, maybe a concert—the Che-
nille Sisters are supposed to be in town next week—then
parking and necking anyplace you say. Just *say*. Please."

Helen's breath caught, slammed out of her with the
force of his conviction; she couldn't think. Damned man.
What was he trying to do to her?

"Dates make me nervous," she whispered. The whisper shook. Damned insane, lunatic man was going to make
her cry; she didn't cry—army brass didn't cry. Under any
conditions she knew of. But here she was, choking, tears
stuck in her throat. How had he known what she needed
him to say? How could she have known what his saying it
would do to her? Her insides were churning. Her heart was
in her brain, her soul in flames, her emotions demolished.
"I can never figure out what to wear and I get all tongue-
tied and don't know what to say."

"Doesn't matter," Nat told her lightly. With affection.
"I can't see what you're wearing, you feel fantastic to me
in nothing at all and you know you can say anything so
long as you say it to me."

That was it, the final straw. Devastated, had he said she
left him? Well, she was downright shattered.

"Damn you, Nathaniel," she said, and her voice broke.

Helen Crockett, the lady colonel who thought up *scenarios* for her sisters to act in, played a meanly physical
game of basketball, let him make love to her in the laundry room and who was capable of leaving hardened-
combat veterans quaking in their boots, was crying.

"Helen? Aw, Helen, don't."

She was crying, damn it, and he didn't know why and he
couldn't reach her, couldn't hold her, couldn't do anything but sit here with the phone in his hand and make
soothing noises in her ear. It wasn't enough, damn it to
hell.

It wasn't enough.

So he began to talk. About anything that came into his head: the kids, Christmas, the letters to Santa Claus the kids had started writing before dinner—including the one Max had wanted to write in braille for Daddo. Plans for the holidays. He asked her what Christmas traditions she'd grown up with, and when she couldn't respond with more than a sob and a hiccough, told her about his growing up, the customs Amanda had observed for Zach and Cara before the divorce. Asked her about Christmas stockings and how she thought they should handle things for the kids this year, make the transition for them, incorporate the traditions.

Told her about Twink casing the house, counting beds and bedrooms; about the kids—Jane and Libby in particular—insisting they wait until Helen got home to go visit Santa at the mall. About the tags their kids had pulled off the parish Giving Tree after this morning's all-school Mass so they could each buy a present for some child needier than they. About how trying to take her place in the household wasn't all it was cracked up to be.

And a little at a time, she responded. The sobs died away; she blew her nose; her voice came back—clogged, then watery to be sure, but usable; she participated in the conversation.

She didn't tell him why the tears; he guessed she couldn't have even if willing. And Nat was surprised to discover he didn't need her to, surprised to learn that understanding her emotion didn't necessarily mean being able to explain it. Surprised to find that it was enough to have her talk to him about nothing and anything merely to have her voice here with him where he lay propped up by pillows piled against the headboard of their bed.

Surprised to chance upon the astonishingly seductive value of the simple discussion of normal seasonal things, like conspiring what to get the kids for Christmas; how to get away Christmas shopping and sneak the gifts into the house without them being the wiser; how to inveigle the grieving, cynical, too-old-for-his-years Zach into having to guess about the reality of Father Christmas's existence for one more year.

They made love to each other on the phone—teasing and raunchy. Lewd and titillating. Tenderly and with mounting passion. And finally with frustration, as well as anticipation of what could pass between them when Helen got home.

A *lot* of anticipation.

Then they held each other quietly, as only lovers could, through an open phone line until drowsiness and the comfort of each other's felt presence allowed them to hang up and go to sleep.

Alone.

Chapter 11

Finnish Independence Day
Feast of St. Nicholas

Toby let him know the minute he heard her car at the top of Ottawa Street, and Nat met her at the back door when she arrived home before dawn December sixth.

His hands were everywhere, unbuttoning her coat, her uniform jacket, yanking at her tie, her blouse.

"I missed you" was the first thing she said when he took his tongue out of her mouth long enough for her to say anything.

"Come to bed" was his fervent response.

"Nat...!" Laughing, giddy, gasping. "Let me get in the house. My stuff—"

"Will keep," Nat muttered, tipping her head so he could access her throat with teeth, lips and tongue. "Right now you've got a real medical emergency on your hands in the shape of a newlywed husband who's been married nine days and hasn't made love to his wife except by phone in four and who may explode from pent-up frustration if he doesn't get to soon.''

"Oh, my, you poor thing," Helen responded with mock concern. "Are you in pain?"

Nat came back to her mouth, voracious. "More than you'll ever know."

"I wouldn't be too sure about that," she murmured, and brought her mouth to his in a long, searing, emotion-filled kiss that poured her soul into him and asked for nothing in return.

Stunned and off-balance, Nat held her away when they finally came up for air, explored her face with sensitive fingertips, seeking expression and understanding.

"Helen?" he asked uncertainly.

She shook her head, smiling crookedly against his fingers, planting a dry kiss in his palm.

"I missed you," she offered softly. It wasn't a lie, but it wasn't the whole truth, either. "All of you—kids, Toby... you. It's been a long week without you. Without this."

She laid a palm on his cheek, slipped her tongue along the seam of his lips, kissing him tenderly and with such longing that the need came crashing into him more immutable than before, tightening in his belly and churning through his lungs in waves bent on drowning him. But this time there was something more endemic mixed with the need, something raw and unconditional, fragile and insidious that didn't feel like it was going away anytime soon.

He wanted to take his time, to love her slowly and for a long time, love her fully and completely, and when he was done, start over and do it again and again.

And again.

Wanted to be waiting for her every time she came home, holding the door open wide to let her in. Locking it behind her for as long as she could stay. Holding on to her with his hands wide open and his heart available and welcoming.

What he wanted scared the hell out of him.

What he needed terrified him even more.

He broke the kiss, breath jarring in his lungs, and leaned his forehead on Helen's for a moment, gathering himself back together.

"Whoa, baby," Helen murmured hoarsely. "That was a little more revealing than I intended."

"No kidding," Nat rasped. "For me, too."

"You don't want to talk about it, do you?" She was anxious not to.

"Not right now." He shuddered theatrically, an imitation of the Cowardly Lion. "Not on your life, maybe later. Maybe never."

"Oh good." Helen heaved a tremulous sigh of relief. "I was hoping you'd say that. Because all I really want to do right now is crawl into bed and have my way with you and vice versa and not think about anything for a long time."

His smile was slow and prurient, monumentally indecent; his kiss was deep and thorough, filled with smoke and flame and heavenly sin; his voice was a rasp shivering down her spine, curling her toes. "I can do that."

He bent to retrieve her briefcase and overnight bag from where he'd dumped them out of her hands when she came in. She collected her uniform bag before he fell over it on the kitchen steps. Together they went through the house and mounted the stairs to the second floor.

"Did the kids polish their shoes and set them outside their doors for St. Nicholas?" Helen whispered as they went.

Nat nodded. "Yup. You get the stuff we talked about?"

"Mmm-hmm. In my bag. A baby Lion King for Jane, a Snoopy watch for Max, red licorice for Libby, a bunch of bright scrunchies for Cara and pirate Legos for Zach.

Wait, I'll find 'em and we can put 'em out on our way to bed...."

His skin was sweeter than she remembered, saltier, more planed and ridged with muscles. His hair was thick corn silk ruffled into damp waves by her hands, wet from the heat of the moment and his sweat-slick skin; his body was hard, firm, a haven of security. She wanted to taste all of him, hold the flavor on her tongue, breathe him into her lungs, savor him. Keep him there.

Her skin was more satiny under his lips than his memory had let him believe, more responsive, her breasts were more sensitive and full, her body more restless, the silk of her thighs more inviting. Her scent was saturated with passion, fragrant and heady, earthy and drugging. He couldn't get enough of her.

He followed her into the bedroom from the hallway, set her cases quietly aside, locked the door and listened to the sough of her garment bag as she tossed it into the chair across the room. Waited for her to come back to him so he didn't have to go stumbling around to find her.

She turned on a light because she wanted to see him, watched the dilatory, purely masculine grin cross his face when he deciphered the switch click.

"I want to see you," she told him, approaching to slide her palms over his chest, down his stomach, under the ragged hem of his cutoff sweatshirt. They lingered on his belly. "I need to...make sure you're not just the dream I've been having the last few nights."

"That's cheating," he said severely, but his face told a different story—that he enjoyed having her eyes on him as much as he did her hands. He caught the left one before she could dip her fingers into his waistband, brought it to his mouth and kissed her ring, turned her hand over and drew a moth-light, nerve-tingling circle in the center of her palm with his tongue. "I'm real, Helen. There's no rush."

A sigh. "Nat..."

"Shh. Stand still. I want to undress you. I've spent the last four nights with this fantasy...."

His hands went to her blouse buttons, slid them one by one from their buttonholes; fingers dusted up under the cotton, along the smoothness of her shoulders, peeled the blouse away. Glided back over the tops of her breasts to the edge of the lace and Lycra teddy covering them. Drifted down around the full, curved sides to spread and span underneath, shaping and lifting.

"So," he murmured, "Colonel Crockett wears sexy undies under her khakis, does she?"

Helen sucked in a breath at the flick of his thumbs across her nipples, and her chest swelled toward him. "I spent this week with my own fantasies."

"Mmm. Did they go anything like this?"

He dipped his head until his lips nuzzled the tight pearl his thumbs had created; she arched a bit, lifting it to him.

He rolled his tongue lazily around it; she shut her eyes and her breath snagged slightly.

He worried the bead gently between his teeth; she moaned and tried to raise herself closer.

He lipped his creation like some luscious fruit, and the rasp of lace and moisture over the delicate skin was both sensual and erotic. To him, to her. She whimpered and tethered him to her with her fingers in his hair, fever rising.

He drew the source of his nourishment, lace and all, suddenly hard and deep into his mouth; she gasped, crying out, feeling the flame.

He suckled, and the lash of his tongue, the force of his hunger was more urgent, more insistent than her memory of four days ago. More loving.

She began to smolder and pant, to clutch at him, holding him to her while her legs threatened to weaken and give way. The way her heart already had.

"Nat, please . . ."

Smiling, he tightened an arm about her waist, supporting her, and wetted her other breast, fastened his mouth
over her nipple to savor and venerate and feed. Nimble
fingers spread over her hip, hiked her against his arousal;
tugged at the zipper of her skirt, shoved the garment down
her legs, hoisted her out of it and kicked it out of the way.

Nothing between them but his ill-concealing gym shorts,
the thin, tantalizing chafe of the lace and the thigh-high
silk, garterless stockings she wore.

Which he wasn't yet aware of.

His hand wandered down her thigh, hooked in stocking
elastic. Paused. Contracted. His lungs seized and he wasn't
in charge of them or anything anymore; his breath shuddered out of him, guttural and heavy.

Desperate.

He raised his head and his heart thudded wildly against
hers. This wasn't the same Helen who did his laundry creatively, treated all their children firmly with love, couldn't
follow a dinner recipe if her life depended on it, contested
practically everything and likened his differences with Zach
to a no-holds-barred, visually impaired game of Horse.
Not the one who polished her brass and did her job better
than anyone else in order to compete with men and keep
and better her distinction in a largely man's world.

It wasn't, he realized, even the same Helen who'd given
herself to him the first time amid piles of laundry and the
rumble of the washing machine, the one who'd waited for
him naked last Sunday night, who'd let the kids wait a few
minutes in order to shower with him Monday morning.
This was a woman making a statement without words, a
woman who'd taken the time to make herself secretly and
completely feminine before she returned to the man—her
husband—who wanted her any way and any where he
could have her. A husband who didn't need her to dress for

him at all, but who found he liked that she had immensely.

A woman who through necessity and habit normally kept her own counsel—but who'd come home to offer a gift and share her secrets with him.

His breathing was erratic, his voice tight and filled with wonder. "You did come home to seduce me, didn't you?"

"Do you like 'em?"

"Yeah." Ragged and nearly undone. "Oh, yeah."

"I didn't know if you would. I wasn't sure if I would, but I saw 'em in this lingerie shop when I was out getting stuff for the kids and I didn't have a St. Nicholas present for you and I just— I just...couldn't stop thinking about wearing them with you. I've never done anything like this before, never imagined...and it felt weird going in to buy them and this teddy, like I was letting the whole world in on some sort of depraved secret I didn't even know I had, and that anybody who saw the bag would know the state I was in and what I wanted to do with you right there in the dressing room when I was trying this stuff on, and I felt so hot and—and wicked, so I hid the bag inside a grocery bag so nobody could see it when I got back to the base, and it was just my secret and..." She was nervous. Uncertain. Vulnerable. "—And I—I'm babbling, aren't I, but are you sure you like 'em?" Her hand moved to the top of one stocking. "I could take 'em off—"

Before she could finish speaking, he captured her hand and sandwiched it tight against his belly between them, tangled his fingers in her hair and silenced her with his lips, his tongue, scorching, burning, branding her mouth with his. Backed her up to drop her on the bed. Loomed over her, dangerous and uncivilized. Achingly tender.

"They're part of my present," he told her fiercely. "When I want it unwrapped, I'll finish the unwrapping. Until then, leave 'em alone, okay?"

She nodded. "Okay," she said in a small voice. Then added inquisitively, "Nat?"

"Yeah?"

She sat up, and her hands slipped under his sweatshirt, pushing it up. Her voice was unsteady. "If you're not ready to unwrap me, would it be all right if I at least unwrap you?"

He shut his eyes and swallowed convulsively. "Yeah."

So she did. Rose and slid her hands up inside his sweatshirt, peeling it slowly off his torso, over his head and arms, discarding it. Then she ran her mouth down him, open and wet, tasting him everywhere the way she'd spent the last several nights wanting to in her dreams. His chest, his back, shoulders, around his sides. Stooping to sample his belly while her fingers snared in his waistband. Kneeling to work his shorts over his hips and down his legs, bathing the trail after them with loitering kisses while his breath went from erratic to harsh and capricious, almost strangling. When she took him in her mouth he was lost.

"Hel-en."

He moved to draw her away, instead found his hands tangling in her hair while his craven body bowed into the sweet torture she wreaked upon him. In the instant before he lost sanity completely, he caught her shoulders and pulled her up his length, mated his mouth to hers.

Breathless, she laughed, joyous, intimate; brought the madness crashing down on him.

Impatient, he stripped the body-hugging lace off her shoulders, skinned it off her breasts and belly, her thighs and legs. Moved to claim every square inch he exposed, imprint his territory in an act as carnal as it was timeless.

As it was loving.

Wild to possess her, he still took his time, found every nerve she had and brought it zinging to life. Her insteps and inner thighs were particularly sensitive; he stroked and nipped and bent to her as she had to him.

"Na-at. Natha-niel."

When she was as wild and mindless as she'd left him, he didn't stop, merely tucked his hands under her thighs and lifted her closer to his mouth, applied lips, tongue and teeth with greater diligence until she was bowing up off the bed, pleading. Frantic and abandoned, flying from the peak he'd pushed her to into the heavens.

He joined them while she was still in flight, impelling her higher than she knew she could go, surging and stroking, stoking a fire hotter than it seemed possible to come out of alive. And then he was the fire and the phoenix, burning with her, flaming out and rising up from the ashes, destroying and rescuing her all at the same time.

She held on and went where he took her, no longer a separate piece of the universe but a piece of him, as he was of her: one heart, one body, one soul.

Just like the marriage vows said.

Did he know she loved him? she wondered, throat tight, watching him across the breakfast table, through the buzz of children's greetings and needs and seasonal enthusiasms. Know love was what had given her the courage to buy that indecent bit of lace, the stockings he hadn't taken off of her until just before this morning's shower? Did he understand what she'd learned about herself since Monday, comprehend the lessons in true human depravity and the underbelly of loyalty she'd been forced and sickened to study while unraveling the jumble of threads binding the representative's son?

Did he know how special he was as a father and a man, but especially as a husband? Did he see what she'd been taught by him and by men who from their beginnings had never been, could never be anything like him? Did he realize how badly his passion and decency frightened her, how terrified she was of loving him the way she knew she did? Would he understand the things she might never be able to bring herself to say?

Would he stay with her as John hadn't when the other side of her life, her career, her ambitions got in the way? And when he left, would he, too, find a judge who'd let him take the children with him?

He passed behind her, pressing close, reaching to grab the milk Jane was directing him to on the counter. His free hand skated lightly down Helen's back and over her rump, his throat loosed a low, satisfied growl of "Hiya, gorgeous, miss me?" when he leaned in to nip her ear.

When she slapped his wandering hand off her hip and shook the pancake spatula at him, "Behave," he gave her a smug, unrepentant, pleased-with-himself grin and a lecherous "I don't want to," and went to pour Jane's milk. Helen wanted to smack him—or love him silly.

Or both.

She turned to set a plate of pancakes on the table in front of Zach, found him watching her and Nat with haunted, wary eyes. Before she could decide how to handle the situation, Zach took the pancakes and turned away, shifting sideways to snatch the syrup out of Libby's hand.

"Hey," she said and snatched it back.

The two of them battled about one thing and another until Helen dropped them off at school, and she didn't have a chance to try to figure out what Nat's son had been feeling. Or to ask him about it. But she had the strange sensation that somewhere deep in their eleven-year-old's aching, terrified heart, Zach was fighting hope.

"Simply put, Captain Crockett, given your medical history and the otherwise healthy shape of your eyes, I think the attending physician made a mistake telling you he doubted surgery would do any good. From what I see, you'd make an excellent candidate for a corneal transplant."

Nat's fists clenched, unclenched. His throat was closed, his chest so tight it hurt. He hadn't been Captain Crockett in over five years. He felt like he'd had the wind knocked out of him and was clawing for air.

Sight.

After nearly six years of telling him vision was but a memory, they were now telling him that maybe within the next few weeks—even by Christmas—he could have the sight back in one eye. That, if all went well, they could give it back to him in the other in maybe a year. That it wouldn't be a perfect twenty-twenty, but that twenty-forty or twenty-fifty was well within reach, and that in time the twenty-forty or twenty-fifty might possibly be bumped up with hard contacts—if he wished.

If he *wished!*

He could see the kids. He could have his cameras back.

He could stargaze and play Horse with the lights on and find out firsthand the color of that damned lace teddy he'd peeled Helen out of this morning.

He could see Helen.

But getting there meant restrictions. No picking up Jane, no wrestling with Max and Libby, no tickling Cara, no roughhousing with Zach. No straining activities or violent movement of any kind for several weeks. No getting bumped or poked in the eye, which meant taking precautions not to be in various situations, for example, around small children, where accidents of the striking and bumping variety could so easily happen. Probably having to return Toby to Leader Dogs so somebody else could use him.

No making love with Helen.

And even if he followed all the rules, the possibility of graft rejection, however slight, remained.

With two minutes to cover the pros and cons, he could hardly think, so much was at stake. The kids had already been through enough, and they were just beginning to get used to having the blind guy and his dog around the house, and while it was frequently inconvenient, Nat was fairly comfortable without his sight. How fair would it be to dump hope on all of them, go through the regimen of further restrictions and inconveniences, the new list of things they'd have to be really, really careful not to do around him, only to have a part of his body over which he had no physical or mental control simply get up one day and say, "*Phht*, forget it, we don't want somebody else's cornea, get rid of it."

On the other hand, taking the risk also meant grabbing hold of the possibility of success, the prospect of not having to be dependent on other people to... to drive the kids to school when Helen was out of town, to take the photographs he needed to supplement his stories. Hell, even to match his clothes or to fold and code the bills in his wallet for him.

Of refuting once and for all Emma's main objections over leaving the kids with him because, even if in only her eyes, he could no longer be considered the half a man her daughter had divorced.

God. His jaw worked and his hands strained around the arms of the chair he occupied across the desk from the doctor who'd dropped the bomb. Why the hell was it that every time it rained, it also poured? Lose his sight, lose his wife, lose his kids. Get back his kids, take a new wife, who was coming to mean something to him beyond his wildest dreams, maybe regain his sight.

And in each case, all in less than two months. Incredible.

Overwhelming.

In the spouse's chair beside him, Helen, of course, had no doubts at all.

Her fingers slid into the crook of his hand, squeezed excitedly. "Nat, that's wonderful! You could see! We could dust off your cameras, we could give you *film* for Christmas. You could teach practical photography as well as photographic and dark-room technique, but you'd still get your pension. I could eventually quit driving the car pool, stop worrying about whether or not a panic attack has me moving the furniture without telling you about it first, and you'd be able to sort the laundry and have no more excuses for not being able to do it. I love it! How soon? When?''

She was infectious; he sucked in air, looking for valor, closed his fist hard around her fingers and found a lop-sided grin to put on. Trust Helen to stamp on his reserva-tions, find the high points and hit them dead on, *bing, bang, bong*—and all without thinking to consult him first.

''When?'' he asked, repeating Helen's question. ''I want to think about it, but if I decide . . . how soon?''

The doctor shrugged. ''When you make the decision to proceed, we notify the eye bank . . . usually one to six weeks.''

Whoa, his brain gasped, agog, while his stomach sank and did cartwheels and tangled in knots and filled up with moths. *Put on the brakes; think about this a minute.*

''That fast?'' he asked. His voice sounded shaky even to him.

Helen's hand tightened painfully around his. ''That's fantastic,'' she said. Then she did something intrinsically un-Helen: leaned over to grab him in front of a witness, kissed him so fiercely his senses reeled and he would have sold his soul for her. Her arms wound around his neck, hugging him for all she was worth; her voice in his ear was ferocious and loving. ''Fantastic,'' she said. And a third time, softer, overflowing and tremulous with emotion, ''Fan*damn*tastic.''

Oh hell, as long as he didn't have to guess how she felt about it . . .

Slowly he reached up to hug the arm Helen had draped across his chest, fed the fingers of his other hand into her hair and pulled her over to brush a pretty damned wobbly kiss on her forehead. Turned back to the doctor.

"Okay." He nodded and his gut churned with dread and hope. "Let's give it a shot."

Second Sunday of Advent—Full Cold Moon

She wanted to tell the kids right away; he wanted to wait and get used to the whole idea himself first.

They waited two days and told the kids after they'd lit the second blue candle in the Advent wreath on the china hutch in the dining room before dinner on the Second Sunday of Advent.

"It's about time," Libby said without missing a beat, clearly unimpressed. "Stupid doctors should have figured this out a long time ago."

She was obviously Helen's daughter. Even without sight, Nat could see their resemblance growing by the day.

"They're going to sew in new eyes so you can see?" Max was trying to understand.

"Sort of." Nat nodded. "But not exactly. You watched that program about eyes with Libby, didn't you?"

A nod, quickly followed by an "uh-huh" Nat could hear.

He swallowed emotion and a smile. Good kids. Resilient. Hell had caved in on them and they'd adjusted. Were adjusting. Nobody could ask to have better children dropped on him even if he'd been intimately involved in each birth and growing stage personally.

Amanda and John had done a good job.

"Well, just like you saw on TV, the doctors are going to lift off the bad part of my eye—" he pointed at the white coating hiding the blue iris of his eyes "—that looks kind of like boards over a window and graft on a new, clear one that'll be like putting in a new pane of glass that I can see through."

"Won't it hurt?" Cara, as always, was kindhearted and empathetic. "I want you to see me again, Dad, but I don't want it to hurt."

"I won't hurt. My eye will be asleep during the operation and I'll have eye drops and stuff for after, and they say it shouldn't bother me much at all."

"And you'll be able to see right away?"

"Pretty much. Soon as they take off the dressings."

"Nat." There was an insistent tug on his hand. Jane wanting to be picked up so she could take part in the discussion. He obliged.

"What, shortie?"

"Getting good eyes?"

"I hope so."

"What color?"

He heard Helen cough, covering laughter. "Same color, sweetie, blue. You'll just be able to see it better."

She poked carefully at his eyes; he flinched. "Don't touch," she said. "Might hurt."

"That's right," Nat agreed, straight-faced. "We'll have to be careful, won't we?"

"Yes." She squirmed to get down, patted his cheek when he planted her on the floor. "Me an' Toby take care of you."

"Well..." Nat cleared his throat and heard the three older children freeze. They knew.

In the sudden, ensuing silence, Toby's tail thumped loudly against a table leg. It hadn't occurred to them before what Nat regaining his eyesight might mean to them all where the dog was concerned.

"You'll have to give Toby back, won't you?" Zach, hurt and accusing. The dog was his lifeline some days, the thing that kept him rooted and made the ache he couldn't get rid of tolerable. Allowed him to live and co-exist with the father he sometimes hated for deserting him merely because his mother had made some judge tell him to. The father he also loved and would have given anything to be able to do things with the way normal kids did.

Whatever normal meant these days.

"We might. He's well trained and he'll make good eyes for somebody else if I don't need him. We won't really have to think about it for a while because it'll take some time to be sure that once I start to see I'll go on seeing, but—"

"But you'll have to give Toby back," Zach said flatly. "You'll have to take him away."

And in the tone of his voice, Nat heard all the things his son didn't say: *You'll take him away just like you went away, just like God took my mother and my other dad away, just like the Colonel goes away and doesn't say anything and I can't stop it. Can't count on nothin' with you, Dad. Can't ever count on nothin'...*

He reached out, wanting to gather Zach in, but the boy wrenched himself well out of range before he could touch him.

Nat released a quiet sigh, kept his voice steady. Trying to salve the wounds Zach wouldn't allow him near. "We don't know that for sure, Zach. The possibility exists that by the time we know for certain I've got my sight back, Leader Dogs won't want Toby at all. He's nearly eight, he's getting old to change masters. Maybe we can make some arrangement, offer to raise and donate a couple of puppies to replace him—"

Zach cut him off. Platitudes had long since stopped doing anything to lessen the heartache when not being able to count on anything was the only thing in eleven years he'd been able to count on. "I don't want you to see if we have to get rid of Toby," he said, and ran from the room.

Chapter 12

Third Sunday of Advent
Saturnalia—Hanukkah begins at sundown

Morning.

Grandma Josephine was standing on the front steps, about to ring the bell, when Helen stepped out to bring in the morning paper.

One hand held the fuzzy collar of a moth-eaten mink coat up around her ears while the other kept a raccoon-trimmed hat of considerable age on her head. The hat's long, draggling red feather drifted constantly into her face, tickling her nose, and her rheumy, ninety-eight-year-old eyes crossed trying to see it well enough to blow it out of her way. On the porch beside her sat a well-traveled, over-size carpetbag and a battered, leather-bound trunk covered with baggage stickers. From the pocket of her coat protruded what appeared to be the bottom end of a large and colorful parrot.

"Oh, hello, dear," she said in a voice reminiscent of Miss Katharine Hepburn's. It took her eyes a moment to uncross and refocus on a gaping Helen. "I'm so sorry I'm late, but we hit a little weather over the Rockies and Janna had to put down for a trice. We spent the night at that new airport in Denver, and it was a bit of a mess getting out of there this morning. They really need to do something about that confusion, but, well, I'm here now and that's not my concern, so let's just forget about it and go in, dear, shall we? It's a bit cold out here for these old bones after Phoenix, you know, even if you don't have much snow yet, but a nice hot cup of cappuccino should fix that in a jiff."

She grasped Helen's arm and helped herself into the front hallway. "Well, don't just stand there, dear, close your mouth and give your old granny a hug and a peck, then get the bags, won't you? Oh, and my cane." She gestured at the heavy, cherry-wood stick with its grotesque carved face leaning against the porch railing. "Wouldn't know what to do without the old gargoyle, there's a love. I understand we have a lot of work to do and not much time to do it, so just point me to my room—I do hope you've fixed up one where there aren't any stairs—and I'll go unpack while you see to the cappuccino. We'll have a nice visit, then we'll get started."

"Get started on what?" Helen felt completely discombobulated. "Grandma Josey, what are you doing here? I thought when you came for Christmas you were going to stay at Ma's."

"Now, now, dear, I couldn't very well do that, now could I? Not when they told me."

Helen's eyes narrowed. She had a feeling that very soon General Greene would have to send someone out from the AG's office to investigate *her* and the murder she was inclined to commit. "Who told you what?"

"Why, your sisters, dear. They all called me—a conference call, just like they have in those huge corporations, so

ve could all talk to each other at the same time, and they
lo, you know, dear. One would think they'd have out-
grown the tendency to all talk at once as they matured, but
ou know, they haven't, they babble just like geese, and
hey're worse than you all were when you were young
heathens dropped out of the sky on me so your parents
ould go off for those Bohemian weekends they wanted
alone. She came back pregnant after every single one and
ou'd think she'd have learned after the first two or three
of you came along, but no, she didn't figure it out until
here were seven of you, and by that time she was headed
or menopause, so I think she finally convinced your fa-
her that if he wanted a boy they'd have to adopt one, but
of course they didn't, or you'd have a heathen brother, too,
and then I'm pretty sure they were a little more careful
about when they scheduled those trips after that.

"And, of course—" She shrugged "—when they told
me the situation here, and your husband needing surgery
and you never knowing when you're going to have to be
out of town and all those little children, well, I couldn't
ignore it now, could I? It wouldn't be Christian, it
wouldn't be right, and I mean, truly dear, I wanted to
come. Your mother is so busy with her life, and all those
other grandparents have theirs, and anyway, it wouldn't be
right to have them coming in here—you need a bit of a
break between the generations. And I, well, you know,
here's a skipped generation between you and me that
makes it all right, and I've reached a stage where, really, it
wouldn't hurt me to settle down a bit for a change, and it's
ood for the heart, you know, dear, so stimulating to be
round the young. I quite look forward to it."

"To what, Grandma Josephine?" Helen asked, aghast,
ot even attempting to sort through the confusion of her
randmother's saga—although she had the gut feeling she
lready knew. "To *what?*"

"Why, I thought I told you, didn't I, dear? I've come to live with you and be your nanny."

And with a gentle pat on her granddaughter's cheek, the aged Mary Poppins collected her gargoyle cane, swept passed Helen and tapped briskly down the hall toward the kitchen.

Nat was in the bathroom shaving when Cara stuck her head in the door to announce, "There's some weird-looking old lady making something weird smelling in our kitchen, Dad, and the Colonel's hiding in the attic and says don't tell anyone where she is, especially her sisters, because if they come up there and bother her any more than they've already done today she's likely to kill 'em."

"Oh?" Nat asked. "That's an interesting statement. And does she know this weird lady is in our kitchen making weird stuff?"

"I'm not sure, but I think she must because she told me to find Libby and tell her to weigh anchor until it was time to go to college unless she wanted all her cheeks pinched, and she wasn't making a lot of sense, Dad."

"No," her father concurred, "it doesn't sound like it. Have you told Libby yet?"

"No, the Colonel was acting so weird I came to you first...huh." There was a thoughtful pause. "Weird Colonel, weird-looking old lady. I wonder if they're related."

"Oh, undoubtedly," Nat said dryly. "If they weren't, Helen probably wouldn't be hiding. Well, you find Libby, I'll go meet the lady in the kitchen, then deal with the Colonel. Did she happen to say where in the attic she planned to hide?"

"Christmas ornaments, I think," Cara replied, and went with considerable interest to see how Libby would take the news Helen wanted her to have. She was back in a second. "Oh, by the way, Dad? Grammy Sanders called. She's

coming over this afternoon to help us decorate the house
the way Mom always did. Okay?''

And even if it wasn't okay, Nat mused bitterly. But Cara
was gone and he wouldn't have told her no anyway.

He wiped shaving cream off his face, ran his hand over
it to make sure he'd gotten all the whiskers, then simply
stood there for a long time trying to think. Had he been
able to see his reflection in the mirror, he would have observed a man who looked like he was about to face the
guillotine on a day they'd forgotten to sharpen the blade
trying to come to terms with all the bad things he'd ever
done in his life to deserve this. Emma was coming over to
make sure Helen decorated the house exactly like Amanda
used to, and Cara hadn't even winced when she'd announced it.

Nuts, he thought. What else can happen?

But this was family, and he should have known better
than to ask.

Contrary to Helen's instructions, Libby beat Nat to the
kitchen by two steps and a heartbeat.

"Great-grama Josey!" she squealed, delighted, and
launched herself enthusiastically into Helen's mother's
mother's arms.

"Is this my young poppet Elizabeth Jane?" Grandma
Josephine asked. "Why, you look just like your mother
and you're as tall as me."

So this was the infamous Grandma Josephine Helen had
told him about. She didn't sound threatening. In fact, Nat
thought, she sounded sharp as the proverbial. Ninety-eight
going on sixty-seven. Maybe.

He held back to listen.

"That's 'coz the vertebrae in your back are compress-
ing and you're shrinking, Great-gram," Libby was saying. "But I have grown. A lot. Probably two feet since you
saw me last."

Grandma Josephine nodded. "I thought as much. And I knew you'd know why I'm so short now when I used to be over six feet tall."

"You were never over six feet tall, Grama!"

"I was. Hasn't your mother shown you my old pictures? Longest legs on a girl between here and Mississippi and taller than most of the boys in my high-school graduating class—except for your great-grandfather, of course. They wanted to take bones out of my legs to make me shorter. You find the pictures, I'll show you."

She turned and her cane clunked the floor toward Nat. "You must be Helen's Nathaniel." Instead of shaking hands, she stumped her way around him, once, twice. Nat felt scrutinized, not unlike a piece of prime Kentucky horseflesh, or the breeding record of a bull whose semen demanded a high price at auction. "You certainly are a handsome boy—blind as a mole, I understand, but well put together—"

All right, so now he understood why Helen was hiding.

Grandma Josephine palpated his chest, squeezed his biceps. "—Good arms, plenty of muscle—" Took his hands and turned them palm up. "—Old calluses, hard worker—" Dropped his hands and circled him, patted his thigh, his rear "—Good strong legs, nice fanny...mmm-hmm." She stopped in front of him and grasped one of his hands in both of her strong, bony and slightly arthritic ones. "Well, I think you'll do nicely, dear. Now so long as you don't let our Helen run roughshod over you, this marriage will work just fine."

Pronouncement made, she clumped matter-of-factly away, calling over her shoulder as she went, "I'm in search of a comfortable chair, dear. Do be a love and bring my cappuccino and help me find one, won't you? It's in a very delicate china mug on the stove, near the front, so don't burn yourself." She collected Libby and her voice trailed off down the hall. "Did you know the Queen Mum gave me that mug personally?"

"She did?" Libby said. "Cool. Who's the Queen Mum?"

"Well, dear, I'll tell you, but first... your mother's hiding in the attic, isn't she?"

Libby sighed regretfully. "Uh-huh. She said to weigh anchor and not to tell you."

"Well, you know, you don't have to tell me because I've known your mother for a long time, longer than you, and she's always hidden in the attic when I first get into town. Something to do with people telling her she reminds them of me and she's not terribly sure what that means and I think it scares her to see what she'll probably turn into when she gets to be as old as me, but then, it scared me too when people told me I was just like your great-great...hmm, let me think, is there one or two more greats in there? Well, never mind, poppet, let's just say it made me plenty wary when people started telling me I reminded them exactly of *my* Grandma Siobhan...."

Trying not to laugh too hard when he picked it up, thus risking joggling and breaking the Queen Mum's delicate china mug and sloshing hot cappuccino over his hand, Nat followed Grandma Josephine on her quest for a commodious stool.

"Helen," Nat called from the attic doorway a short time later. "I met her and she knows you're up here, so why don't you quit hiding and come out and face her."

"Don't want to," Helen grumped gloomily. Her muffled voice came from somewhere off to his left. "If I do she'll make me *do* things. Terrible things. Things nobody should have to do."

Nat snorted, moved toward her voice. "She's ninety-eight years old, sharp as a whip and she seems like a good old bat—her word, not mine—to me. What kind of terrible things can she make you do?''

"You don't want to know," Helen assured him earnestly. "You can't even begin to imagine, they're that bad. And it's not like she even really tries, it's just—just...well, you have no idea what kind of genetics I've passed on to Libby, and that woman will let you see them all."

With an effort, Nat cleared laughter out of his throat, attempted empathetic commiseration. "If you mean she's blunt and tactless, I already know that about you *and* Libby. I like it. If you mean she's definite and reminds you of an indestructible Tiger tank charging across a desert, I already know that about you and Libby, too."

"Oh . . ." Helen sighed moodily. "That's part of it, but there's more to it than that."

Nat picked his way cautiously among piles of trunks and boxes, getting closer to her by the sound of it. "Like what?"

"Oh, like she's..." Another morose sigh. "Come to live with us and be our nanny."

Nat stopped. "Excuse me?"

"Oh, yeah," Helen said, gloom deepening, "You heard me. My sisters called her. She's come to stay, bag and baggage, so we don't have to worry about the kids after your surgery or during it or any other time if we have to be gone."

"She's ninety-eight years old. She could die any minute. The kids'll get used to her and she'll be gone. How much time could she possibly have left?"

"Oh . . ." Yet another heavy sigh. "Fifteen or twenty years. Her own mother didn't die till she was a hundred and twelve—or so the story goes—and she might have been older than that. It's hard to say, since her birth certificate went up in smoke during the Chicago fire or something—"

He was laughing again. Couldn't help it, Helen sounded so deathly glum. Which meant he should really try to be at least a little sympathetic, shouldn't he?

"—And her mother's mother was at least a hundred and six, but we're not sure about that, either, because she had a tendency to lie about her age, make out she was younger than she was—"

Oh, God, if he laughed any harder he'd choke.

"—And I'm not sure that's really the kind of genetic background you want nurturing your kids—"

He got hold of himself enough to murmur, "Oh, I don't know, I let you nurture my kids and you seemed to turn out okay despite the influence of genetics, and she seems pretty spry. If it wouldn't solve 'em permanently, having her here might at least sidetrack a few problems for a while."

"Oh, sure, you say that now, but just wait till she starts telling the kids the story of her life."

"The stories she was telling Libby when I came up here were pretty good, creative exaggerations, entertaining tall tales—"

"Not tall tales."

"What?"

"Not tall tales," Helen repeated darkly. "True."

"True?"

"Mmm-hmm. Every one of 'em. And she's probably started with the tame ones. Wait'll she starts telling 'em she was a suffragette and went to jail with Emmeline Pankhurst and gets them all charged up about some cause and gets Janna to jet them off to save the rain forest or the dolphins or Antarctica or something. Or tells them how she used to go leprechaun hunting with her sisters in Ireland in the middle of the night, sneaking out with no parent the wiser—or how she once married a Baptist and brought scandal to the Church. Or—or wait until she hangs the nude portrait Picasso painted of her over the living room couch and tells the kids how they were lovers or—"

The laughter would kill him if he didn't stop her, so he did. Cut her short with the most sobering news he could find.

"Emma's coming over after lunch to decorate the house the way Amanda did it for Christmas last year to make sure nothing's changed."

"Oh, geez," Helen moaned.

When her sisters planned a disaster, why was it God forever seemed to want to dabble in it, too, and guarantee success?

Third Sunday of Advent—Day

Helen's brothers-in-law showed up just before lunch with Grandma Josephine's orthopedic bed and a few other...items...she'd had Janna crate up and jet in with them.

By the time the bed arrived, Helen had brought most of the Christmas ornaments down from the attic and reluctantly turned the main floor's company-best but also smallest and most-private living room into Josephine's bedroom. The guys, under Josephine's and Libby's decided direction, moved her in. Then Josephine and the kids unpacked her. Even Zach, intrigued in spite of himself, helped.

It took longer than one might reasonably expect because every unpacked item had a story to go with it and every story had to be told. Helen carted Christmas ornaments and ignored everything else; Nat nearly exploded trying not to laugh himself sick, then nearly wept when he heard Zach guffawing loudly in his place.

After they'd unpacked her, Josephine and the great-grandkids fixed lunch. Great-gram, as she readily told them, was a terrible cook, which meant that kids had to do the fixing so whatever they were going to eat would be edible. And they did, gravely and precisely—with a little lunacy thrown in for spice—fix a mostly edible meal.

Nat thought Josephine was wonderful and told Helen that if genetics was going to force her to grow up to be like her grandmother someday, he might be tempted to stay married to her forever strictly in order to find out what would happen next.

With grand and dire foreboding, Helen advised him to "Just wait."

As foretold, Emma arrived immediately after lunch, impeccably dressed as ever, but looking a trifle vague and confused and...lackluster. She didn't sound or behave entirely like herself, either, but appeared almost... docile, picking dilatorily through the boxes of ornaments and decorations as though searching for something she couldn't quite recall losing. And instead of taking over the decorating as planned, she was almost diffident in suggesting that she, Helen and Nat might take the kids to the mall to visit Santa together, give Grandma Josephine a little time to rest after her trip and settle in.

Helen had assumed Emma would object to Grandma Josey and her Mary Poppins plans out of hand, but Emma merely shrugged and said that it might be nice for the children to have a great-grandmother in the house.

Neither Helen nor Nat could put a finger on the trouble aside from the outward differences in Emma's manner, and since that seemed mostly for the better, they couldn't find a reason to object to taking themselves and the kids out with her.

With some misgiving and the children's enthusiastic encouragement, they agreed to the trip.

Leaving Grandma Josephine waving from the doorway and taking Toby in harness with them, they piled into Helen's and Emma's cars and went.

* * *

"Stop those coats!"

Standing in the long, noisy Santa Claus line behind the fountain between Montgomery Wards and the Kay-Bee toy store with five children, Emma, Nat and his big yellow dog, Helen heard the shout and turned in time to see a rack full of fur coats barreling toward them, antitheft rings clanging from every sleeve. Behind the furs a straggly line of uniformed security officers gave inefficient chase—not for lack of heart, but because to a person they wore shoes that looked great but weren't designed for running on slick mall floors. Without hesitation, Helen plopped Jane into Libby's arms, grabbed her big, heavy purse from her shoulder and darted out to cut off the furs.

"Come on, Toby, get 'em," she yelled.

Responding to the urgency of her tone, the dog cast one apologetic glance over his shoulder at his harness and Nat before lunging after the woman who gave peanut-butter cookies to the three-year-old he adored and could always count on to share them with him. With a startled, "Hey!" Nat went along. It was either that, have his arm jerked out of its socket or go sprawling headfirst into who knew what if he let go of the harness. Almost anything was preferable to that.

Almost.

Unfortunately, Toby took the high road.

The velvet rope around the Santa Claus igloo tangled around Nat's thighs. The movable posts the rope was fastened to went down with a clang. Nat stumbled, but years of athletic training of one sort or another—including rock climbing while blind—kept his feet under him; reflex and terrific inner-ear balance enabled him to get out of the rope and kick it aside.

"Daddo, Daddo, step up, step up," Max screamed from somewhere behind him.

"Right foot, eighteen inches, right *now,*" Zach hollered from off to the side, keeping pace. "Put out your hand, he's goin' through the igloo and over the fountain. Step up again, three feet, a step and a half across, jump down three feet—"

Splash, slosh, slosh, running through the fountain, cold water sluicing off his jeans and gushing from his shoes. What the hell was going on?

"—Two more steps, step up and *over* right now, eighteen inches, you're going out of the fountain. Get out of his way, people, get out of his way! You're clear, Dad, go get 'em! Catch 'em, Toby."

Catch who? Nat wondered, but that was all the time he had to devote to any activity except concentrating on not slipping and getting himself killed or killing anyone else before he had a chance to throttle Helen for starting whatever this was.

He felt a whoosh and whistle of air beside his head; heard the rattle and roll of small wheels, the clank of metal on metal, Helen's fervent, muttered "Hit it, hit it, hit it!" and the solid *thwack* and *oof* of someone getting hit by something heavy. Detected the gathering of canine muscles in the dog in front of him, loosed a succinct expletive and prepared himself for Toby's spring.

When the dog launched himself, Nat simply trusted him and hung on, hoping for the best. Stupid, perhaps, when he had time to think about it later, but at the moment he was well beyond figuring out the logic of why he didn't just let go of the damned harness instead of letting himself be dragged along for the flight. Together he and Toby hit the insubstantial wall of fur coats, the solid but already off-balanced body of the person hiding in the middle of the furs in an attempt to steal them. Together they crashed into a storefront—not glass, thank God—and went down atop the thief among the furs.

It was a relief to come to a stop at last, but relief was short-lived. The fur thief struggled, kicking out from underneath Nat and Toby despite the dog's snarling and Nat's determined effort to hang on to whomever Toby had taken in such dislike. He lunged up after the flailing feet of the person he and Toby had taken down, ducked instantly when Helen commanded, "Stay down." Heard a sound he could only identify as cracking cartilage and felt the would-be thief topple across his back, land flat on the floor and lie still.

The next morning's headlines were great: Woman, Blind Man and Leader Dog Capture Runaway Furs Eluding Mall Security.

But that was tomorrow, and although they had yet to discover why, tomorrow neither Helen nor Nat would have the desire to bask in headlines. And they still had today to get through.

In the mall, security officers converged on the pile of now-disheveled furs and their thief; excitement and babble reigned, radios crackled, the Waterford Township police, a couple of Oakland County sheriffs and a newspaper camerawoman and reporter arrived to question everyone in sight.

"Nat, are you all right?" In the midst of the hubbub, Helen came down on her knees beside him, frantically running her hands over him, checking.

"Fine," Nat snapped tersely, brushing her hands aside. "But what the hell am I doing here in the first place?"

"You didn't let go of Toby's harness when you should have, you big idiot, that's what."

"I'm not supposed to *have* to let go of Toby's harness when he's in it," Nat retorted somewhat testily—but who could blame him? "That's why he's in it—so I can hang on. Where is he? Is he all right?"

Toby answered that himself by sticking his wet nose in Nat's face and giving it a rough and thorough tongue-lashing. Resigned, Nat worked a hand into the dog's ruff and scratched energetically.

"Dad, that was great! You should have seen the Colonel slug that guy with her purse, it was *awesome*." Zach dropped to the floor and slapped his father's knee, threw his arms around Toby's neck. "Good dog, Toby! You caught a robber, you're a hero."

"Daddo, Daddo, Daddo!" Max dashed up and flung himself into Nat's arms, rocking him back to the floor. "You okay? I couldn't say the directions, I didn't know how, Zach had to do it and he was *good,* he did it 'xactly right and you didn't get hurt and he's a *hero*."

"Yes he is, he did it perfect," Nat agreed with heartfelt emotion. He reached for where he could still feel Zach hugging Toby, squeezed his son's neck and ruffled his hair. "Thanks, Zach. I wouldn't have made it without you."

"No problem, Dad," was all Zach said, but he did so with shy dignity, more than a little pleasure and no defiance whatever.

Before the scene could get mushier, Libby puffed up, lugging a tearful Jane.

"Mom, she's wet."

"Tern'l," Jane sobbed, crossing her legs and squirming hard. "Have to doe potty right *now*."

Helen was on her feet instantly, lesson learned weeks ago the uncomfortable way. "Oh, great, okay, I'll get you there. Can you hold it a minute, babe?" She hoisted Jane into her arms. "Oh, yuck, you are wet, aren't you?"

Nodding, Jane buried her face in Helen's neck and wailed. Helen rubbed her back soothingly. "Don't worry about it, love, there was a lot of excitement and you couldn't help it. I'll take you down to the bathroom and get you cleaned up, we'll rinse out your clothes and dry them under the hand dryers—or maybe I'll just let you wear my sweatshirt, how 'bout that, huh? You want to be an army kid?"

Jane waggled her head against Helen's shoulder, indicating her agreement.

"All right, that's what we'll do then." She started walking backward down the mall, talking to Nat as she went. "I'm taking Jane down to the bathroom. You guys want to get back in line and we'll come find you? Libby, where's Cara and Emma? Maybe they've still got a spot...."

Twenty minutes later she and Jane returned to find a grim Nat waiting for her in front of the fountain with three worried-looking kids, one panting dog and no Cara or Emma. Every instinct she possessed—of army officer, adjutant general's investigator and mother—fizzed to instant attention.

She put Jane down next to Toby, straightened and touched Nat's arm. "What?" she asked.

"We didn't find 'em," he said shortly. "Kids looked, Toby looked, not a sign of either one of them."

Her response was automatic. "Are you sure? Maybe if I..."

"I hope so," Nat agreed. "Go."

She pressed his hand. "Back in a minute."

She took fifteen and still came back empty-handed. Stooped in front of Libby. "Lib, did Grammy Sanders say anything, go anywhere before you came to find us with Jane?"

Libby shook her head. "No. She was just standing in the line with us waiting."

"What about Cara?" By sheer will Helen managed to keep her tone calmer than her churning insides. "I know it's not like her, but did she maybe wander off anywhere, see something she wanted to look at in a store window, tell you she'd be back in a minute?"

"Uh-uh."

"Did anything peculiar happen?" An edge of panic crept out from under Helen's facade, stuffed forcibly back in.

Libby cocked her head, clearly thoughtful. "You mean besides Nat running through the fountain?"

Helen shut her eyes, prayed for patience. Ignored Nat's somewhat strangled but edgy cough above her. "Yes, I mean besides that."

"Well...I don't know if it's *peculiar* 'coz she does it sometimes accidentally 'coz Cara looks like her, but it's usually only once and then she doesn't do it anymore..."

"Lib." Helen displayed extreme forbearance, excessive calm. "Don't do me or Grandma Josephine right now. Don't make me crazy, 'cause this is important. Say it once and be clear about it."

Libby sighed. "Well, Grammy called Cara 'Amanda'—"

Nat sucked in air and gripped Helen's shoulder.

"—And she didn't do it once like a mistake the way she usually does, she did it a lot like it was Cara's name—"

"She called Cara 'Mandy' on our way over here in the car," Zach interposed suddenly. "Twice. She never did that before." His face paled and twisted and he turned to Nat. "She was talking to Cara like Cara was her little girl, like maybe she was Mom—" His voice broke, steadied. "It was kind of strange, but then she went back to talking to Cara like Cara and the rest of us, and I didn't pay attention anymore. I'm sorry." Another painful break in his voice. "Was it important, Dad? Was it?"

Nat dropped an arm around his shoulders. "No, I'm sure it's not important, I'm sure it's fine, Zach. Don't worry, it's fine."

"Maybe we should try having them paged," Helen suggested.

Nat nodded. "You want to go do that? I'll wait here with the kids in case they come looking for us."

"On my way."

Twenty minutes, half an hour, forty-five minutes passed. Three times the pager called for Emma Sanders and Cara Crockett to meet their party at the Santa Claus fountain. Three times Cara and Emma failed to show. Helen returned several minutes after the third page, pulled Nat away from the kids with strict instructions to Zach and Toby to stand right there and keep track of the younger ones.

"I went outside to check," she said without preamble. "Emma's car's gone, Nat."

Panic struck with tidal force. "God, Helen."

She put a hand to his mouth. "Don't scare the kids, Nat."

"Don't scare..." Incredulous. Impotent. A parent's worst nightmare. "God, Helen, where's my daughter? You're terrifying me."

Helen rubbed her eyes; the hand she laid on his arm trembled much like her voice. "I don't feel so calm myself, babe, but there's more and you've got to hear it. I called Jake on the off chance, but they're not there, either. He said he found a couple things this afternoon he thinks we should see. He'll meet us at the house."

Saturnalia—Evening

They should have been in the other rooms helping Grandma Josephine sidetrack the kids by decorating the house, Helen thought, or putting up the tree, stringing popcorn, baking cookies, appointing a lord or lady of misrule, attending the Christmas concert up at the church—anything but waiting for the police to arrive in order to report a missing nine-year-old child.

She studied Nat, who was looking haggard, sitting alone at the dining room table, head bowed over the fourth-grade school pictures he couldn't see of his late ex-wife and his daughter, each at age nine, each dressed in clothing of similar colors, blond hair long and fine and similarly parted, their faces identical. In front of the dining room window looking out to the street, Jake stood holding the Walt Disney World brochures he'd also brought along to show them.

"When Cara gave Emma her school pictures after the wedding, Emma started talking about Amanda and how many things we hadn't done and now it was too late and how like Amanda Cara was. I said no, Cara was Cara, looks and all, and Emma got mad and went and got out Amanda's school pictures and found that one, fourth grade, same as Cara, and stuck it in front of my face to prove to me I was wrong."

He swallowed, Adam's apple bobbing convulsively, not only a worried grandfather but a frightened husband who'd loved his wife for more than fifty years and was suddenly on the verge of losing her. "She started saying how much Amanda wanted to go to Walt Disney World when she was Cara's age, and how we never took her. I don't remember Mandy ever saying anything about it except in passing, but Emma was certain. She said if we didn't take Amanda now, we'd never have the chance. She was looking at Cara's picture, not Amanda's, and it bothered me some, but I guess I didn't want to think about it much. Emma gets confused sometimes lately, but it's only for a minute and it always passes. I guess this time it didn't. I'm sorry, Nat. If I'd realized what was happening, I never would have—"

Nat jerked a hand, cutting him short. "I know, Jake, I understand, it's not your fault, thanks. And at least she loves Cara and will do her best to keep her safe no matter who she thinks Cara is." His throat tightened against voicing the unthinkable. He forced it out anyway. "Unless she's so confused she can't remember..."

"Nat, don't do this," Helen said fiercely, flying over to drop to her knees beside his chair. "Don't go there, it won't help Cara or any of us. She's a smart kid. If Emma's too confused to remember what she's doing, Cara will try to help her figure it out. She'll find a way to get to a phone, call us, call for help. She'll be fine, Nat, she'll be *fine*. The police will take Emma's license-plate number and they'll give it to all the state police between here and Florida and they'll find her. It's a straight shot, I-75 all the way from here to Walt Disney World. As long as Emma sticks to the expressway, they can't miss her. Cara'll be home tonight or maybe tomorrow, and she'll be fine, Nat, you'll see." She locked her arms around his waist and buried her damp face in his chest. Her shoulders shook. "You'll see."

Bleakly Nat stroked her hair, then put his arms around her and buried his own face with his own tears in the crook of her neck and held on for dear life.

You'll see....

Chapter 13

But there was no sign of Emma or Cara anywhere along I-75 Sunday, Monday or Tuesday; no trace of them at gas stations or truck stops or McDonald's restaurants or Walt Disney World. The police moved phone-tracing equipment into the house and deployed a rotating shift of single detectives to man it.

By Wednesday the house was permeated with the fragrance of Christmas spices and Christmas baking; was dressed in artificial snow, cedar roping and lights, in vivid-hued frocking of red, green, gold and silver, with mistletoe and angels everywhere; was riddled with fading hope and the encroaching pall of grieving.

Jane and Max clung to Helen and Nat, not wanting to let them out of their sight even to go to school Christmas parties, so Helen kept them home and let them keep track of Great-grama Josey, make sure she stayed out of trouble. Josephine let them into her fascinating bedroom and, without leaving it, guided them around the world and took them on adventures that captured and distracted their young minds, dragged them away from their fears.

Zach and Libby, older, were harder to protect.

Zach was subdued, trying to be manly, but obviously frightened by the tumbled world he was supposed to maintain his balance in. He called home from school so often Monday that Nat, in despair, finally sent Helen to bring him and Libby home where they could at least see that nothing was happening that they weren't being told about. Once there, Zach spent his time in Nat's shadow and kept Toby close to his side, one hand clenched constantly in the dog's soft ruff, holding tight. On Wednesday morning Helen found him huddled under his quilt on the love seat in her and Nat's sitting room with a pillow clutched tight to his stomach and his hand flung over Toby on the floor below him, unhealthily asleep with his eyes open wide.

Libby curled herself into the smallest ball she could form in the darkest corner she could find and took losing Cara straight to heart; spent her days living in guilt and haunted silence, trying to deal with a havoc she refused to believe she hadn't wrought.

"I should have paid attention," she sobbed when Helen found her behind the clothes in her closet after she and Nat spent most of Tuesday afternoon searching for her. "I shoulda seen where they went, but I was watching you and Nat and I didn't take care—"

"Libby, don't, shh." Helen crawled into the closet, lifted her daughter into her lap and hugged her close, rocking her. "It's not your fault, shh, there was so much confusion and you took such good care of Jane. If anyone's to blame it's got to be me because I'm the one who didn't think before I went after that guy with the coats. I'm so sorry, I just handed Jane to you and went, and you took care of her like I knew you would and—"

"It's your training, Mom," Libby cried, grabbing a fistful of Helen's camouflage T-shirt and rubbing her face on it, understanding far too much for her years. "You couldn't help it, you're s'posed to do stuff like that."

"Oh, geez, Libby." Helen bit her tongue and looked at the closet ceiling, fighting emotion. "Don't excuse me for all the stupid things I do, I won't love you any less if you don't. When I'm with the army, that's when I'm supposed to use my training. When I'm with you and Zach and Cara and Jane and Max I'm supposed to be the mom—or at least a reasonable facsimile of a mom, and if I'm not, that's *my* fault. I'm the grown-up here, you're the kid and we should each be able to behave not only like who we are, but like who we're supposed to be at the time. You *did* your job, you behaved like the kid who was given her baby sister to watch and you did that so well. Me, I behaved like Peter Pan when I was supposed to be acting like Wendy, so don't tell me losing Cara was your fault. Nat and I know damned well it's not."

"I don't want Nat to hate me, Mama, because I didn't see where Cara went. Don't let him hate me, Mama, please."

"He doesn't hate you, baby, he loves you. I love you. It'll be okay, baby, Cara'll be fine, we'll all be together, shh, shh...."

When she finally got Libby quieted and out of her closet, sent her down to help Josephine play with Jane and Max, Helen went looking for Nat. Crept into his arms, held him tight and cried.

Wednesday morning, because she had to do something, had to make something normal no matter how difficult it was to feel it, Helen forced herself to go out and finish her Christmas shopping, come home and go scrounging through the attic for the wrapping paper she thought she'd seen up there last week. It was when she was pawing through one of the old steamer trunks in search of something special to use to wrap Cara's "from Santa" gift that she found the presents from Amanda.

Lovingly wrapped and ribboned in Victorian paper with intricate, hand-tied bows, bearing hand-cut and hand-lettered angel cards, there were eight boxes of varying sizes and shapes, one for each of the children, for John and for Jake and Emma. Swallowing hard and feeling like an intruding spy, Helen lifted each box out of the trunk and read the attached card. Each bore the intended recipient's name, a couple of lines of poetry that were both loving and funny, and the inscription With Much Love from your Guardian Angel.

Hand to her mouth to keep her heart from escaping her throat, Helen rocked back on her heels and stared at the gifts. She was still sitting there staring a short while later when Nat tapped up the attic steps looking for her.

"Helen?"

"Here." A sniff and a gulp straight ahead and to his right. "Whatchya need?"

"Someplace to hide and you to hang on to."

He came to her, held out a hand and let her guide him down to her. Reached out to gather her close and shield his face in the harbor of her neck.

"Nat?" Her arms swept around his shoulders, cradled his head. "What's happened?"

He shook his head, tightened his hold on her. "Nothing. I hate not being able to do something, break something, find her. Bring her home. Music Minister just called wanting to make sure Cara would be there to play Mary at the children's Mass on Christmas Eve. I told her I hoped so and hung up on her." His shoulders shook and her neck felt wet. "Damn, you'd think there wouldn't be any more tears after a while, wouldn't you? You'd think they'd dry out and stop stinging and just leave the ache."

"Nat." Gently she stroked his hair, rocking him. Loving him. "Nat."

He gave himself a few more seconds of her comfort, then pushed away to wipe his face on his knuckles. Shook his head, trying to clear the fog, jaw working, face wry. Tried to smile. "Well, that accomplished a lot, didn't it? So, what're you doin' up here? I don't think the house can take any more decorating. Cara gets home, she's going to wonder what we were thinking."

"Sometimes I wonder myself, but Grandma Jo and Jane and Max enjoyed themselves so much I didn't have the heart to tell them that in my opinion less is usually more. No, I was looking for wrapping paper for the Santa Claus presents—you know, something we haven't used to wrap anything you and I are giving them—and I found..." She hesitated. "Amanda left presents for them, Nat."

"For who, the kids?"

"The kids, John, Emma, Jake. Wrapped and labeled and signed with love from their guardian angel."

His laughter was humorless and hurting. "Geez, Helen."

"I think we should put them under the tree, Nat. I think maybe we should send John's to Henry and Ida, and make sure Emma and Jake get theirs. Maybe it'll help, let them all know how much she loved them even though she and John couldn't take the time to say goodbye. Maybe..."

He lifted a hand, caressed her cheek. Nodded sadly. "Whatever you think, Helen. Anything you want..."

The call came a little after the midnight turn of the calendar page to December 22, a scant few minutes after Nat had desperately and convulsively poured himself into the haven that was Helen.

Still holding on to her with bruising force, he rolled away to snatch the receiver off his bed stand.

"Daddy?" Cara's voice sounded tired but strong, not frightened.

He was up, alert, crushing the breath out of Helen with one arm while his other hand strangled the phone. "Cara?"

Startled, hopeful, terrified, Helen came equally alert, struggled up Nat while his grip on her tightened, leaning against him to press her ear into the receiver beside his. "Cara?"

Laughter came from her end, a nervous giggling, the relieved edge of hysteria. "Hi, Daddy. Hi, Colonel. I don't know where I am. Can you help me find out and come get me?"

"Yes, of course we will, right now, baby." Nat felt pressure in his lungs, tension in his heart, relief and fear mingling. "First, are you all right? Where's Emma?"

"Asleep in the car back there," she answered vaguely. "I got out and walked. I'm hungry, Daddy, and my feet are cold. Could you bring me my warm boots and some food?"

"Boots, socks, the refrigerator and your whole wardrobe if you want it, darlin', but you've got to help the Colonel and me find you first." He let go of Helen, sketched a violent *Go!* gesture in the air.

She scrambled to get dressed, bent to press her lips to his unoccupied ear. "I'm going to make sure that cop downstairs is awake and tracing this, then I'm going to use the other line and wake Caroline and have her put a plane and a helo on standby. Soon's we get a general location, you and I are in the air and Caroline moves in a ground team to help the police find the actual."

Nat nodded, jerked his thumb hard at the door as if to say *Don't stand there telling me about it, damn it, just do it!* and again spoke to Cara. "Honey, tell me where you're calling from. Are you at a gas station? Is there a sign? I'm going to keep you on the phone to help the police find you so the Colonel and I can come get you as fast as possible. Describe where you are to me...."

Cara and Emma were marooned in a snowstorm in southern Utah just west of the Colorado border—on their way to Disneyland, not Walt Disney World.

When Helen finished talking to the police and General Greene, she hung up and called Jake.

"Jake? Nat's got Cara on the phone upstairs—"

"Is she all right? Is Emma all right? Where—"

"We're working on getting their location now. Soon's we have it, Nat and I are flying out—"

"I'm coming, too," Jake interrupted brusquely and hung up before Helen could finish.

Understanding completely, she pushed down the phone button, released it and called her mother to come stay at the house with Grandma Josephine and the other kids, then went to wake her grandmother and tell her what was happening. Back upstairs, she woke Zach and Libby to fill them in, nodded in empathy when they were too excited to go back to sleep and instead followed her down the hall to Nat. While they were talking to Cara, Helen gave in to an unexplainable impulse and climbed into the attic to collect Amanda's gifts for Emma and Jake.

Shortly thereafter, Jake arrived, followed closely by Julia Brannigan. Leaving Julia, Josephine, Zach and Libby to take turns making Cara stay awake and talk to them so she wouldn't freeze, Helen, Nat and Jake headed for the airport.

It took a little time and the cooperative efforts of the local sheriffs, the search team General Greene pulled together at Helen's request and a ski patrol to locate the abandoned store with the ancient pay phone Cara had found to call from. When the ski patrol got to her after a hard two hours of looking, Cara was sleepy, snow-covered and nearly frozen, huddled in a car blanket on the ground against the phone kiosk.

Emma was two miles down the road, asleep in the car, which was out of gas and partially buried in a snowbank. Both were suffering from exhaustion and some minor frostbite; Emma was also suffering from the effects of depression and a type of confusion that often afflicted aging persons but had nothing to do with Alzheimer's. Time and treatment for the depression symptomatic of her extreme grief could be her only healers.

By the time Helen, Nat and Jake were able to get through to them later that afternoon, Emma and Cara had been taken by chopper to the nearest hospital for treatment. In the hospital, Cara was still being examined, so they saw Emma first.

Attached to a precautionary heart monitor because of her age and tied to IVs, she appeared shriveled and shrunken, lost, far less than her usual self. She recognized Jake, but didn't know either Nat or Helen, asked for Amanda. When the attending physician pressed her, trying to jog her into identifying them, she turned on her side and burst into tears.

Despite the pain Emma had brought them from the beginning, Helen's heart wrenched at the sight of the lonely, suddenly elderly woman who had lost her daughter and was now apparently losing herself. She watched Nat's lips harden and compress as he listened to his former mother-in-law cry, watched him struggle not to forgive her, then finally take her hand and forgive her anyway, silently, without the words she wouldn't, for the moment at least, comprehend. When he stepped back and turned to her, Helen squeezed Nat's hand, left Amanda's final Christmas gifts to her parents on the bed table where Jake wouldn't miss them and guided Nat down the hall to his daughter.

Cara was overjoyed to see them, drowsy but full of her adventures, anxious for hugs, in need of kisses—and sleep.

Tied as Emma was to IVs, and with her frostbitten fingers and toes wrapped, Cara looked pale and a trifle thin. Helen supposed the thinness was simply a mother's imagination, superimposing a waiflike demeanor on the child who had been strong enough not only to survive a bewildered grandmother, a scary cross-country odyssey, a heavy blizzard, freezing temperatures and a couple of days without food, but had also been resourceful enough to rescue herself and her grandmother despite the odds against her.

Unable to see her, to assure himself through nonphysical channels that Cara was indeed all there—ten fingers, ten toes, two hands, two feet, two ears, two eyes and one nose—he needed to touch her, but was half-afraid to because he didn't know where to put his hands so he could hold his daughter without unintentionally hurting her or getting tangled in the IVs.

"Help me, Helen," he whispered, so she did. Dropped the bed rail for him, moved things out of the way, moved the recliner one of the nurses had brought down from Pediatrics next to the bed and guided him to it. Let him settle himself, then placed his child in his arms.

Holding Cara at last, Nat relaxed for the first time in a week, resting his cheek against her hair and cuddling her close, smiling while his little girl slept.

Heart full and unable to take her eyes off them, Helen realized that everybody's favorite Madonna and Child told only half the story. This was the picture she would keep in her heart: Father and Child, safe together at last.

From the bits and pieces Cara told them in between naps, Nat and Helen slowly gathered what had happened from, er, mall to call.

When the mall commotion began, Emma had taken Cara's hand and pulled her out of the way of the curious crowd. At some point, they'd begun walking, looking in store windows and picking out things they liked. Cara had forgotten about not having the others with her, hadn't paid much attention when Grammy Sanders walked her out to the car to go home. They'd been pulling out of the parking lot when Cara suddenly remembered they'd left everyone else in the mall, but when she'd said something about it, Emma had looked at her strangely and said, "That's okay, darling, Mama will take care of it, fasten your seat belt, there's a good girl," and continued driving.

They'd driven long enough for Cara to fall asleep, trusting Emma to bring her safely home despite the fact that the drive back home from the mall seemed an awful lot longer than the drive there had been. When she woke up, Emma had laughed and said something about taking the scenic route and a wonderful surprise waiting for Mandy at the end of it.

Though somewhat apprehensive about being called by her mother's name so often, Cara had simply written it down to the silliness of age and politely ignored it the way she and the other children always did whenever one of their older relatives confused them with someone whose genetic bone structure they'd inherited. Even Jane and Max had occasionally been called by somebody else's name by aunts and uncles a generation older than their parents, so why should it concern Cara to be mistaken for her mother once in a while when even she knew how much she resembled Amanda?

Cara thought she'd slept a long time. When she'd wakened a second time it was black outside, real night, and there hadn't been any streetlights to hide the stars. Emma had parked at the side of the road with the interior car lights on; she'd looked a little anxious and had been studying a map. Cara didn't recognize anything about where they were, but when she'd asked, beginning to feel frightened, Emma had patted her hand reassuringly and told her that Mama was a little lost but not to worry, go back to sleep, they'd get straightened out in no time. It wasn't until Cara woke up and it was light outside again that she'd understood how wrong things really were.

As nearly as she could figure, she and Emma had driven for the most part of five days, stopping occasionally to get gas, to wash up in gas-station bathrooms. Cara had started looking for a way to get to a phone sometime Monday. She'd even asked Emma about calling Daddy, but Emma had seemed confused about who Cara's daddy was, had grown more agitated and fearful the longer they'd been on the road, had been afraid not only to let Cara out of her sight but to let go of her at all for fear somehow they'd get separated and Amanda would be lost.

Cara told them Emma had started looking over her shoulder a lot, becoming more and more fearful by the day and wanting as little contact with people other than Cara as possible; had started crying and had told Cara she couldn't remember their phone number and anyway was a little afraid of what phones could do to people, and oh, my, wouldn't Daddy be angry with Mama for getting them so lost when all she'd meant to do was drive down the road a little way to Disneyland, and oh, there, she'd gone and spoiled Amanda's surprise, don't tell Daddy, dear, don't tell Daddy.

And Cara, older sister to three younger siblings, her mother's and now the Colonel's responsible helper, had realized that Grammy Sanders was no longer the adult in this situation, that something had happened to her and she badly needed someone to take care of her. Cara had done the best she could to do just that.

Since Emma seemed to become more herself while they were driving, Cara hadn't tried to talk her out of doing so, but had simply kept her eyes open all the time for the opportunity to find Grammy some help. By Thursday, Cara said, Emma had stopped talking period, and all they'd done was drive without stopping, except once at the side of the road in the middle of nowhere when Cara had to go to the bathroom. Driving into the blizzard and running out of gas had seen the end of Emma's reality reserves. Before Cara's eyes her grandmother had seemed to become drained of life, to give up, shrink and fade, unable to handle more. Crying, but without saying a word, Emma had simply shriveled up in her car seat and refused to move.

When Emma had fallen asleep at last, Cara had taken the car keys and looked in the trunk for blankets or something to keep them warm. She'd found the big heavy metal lantern Jake kept in the trunk, two blankets, some too-big boots, an extra jacket, scarves, mittens and a shovel, water and a stash of dried figs and some flares. For one of the safety classes at school, she'd read newspaper stories about people who'd been stranded in blizzards, knew it was always best to stay with the car. So she'd eaten some figs, then read the instructions on the flares and lit them.

Snow buried the flares, so she'd gotten out the shovel and tried to unbury them, but the snowfall was heavier and faster than she could keep up with. She'd gotten back in the car, stuck the keys in the ignition and switched them backward the way John had once shown her so she could play the radio without turning on the engine. She'd found a talk station on the radio and in between listening to it and trying to keep herself and Emma warm under the blankets, had honked SOS with the horn, three shorts, three longs, three shorts, the way Libby said Nancy Drew did it—Cara was more into the Baby-sitter books and Sweet Valley High, herself—until the car's battery went dead.

By that time it was starting to get dark again, she had to go to the bathroom because of the figs and the water she'd consumed and the snow was letting up a little. Emma hadn't moved for such a long time that Cara kept feeling her mouth and chest to make sure she was breathing; the

blare of the car horn hadn't disturbed her even once. Nobody came to find them.

Cold and more afraid of not doing anything than of at
least trying to do something, Cara had finally decided it
couldn't be too much worse for her to get out in the snow
and relieve her body than it would be for her to try to sit
in the car any longer, uncomfortable as she was. When
she'd gotten back in the car that time, Emma seemed to be
sleeping deeper than ever, and her breathing was more ir-
regular and shallow. It was at that point that Cara had determined her grandmother couldn't wait much longer for
help to come to them and had resolved to go out and find
it. She'd taken the flashlight and what little money was left
in Emma's purse, collected one blanket, donned the jacket
that came down to the tops of her boots, put on an extra
hat and mittens and struck out for parts unknown.

Since there'd been nothing for hours back in the direction they'd come from, she'd headed the way the car was
pointed, doing her best to stay on the road and out of the
drifting snow. She had no idea how long it had taken her
to find the abandoned store with the ancient rotary but
still-working pay phone out front, couldn't explain what
had made her turn off the road just *there* when she
couldn't see anything through the blowing snow, but that's
what she'd done. There'd been enough change in Grammy's purse to start the collect phone call and she'd even
remembered her area code. Dad and the Colonel had taken
care of the rest.

Simply grateful to have her back, Nat wasn't concerned
about the hows and whys, but Helen thought of the angel
presents back home in the attic and offered a word of
thanks to Amanda and the legions of heavenly beings who
must have worked extra hard to lead a little girl home.

Chapter 14

December 24

The entire family was there to greet them when they got home late Sunday morning: Blocks and Brannigans, Maximoviches, Crocketts and Block-Brannigan relations from far distant zones of reality and somewhat scattered dimensions of time. Fortunately the B-B reality and time impaired were largely a feather-boa-wearing, kindly, eccentric, tactless and gently benevolent faction, eliciting rolled eyes and disbelieving laughter rather than fear.

Cara was the center of everyone's attention, especially—at first—her siblings. After Nat established her on one of the living room couches in the heart of the festivities, Libby, Max, Jane and Zach couldn't wait to be of service, fetching and carrying, giving her unexpected hugs and lavishing on her presents of some of their favorite toys until Cara was nearly suffocated beneath the literal weight of the stuffed animals, books, games, trucks, pens, etcetera, of their love.

Having her home got old after a while, however, and within a couple of hours—after her story had been told and embellished so many times her siblings stopped being able to suspend their disbelief and started picking it apart—the old pecking order was reestablished and Cara was once again merely the not-feeling-well kid on the couch, the butt of Zach's worst jokes, the long-suffering lieutenant-secretary to Libby's general, Max's favorite person to bug and Jane's resigned designated reader of *Green Eggs and Ham*—over and over and over.

It was a crowded day, full of food and laughter and way too many hovering people. By early afternoon, Cara was exhausted, so after letting the cousins exchange and open their name-drawing gifts to each other, Helen kicked everybody out. With a great deal of understanding and only a few teasing comments from her sisters about the poor extent of her hospitality after all the trouble they'd gone through to arrange this party at her house, everybody but Grandma Josephine went.

A family, they spent the rest of the day in unhurried, joyful preparation for the evening's and following day's celebrations.

In spite of the bandages on her hands and feet, Cara was determined to still play Mary in the Christmas pageant and following tableau, so after a hurried conversation with the Music Minister, Helen made a hurried dash up to the church to bring Cara's costume home for a quick fitting. And it was a darned good thing that the alterations to the shapeless blue robe could be accomplished with a few strategically placed safety pins and a rope belt, or Cara would have been up the creek without a seamstress.

Amid a flurry of flour, powdered sugar and food coloring, the Christmas cookies Zach, Libby, Max and Jane hadn't wanted to make until Cara came home were mixed, rolled, cut, baked and creatively painted. Grandma Josephine, the self-designated kibitzer on the project, encouraged the children to suggest stories for each of their creations, then told them tales of the real people she'd met in her travels through life who reminded her of each of their cookies. Albert Einstein was the sheep with the wild hairdo Libby gave it. Other twentieth century historical and celebrity figures with whom Josephine professed modest acquaintance fared less well. Stephen Spielberg, for example, was the purple goat whose horn broke off and who needed Josephine to glue it back on for him—and then introduce him to George Lucas—and tell him that special effects were the wave of the future. And *Jurassic Park*'s Michael Crichton—according to Great-grandma J—was the blue elephant who originally wanted to write a sweet little story about cute and scary little mice until Josephine Block set him straight.

The children were delighted with the chronicles. Helen swallowed them with several grains of salt and a lot of eye rolling, and Nat tried not to wonder which parts of the fabrications might or might not be true.

And probably guessed wrong every time.

The children's Christmas Eve Mass was scheduled for five, so after the cookie baking—and consumption—everybody bathed or showered and dressed for Christmas.

The church was packed to the rafters, standing room only. Fortunately, pageant and angel families were needed early, so Nat, Zach and Grandma Josephine found seats for eight in a front pew and scattered coats to reserve the spaces for the other family members.

Stationed in the church vestibule helping angels and shepherds dress, Helen watched the parish come in, families gather. Dress ranged from blue jeans and sweaters to gorgeous and sparkly. Mothers and grandmothers had dressed infants in darling, beautiful outfits that would never be worn again but would be preserved in the family photograph albums forever.

Fathers carried toddlers, held newborn babies in nervous arms. Teenagers stood close to current inamoratas; younger children who were no longer in arms but were still young enough to take the Night Before Christmas literally went big eyed to the crèche, petted or kissed the head of the representative ceramic Baby Jesus. Children too young to date but too cynical to believe in Santa anymore found friends and talked about what they might be getting in the morning. And everyone smiled and greeted everyone else, laughed and shared a moment regardless of how good or bad their lives outside of this place and time might be.

Mass began in darkness, moved to blaze with light as candles were lit from the ends of the pews inward. The children's choir sang their specially prepared songs; the listeners joined in wherever they could. The angels, Jane and Max among them, twirled up the aisles during the Gloria, stumbling and serious to the joyous ringing of bells and rattling of keys, the whir of camcorders and the grins and covered faces of their enjoyably embarrassed families.

During the reading of the Gospel, Cara's Mary rode a borrowed child's wheelchair covered by a gray robe into Bethlehem. The shepherds on the hillside were properly—and probably literally—sore afraid when Libby's announcing angel, cockeyed halo, skewed wings and all, shouted, "Hey! Unto you a Child is born!" The bearded wisemen presented their gifts of gold, frankincense and a basket of canned vegetables, bread, fruit and canned ham with almost the right amount of reverence. Once the pageant was presented, the participants stood in tableau without moving a whisker until the Music Minister signaled them to join their families.

The Mass progressed, the host and wine consecrated, the Our Father recited, the sign of peace lengthily and cheerfully exchanged, communion distributed. When everyone had settled back for the moment of silence following communion, the lights were turned out and parents in the know aimed their children's eyes toward the doors. In a moment, Father Christmas appeared; the hush grew as he moved up the aisle to the crèche, knelt on one knee before it and removed his hat for a long instant of silent meditation. Then he left as silently as he'd come and the wide-eyed children exhaled held breaths. The adults with them inhaled, their own sense of wonder momentarily restored and engaged.

Then the Mass was over and the exodus began, with more greetings and visiting and dispersing until, finally, the last of the families went home.

Nat ordered pizza before they left church, and they stopped to pick it up on their way to the house. The children, Zach included, were wired to the gills from Christmas expectations, more than a little rowdy. Libby and the boys, with far more energy than necessary, toppled a willing Nat off the couch after pizza, while Helen built a fire in the fireplace. The ensuing wrestling match was noisome, filled with Max's shrieks, yells of "Dad, no fair, you're bigger than me" from Zach, and hearty laughter and giggles from Libby, who was the most ticklish of the bunch.

When the fire was burning brightly, Helen turned to find a pouting Jane wanting to take part in the tussle with Nat, but afraid of getting in the way of flying arms and feet. However, she was perfectly willing to let Helen sweep her wildly off her feet, blow raspberries on her rosy cheeks and neck and tickle her until she was squealing with delight and had to go to the bathroom. In the big chair in front of the fire, Grandma Josey sat with Cara, enlightening her about the whys and wherefores of collecting African masks via pirate traders in Fiji until Helen caught the gist of the lesson and put a stop to it. Her children she informed Josephine firmly, were much too young to need to know how to bargain with pirates.

With some misgiving, Nat decided this must be one of the true stories Helen had referred to and wondered exactly how responsible a parent he was for letting Josey tell his children things he wasn't around to edit. Decided that if they learned anything at all about living long and fully from Josephine's...parables, then the parables—no matter how blatantly outrageous—were well worth the later questions.

At long last—later than the parents wanted but earlier than the kids felt necessary—everyone was readied for bed, Nat read *A Visit From Saint Nicholas* and it was time to hang stockings. After hanging their own stockings—Victorian style, lovingly and painstakingly embroidered by Emma for each of them as they joined the family—the five kids disappeared in a bustle of whispers and *shushes*. Came sidling back a few minutes later wearing silly grins and shyly expectant faces, hiding things behind their backs.

Helen touched Nat's arm, whispered, "Uh-oh. They look goofy and they're hiding something behind their backs."

He pressed his lips to her ear, whispered wickedly and very quietly, "I'm not hiding what I've got for you behind *my* back, in case you're interested."

The heat spread instantly. "Very interested," Helen murmured, "but cool your shorts for a bit, would you? We've got other things to do first."

Nat sighed, hand to his heart. "I guess the honeymoon's really over. You're no fun anymore."

"Wanna bet?" Helen asked, then, before he could do more than grin appreciatively, turned to the kids. "What's up?"

"Umm," Cara said diffidently, "We, umm—"

"Umm, we have something . . ." Zach shuffled his feet.

"We have something for you," Libby said, shooting her older siblings disgusted looks. She'd never quite understand how it was so many people had so much trouble putting five words together without hemming and hawing. *She* never had trouble spitting out what she intended to say. "Max?"

She gave him a poke and the five-year-old stepped forward, took a deep breath and cleared his throat. Brought his hands out from behind his back and held out four large, brass cup hooks to Helen.

"Kern'l, we need you to put these on the fireplace for us. Right here—" gravely he pointed out the bare spots at each corner of the mantel framing the hung stockings "—and here and here." He showed her the space between his stocking and Libby's in the mantel's center. "I brought you a little hammer and a nail so you could start the holes." He went back to the couch, reached underneath to pull the tools out. "I wanted to do it for you, but Libby said you'd catch us if we did it early and we wanted it to be a s'prise, so I didn't. I will now, though. If you want."

Helen fetched a dining room chair for him to stand on. "I'd like that very much."

When he'd finished screwing the hooks into the mantel, he marched solemnly back to his place in the row of children and Helen put the chair away. Unable to contain herself, Jane danced and twirled excitedly.

"Now?" she whispered loudly, nodding, eyes alight. "Me do it now?"

"Go ahead," Zach said.

Wiggling with pleasure, she bounced across to Nat and tugged on his hand. He picked her up.

"Whatchya got, sweet cheeks?"

"Me have stocking for Toby, see, Nat?" She shoved the fuzzy red-and-white stocking into Nat's cheek and rubbed so he could feel it. "Me put his name on it, *there*—" she grabbed Nat's hand and traced his finger over the glittery letters that might possibly have spelled Toby—in Martian. "—an it's *bootifool*. See, Tern'l?" She swung the stocking at Helen, then nudged Nat's chest impatiently with her knees as though he were a horse. "Move, Nat. Needa hang it up."

Ceremony completed, she squirmed down and jumped about, waiting for the rest of it to take place. Zach stepped forward, shoved a stocking into Nat's hand.

"It says Pop and you're supposed to hang it here." He guided Nat to a hook at the end of the mantle. Turned to Helen and Grandma Josephine. "We have 'em for you guys, too."

Cara and Libby brought matching stockings out of hiding. Libby handed hers to Josephine.

"It just says *GGJ*," she said, "'cause your name is too long to put it all on."

"That's true," Josephine agreed. "It was never meant to be monogrammed on anything."

"That's what I thought." Libby nodded. "Here, I'll hang it up for you." She did.

Shyly Cara brought her stocking to Helen. "It says Mom," she said hesitantly. "I hope that's okay. I wanted to put Colonel, but Libby said not to because you could get demoted or promoted and might not always be a Colonel, so we should put something less..." she hunted for the word "less *unique*. You hang it at the other end from Dad's."

Overwhelmed, Helen held the stocking, looking at the glittering gold letters, tracing them once while her throat closed. She leaned into Nat and he kissed her temple, slipped an arm about her shoulders and squeezed.

"Is it all right?" Zach asked anxiously.

Helen nodded, eyes bright. "Oh yeah," she said. The smile that crossed her face felt big and brilliant and about to crack. "Yeah, it's definitely all right."

Then she hung the stocking on the remaining hook and, hand to her mouth, admired the way the letters sparkled in the firelight.

Mom.

Christmas Eve—11:23 p.m.

Kids and Josephine in bed asleep at last, Nat and Helen skulked down the upstairs hallway and staircases like thieves, dragging sacks of booty behind them.

"Shh, Nat, don't rattle the packages, you'll wake the kids."

"Me? Who the hell's great idea was it to hide all this stuff in the attic where we'd have to sneak it past the kids' bedrooms anyway?"

"Oh, just shut up. Next year I'll know better and we'll hide 'em in the basement."

"A likely story," Nat whispered, then nearly tripped over Helen, who'd stopped short at the girls' doorways to listen.

"Be careful," she breathed.

"Tell me when you're going to stop," he hissed back, "or let me lead."

"You could lead me straight down the garden path to hell," Helen whispered back, "and I'd go."

He slipped passed her, started down the steps to the main floor. "Is that a threat?"

Helen followed him. "Or a promise."

Downstairs they put out the gifts, filled the stockings. Toby's got a rawhide bone—made in the United States, as per Zach's insistence—and a big box of dog cookies. Josephine's got a bunch of tall, multihued ostrich feathers and a new fake-sable-trimmed hat with a bunch of orange poppies sewn onto the side. The kids' stockings were filled with assorted oddments of things they each liked, then

Helen stuck one small gift in Nat's stocking and he tucked one into hers.

When they were finished, they snuggled together in the big chair in front of the fire, enjoying the peace and each other. Outside the snow drifted gently to earth. Inside, Nat kissed Helen long and deep, fiddled loose the buttons of her heavy silk blouse, drew the fabric open and slipped his fingers under it to outline what lay beneath.

More heavy silk ridged in feather-light lace lay under his hand, molded gently to Helen's breasts. He grinned against her mouth.

"New teddy?" he asked.

Helen nodded. "Siren red. Thought you might like a little seasonal packaging if you were going to unwrap this gift under the tree."

Nat pulled her blouse out of her pants, finished unbuttoning it and laid it open, dragged his hand from her breast to her hip, hauled her close. "You're going to let me open a present before midnight?"

In the front hallway the grandfather clock chimed the hour.

"It's midnight," Helen said, gathering his shirt collar in her fist and pulling him into her kiss. "Merry Christmas."

"Merry Christmas," Nat whispered. Then they didn't speak again for a long time.

When they next came up for air, they were both somewhat flushed and heated, their clothing in open disarray.

"I think maybe we should move this upstairs," Helen murmured, pushing herself up on his chest, tugging him after her. "Don't you?"

"Unless you want Grandma Josey walking in on us when I make you scream." Nat grinned, pure arrogant male.

"I never scream." She was affronted. Then she amended for the sake of honesty, "Well, almost never."

Nat slipped his hands under the hair on her neck, kissed her lingeringly. "Yeah, but only because I keep your mouth so busy you can't."

"Nathaniel." Helen sighed. "Let's go upstairs."

He caressed her jaw. "In a minute, okay? First I've got something I want to give you now."

He got up, went out to the dining room hutch, came back.

"Nat, you don't—"

He hushed her with a finger to her lips. "I want to, Helen." He pressed a tiny velvet box into her hand.

She looked at him, uncertainty in her voice. "What—"

"Open it and see."

With shaking fingers, Helen snapped the box open. An emerald engagement ring gleamed up at her from the depths of the deep red velvet.

"Oh, Nat." Stunned, she looked at him. "I—I...oh, *Nat.*"

He smiled. "Jed says it matches your eyes. That's what I wanted."

"But I—oh, Nat, I don't..." She gulped.

He went down on a knee in front of her, fumbled for her hand. "I love you, Helen Crockett," he said simply. "Marry me again."

She'd thought the revelation would frighten her, would come into being like a thunderbolt the way the initial libidinal hunger always had, but it didn't. It was an insidious hungry delight that filled her to brimming and wouldn't go away. It was choking tenderness and roaring passion and peace. It was five kids and Toby and Grandma Josephine. And always, on top of it and underneath it and around it, it was Nat. She slid forward in the chair toward him.

"Yes," she whispered. "I will. I love you, Nat."

Then, because it was so ridiculously simple now that she wasn't afraid of it anymore, she stretched her arms around his neck and, laughing, said it again. "I love you, Nathaniel Hawthorne Crockett. I love you. Now get off your damned knees and take me to bed."

Post Script

December 31, VA Hospital
Ann Arbor, Michigan

"You ready, Captain Crockett? We'll take the patch off and see what we've got."

Nat's fingers twitched nervously; his mouth felt dry. He didn't think he'd ever been so afraid of a single moment in his life.

"Where's Helen?" he asked.

"Here, Nat." She stooped at his side, understanding perfectly. "You want me to go?"

"No." He grasped her hand hard. "You stay. Where're the kids?"

"In the waiting room with Josephine. You want them here?"

"No." He took a breath, blew it out. "Okay, Doc, let's do it."

The doctor picked at the tape over the patch, peeled it back. "Now, it'll seem bright in here and it'll take your eye a few minutes to adjust, so don't be concerned if you can't see anything at first."

He lifted off a layer of gauze, dropped it onto the treatment tray to his right. "We'll take a look here, and if everything's working, we'll stick you in a perforated metal patch. I want you to wear the patch all the time for the first three months to make sure none of those kids can stick a finger in your eye."

He took off another layer of gauze. "No bending for at least a couple of weeks, no stairs today, after that be careful. If you have to sneeze or cough, do it with your mouth open so you don't jerk the wound. We'll send you home with a post-op instruction sheet, antibiotics and steroids for your eye. Don't skip any doses. You shouldn't feel too much discomfort, if any at all, but if you need something for minor pain take acetaminophen, not aspirin. If you feel any sharp or persistent pain, I want to know immediately. Well..." He picked up the last piece of gauze. "I think we're there." He lifted off the patch. "Blink a bit and tell me what you think."

Tell him what he *thought?* Nat wondered, incredulous. How could anybody think?

Instead of thinking, he simply blinked his right eye—his clear *blue* right eye—and let the marvels come to him.

Light, white and watery to begin with.

Snatches of color: chrome, steel, blue, pink, green, white.

The doctor's face, hazy and out of focus, younger than Nat would have thought, freckled pink scalp showing where his hairline receded.

Helen's hand, warm and tight in his.

He turned his head slightly and she was there, vibrant and vivid, more beautiful than his last sight of her so many years ago. Fair black-Irish skin. Fuzzy, dark curly hair that wouldn't stay put no matter what she did with it. Freckles bridging her nose. Generous mouth, straight nose except right there at the tip where sight confirmed what touch had told him about that sassy upturn.

Her hands, slim and strong in his, his rings on her wedding finger, one plain gold band and one emerald to match her eyes.

He brought his gaze to her face and found those deep green pools waiting for him, brimming with hope, with love. Smiling. Knowing. Waiting for him to say it.

So he did.

He reached up a finger to brush her cheek and grinned, with his heart printed plainly on his face.

"Damn," he said dryly, fervently. "It's good to see you."

National Pickle Day—Fourteen months later

It was a beautiful day, sunny, clear, an early promise of spring. Inside, the family courtroom at Oakland County's district courthouse was unusually full of Brannigans when the judge emerged from her chambers to take the bench.

"All rise," the judge's assistant said.

In a great clatter of sound, everyone did—except for Helen, who was busy brushing children's suits and dresses into place and whispering admonitions.

"Helen," Nat growled. "Get up and quit fuss-budgeting, it's time."

Helen stood, stared earnestly into his one deep blue, sparkling eye and its opposing hole-filled metal eye patch. "I just want them to look nice, make a good impression."

Nat swiped his palm across her rump, flicking down the folded ends of her uniform jacket. "What about you, Colonel?" His eyes skimmed down her, head-to-toe, paused on her legs. "You've got dust on your hem." He pressed his mouth to her ear. "And are those my favorite thigh highs you're wearing?"

"That's for me to know and you to find out," Helen told him smugly. "Later."

Counting heads, she looked down the row of children in front of her—seven of them now, since the same group that had found Jane and Max for John and Amanda had called Helen and Nat six months ago, desperate to place orphaned, ten-year-old Arkady, who'd needed a lifesaving surgery, and his sister, Anna, with a family who would take them both. It was a rich life she and Nat had found for themselves, one that would continue richer still after today.

On the bench the judge pulled her glasses down her nose and looked them over: uniformed, untraditional-looking mom; tall, rangy dad in an eye patch, holding her hand. Funny-looking old lady with a gargoyle cane and some kind of hugely feathered hat on her head. One oversize yellow dog wearing a red bow who shouldn't have been allowed in the judge's courtroom at all. Six kids standing uncomfortably stiff and straight and apprehensive. The seventh child—Libby, of course—who looked the judge straight in the eye and dared her to say no to this group adoption.

"You're here to adopt all these children?" she asked sternly.

"Yes, Your Honor," Nat responded.

"Yes, ma'am," Helen said firmly. And grinned.

The judge ignored the grin, glanced at the paperwork she'd already studied at some length in her chambers. Looked over her glasses at the court and enjoyed the hush of bated breath from the spectators. Pursed her lips and rubbed her chin. Eyed the children.

"You're all here to be adopted by these people?"

"No, Your Honor," Max said gravely. "Just by Kern'l and Dad."

The judge shut her eyes and refused to smile. Figured the hell with it and smiled at them anyway. Wasn't often she had a happy courtroom, be a shame not to enjoy it while she did.

"Well," she said, "if that's what you want, I don't have a problem with it. So, let's see now, we have here Colonel and Mr. Crockett, Zachary Crockett, Cara Crockett, Elizabeth Crockett, Maximilian Crockett, Jane Crockett, Arkady Crockett and Anna Crockett. Is that correct?"

"Yes, Judge."

"Good. That's it then. Congratulations, pick up your paperwork and get that dog out of my courtroom. Dismissed."

In the ensuing pandemonium, amid kissing and crying and congratulations, Nat pulled Helen to him. While his lips and tongue kept her mouth too busy to protest, his wandering hand skimmed lecherously down her hip, rounded her bottom and drifted over her thigh, confirming to the sinful, throaty taste of her laughter, her stockinged invitation for their locked bedroom door and *Later*.

* * * * *

COMING NEXT MONTH

MILLION DOLLAR SWEEPSTAKES (III)

No purchase necessary. To enter the sweepstakes and receive the Free Books and Surprise Gift, follow the directions published and complete and mail your "Win A Fortune" Game Card. If not taking advantage of the book and gift offer or if the "Win A Fortune" Game Card is missing, you may enter by hand-printing your name and address on a 3" X 5" card and mailing it (limit: one entry per envelope) via First Class Mail to: Million Dollar Sweepstakes (III) "Win A Fortune" Game, P.O. Box 1867, Buffalo, NY 14269-1867, or Million Dollar Sweepstakes (III) "Win A Fortune" Game, P.O. Box 609, Fort Erie, Ontario L2A 5X3. When your entry is received, you will be assigned sweepstakes numbers. To be eligible entries must be received no later than March 31, 1996. No liability is assumed for printing errors or lost, late or misdirected entries. Odds of winning are determined by the number of eligible entries distributed and received.

Sweepstakes open to residents of the U.S. (except Puerto Rico), Canada, Europe and Taiwan who are 18 years of age or older. All applicable laws and regulations apply. Sweepstakes offer void wherever prohibited by law. Values of all prizes are in U.S. currency. This sweepstakes is presented by Torstar Corp, its subsidiaries and affiliates, in conjunction with book, merchandise and/or product offerings. For a copy of the official rules governing this sweepstakes offer, send a self-addressed, stamped envelope (WA residents need not affix return postage) to: MILLION DOLLAR SWEEPSTAKES (III) Rules, P.O. Box 4573, Blair, NE 68009, USA.

SWP-S1295

Are your lips succulent, impetuous, delicious or racy?

Find out in a very special Valentine's Day promotion—THAT SPECIAL KISS!

Inside four special Harlequin and Silhouette February books are details for THAT SPECIAL KISS! explaining how you can have your lip prints read by a romance expert.

Look for details in the following series books, written by four of Harlequin and Silhouette readers' favorite authors:

Silhouette Intimate Moments #691
Mackenzie's Pleasure by *New York Times* bestselling author Linda Howard

Harlequin Romance #3395
Because of the Baby by Debbie Macomber

Silhouette Desire #979
Megan's Marriage by Annette Broadrick

Harlequin Presents #1793
The One and Only by Carole Mortimer

Fun, romance, four top-selling authors, plus a FREE gift! This is a very special Valentine's Day you won't want to miss! Only from Harlequin and Silhouette.

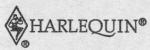

VAL96

INTRODUCING...

A collection of award-winning books by award-winning authors! From Harlequin and Silhouette.

Falling Angel
by Anne Stuart

WINNER OF THE RITA AWARD FOR BEST ROMANCE!

Falling Angel by Anne Stuart is a RITA Award winner, voted Best Romance. A truly wonderful story, *Falling Angel* will transport you into a world of hidden identities, second chances and the magic of falling in love.

"Ms. Stuart's talent shines like the brightest of stars, making it very obvious that her ultimate destiny is to be the next romance author at the top of the best-seller charts."
—*Affaire de Coeur*

A heartwarming story for the holidays. You won't want to miss award-winning *Falling Angel*, available this January wherever Harlequin and Silhouette books are sold.

We've got more of the men you love to love in the Heartbreakers lineup this winter. Among them are Linda Howard's Zane Mackenzie, a member of her immensely popular Mackenzie family, and Jack Ramsey, an *Extra*-special hero.

In December—HIDE IN PLAIN SIGHT, by Sara Orwig: Detective Jake Delancy was used to dissecting the criminal mind, not analyzing his own troubled heart. But Rebecca Bolen and her two cuddly kids had become so much more than a routine assignment....

In January—TIME AND AGAIN, by Kathryn Jensen, *Intimate Moments Extra:* Jack Ramsey had broken the boundaries of time to seek Kate Fenwick's help. Only this woman could change the course of their destinies—and enable them both to love.

In February—MACKENZIE'S PLEASURE, by Linda Howard: Barrie Lovejoy needed a savior, and out of the darkness Zane Mackenzie emerged. He'd brought her to safety, loved her desperately, yet danger was never more than a heartbeat away— even as Barrie felt the stirrings of new life growing within her....

You're About to Become a
Privileged Woman

Reap the rewards of fabulous free gifts and benefits with proofs-of-purchase from Silhouette and Harlequin books

Pages & Privileges™

It's our way of thanking you for buying our books at your favorite retail stores.

Pages & Privileges ™

**Harlequin and Silhouette—
the most privileged readers in the world!**

For more information about Harlequin and Silhouette's PAGES & PRIVILEGES program call the Pages & Privileges Benefits Desk: 1-503-794-2499

Silhouette®

SIM-PP86